"I don't
abo

John reached out and gently touched Elizabeth's cheek. Their eyes met, and the realization of how much she liked him scared Elizabeth into jumping up from the park bench.

"Elizabeth. I didn't mean to upset you. I—"

"You didn't. But—" She couldn't let him say he was sorry for the tender moment. She didn't want to hear that. "It's just getting late, and we should get back."

He stood from the bench, and she slipped her hand through his arm before they began their walk back.

"Thank you for listening, John."

"Anytime. I mean that, Elizabeth. I've opened up to you in ways I never have with anyone else."

His words warmed Elizabeth's heart. This man whom she'd sparred with for over a year had suddenly become the person she shared all her deepest hurts and fears with. He was truly her best friend. But now she wanted for more.

Books by Janet Lee Barton

Love Inspired Historical

Somewhere to Call Home
A Place of Refuge
A Home for Her Heart

*Boardinghouse Betrothals

JANET LEE BARTON

was born in New Mexico and has lived all over the South, in Arkansas, Florida, Louisiana, Mississippi, Oklahoma and Texas. She loves researching and writing heartwarming stories about faith, family, friends and love. Janet loves being able to share her faith and love of the Lord through her writing. She's very happy that the kind of romances the Lord has called her to write can be read and shared with women of all ages.

Janet and her husband now live in Oklahoma and are part of what they laughingly call their "Generational Living Experiment" with their daughter and her husband, two wonderful granddaughters and a shih tzu called Bella. The experiment has turned into quite an adventure, and so far, they think it's working out just fine. When Janet isn't writing or reading, she loves to travel, cook, work in the garden and sew.

You can visit Janet at www.janetleebarton.com.

A Home for Her Heart

JANET LEE BARTON

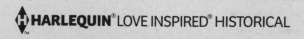
HARLEQUIN® LOVE INSPIRED® HISTORICAL

Recycling programs
for this product may
not exist in your area.

LOVE INSPIRED BOOKS

ISBN-13: 978-0-373-28281-4

A HOME FOR HER HEART

Copyright © 2014 by Janet Lee Barton

www.Harlequin.com

Printed in U.S.A.

Debate thy cause with thy neighbor himself;
and discover not a secret to another.
— *Proverbs* 25:9

To Dan for encouraging me every step of the way,
To Tina James for seeing the possibilities for this series,
To Giselle Regus for helping to make this story better,
To Tamela Hancock Murray for being such a great agent,
& always to my Lord and Savior for showing me the way.

Chapter One

New York City
June 1896

John Talbot had barely reached the top step leading to Heaton House before Elizabeth Anderson rushed out the door and slammed into his chest. He reached out to steady her.

"Whoa there! Are you all right, Elizabeth?"

Her hazel eyes appeared a little dazed as she looked up at him and she seemed to be trying to catch the breath he was certain had been knocked out of her. He was nearly a foot taller than her and she was a trim woman. She had to be shaken by the collision. He felt a little breathless himself, looking down at her.

"Elizabeth, are you all right?" he repeated, keeping a firm grip on her slender arms.

She gave a short nod and took several deep breaths before finally finding her voice. "I'm fine. I think."

She looked fine—better than fine actually. He'd never been quite this close to her, near enough to notice how thick and long her eyelashes were or how much green shot through her hazel eyes. "Are you sure?"

She gave a little nod.

"I'm sorry. I didn't expect you to come flying out the door that way."

"I know. It's not your fault."

"Where are you off to in such a rush?"

"I just received a call from my aunt letting me know my father is in town and insisting I come to dinner. I'm in a hurry."

"Would you like me to accompany you?" Mrs. Heaton had a hard-and-fast rule that none of the women boarders were to be out alone after dark and that if necessary, one of the male boarders would accompany them.

She shook her head. "No, thank you. It's still light out and I'll be fine."

She still looked a little bemused and he felt responsible. "Do you need me to come get you later?"

Elizabeth pulled away from his grasp. "No. I'll be staying the night with her."

Obviously she didn't want his help. He nodded and took a step back. "Have a good evening."

"Thank you. You have a good evening, too." Elizabeth hurried down the steps and headed toward the trolley stop.

John watched until she boarded the trolley that pulled up just as she arrived at the corner, trying to figure out if there was a way to follow her and find out once and for all where this aunt of hers lived.

All he knew was that the trolley she took would take her to Fifth Avenue where some of the luxury apartment buildings were. And that opened up more questions than it gave answers to. Elizabeth lived at Heaton House and was employed at a women's magazine called the *Delineator,* but why would she need to work if she had relatives who could afford to live in that kind of luxury? If her aunt did live on Fifth Avenue, why wasn't Elizabeth living with her? And this was the first time he'd ever heard her mention her father. Why didn't she live at home?

A sudden clap on his shoulder brought him out of his thoughts and he turned to find Benjamin Roth, another of Mrs. Heaton's boarders, grinning at him. "What are you standing here woolgathering about, my friend?"

John gave a small shake of his head and shrugged. "This and that."

"Hmm. Woman problems?"

"Now why would you say that? There's no woman in my life to be a problem and that's the way I want it. I've been down that road before and I have no intention of putting myself in that position again." After the debacle that'd cost him his job, John had decided his instincts where women were concerned were pretty much non-existent and he'd never trust one with his heart again.

"I see. That was Elizabeth I saw hurrying away, wasn't it? Didn't make her mad, did you? You always seem to be trying to get a rise out of her."

"No, Ben. I didn't make her mad. She's going to see that aunt of hers again."

"Ahh, I see," Ben said.

"No, you don't."

Ben threw back his head and laughed. "Whatever you say, John. But I think you protest too much. You care about that woman. It's plain as the nose on your face."

"Of course I care about her. Just like I do everyone at Heaton House. But you have to admit, she keeps part of her life separate."

"We all have lives outside of Heaton House, John."

"I suppose." Others did, he knew that. But John's life seemed to revolve around his work and living at Heaton House. His mother had passed away when he was only five and his father had died when John was around seventeen. He'd been on his own since then.

"However, I will concede that I've wondered about where Elizabeth's aunt lives, too," Ben said. "Michael probably knows, but I've never asked him. He'd think I was being nosy or that I was interested in Elizabeth in a more than friendly way, and I'm not."

"I know. That's why I haven't asked, either. He'd probably say it was none of my business or tell me to ask her myself and I can just picture how that would go over."

"Yes, but you—"

"No buts, Ben." He slapped his friend on the back. "We seem to have come to a dead end with this conversation. Let's go see what's for dinner."

Elizabeth stepped on the trolley, paid her money and took a seat that'd just been vacated near the driver, all the while trying to calm her pounding heart. She'd never been quite so close to John before and her response to his touch frustrated her almost as much as the telephone call from her aunt had.

She and John clashed more often than not. He worked for the *Tribune* and she worked for the *Delineator,* and over the years they'd often sparred about the similar stories they sometimes found themselves covering. It was always clear to her that he thought her writing was inferior to his—the *Delineator* was a woman's magazine, after all—and he'd even referred to her writing as *fluff* in the past.

Somehow he thought his articles on the same social scene she wrote about were much more worthwhile. And now that his editor had asked him to do more serious pieces, following his article about the Ladies' Aide Society and the child-care homes they were starting, he'd be even harder to be around. Everyone knew that John Talbot wouldn't rest until he broke a story that would put his byline on the front page and promote him to a lead reporter for the *Tribune*. It seemed to be all he cared about.

Elizabeth let out a deep breath and tried to put John to the back of her mind as had become her custom. She was already upset that her father had demanded she visit her aunt's on such short notice. Thinking about John's attitude toward her work wasn't going to calm her any.

Leaning her head back against the seat, she looked out the window at the passing scenery. The quietness of Gramercy Park gave way to more and more traffic noise as they reached Fifth Avenue and turned amid all manner of vehicles—hacks, omnibuses, landaus and carriages of all sizes going in all different directions. It was especially busy this time of day.

She tried to tell herself to calm down. She wasn't upset at her aunt, loved spending time with her, in fact. But to be summoned to her home because her father, Charles Edward Reynolds, had come into the city and wanted her there for dinner on such short notice was just…irritating.

There was so much going on at Heaton House right

now, she hated to miss out on anything. But she'd promised to be available whenever her father came to town—it was the price she paid to have her independence. She shouldn't really be upset at him, either. But she was. All he seemed to be interested in was getting her married off—but only to a man of his choosing.

Well, catching his first choice in a very compromising position with another woman—at their engagement party, no less—had ended with a broken engagement, her heart shattered and had soured Elizabeth on men in general. She had no intention of letting her father choose a mate for her again, not even if she wanted one—which she didn't. She released a huge sigh loud enough to capture the driver's ear.

"You have a bad day, miss?"

She really hadn't had a bad day until she'd found out she'd been ordered to have dinner with her aunt and her father. Her father wanted to see her. Was that really so bad? She did love him. And besides, it was just for the evening, not the whole weekend. "Not so much a bad day... Perhaps it's my own attitude making me so—"

"Downcast?"

She should be ashamed for giving that impression to anyone. There were much worse things in life than having to change her plans to spend time with family. "Maybe a little, but not anymore."

When she got off the trolley at its stop just a block from her aunt's apartment, she turned to the driver and smiled. "Thanks for making me realize I have absolutely nothing to be downcast about."

His face fairly beamed. "You're welcome, miss. I'm glad you're feeling better."

"Thank you. So am I."

By the time she knocked on her aunt's door, she was looking forward to telling her all about the happenings at Heaton House.

The door opened and her aunt's maid, Amanda, smiled. "Miss Elizabeth, it's wonderful to see you. Mrs. Watson and your father are waiting for you in her study."

Her heart sank. She'd hoped for some time alone with her aunt. "Thank you, Amanda. It's good to see you, too. Will you let them know I'll join them as soon as I freshen up?"

"Certainly."

Elizabeth hurried down the hall and let herself into a room her aunt had decorated just for her. It was beautiful and she loved the view of the avenue below and even a bit of Central Park. But she didn't have time to enjoy that view right now. She hurried to choose a gown for dinner. There was a new yellow silk dinner gown hanging in her wardrobe. She quickly selected it. She never had to worry about packing for an overnight stay. Her aunt kept her wardrobe filled with the latest styles—so much so that Elizabeth had been able to give clothes away to those less fortunate.

She was blessed in so many ways and she had no right to feel put out by a visit from her father. She sent up a prayer, asking for forgiveness for being upset by his unexpected visit. She also prayed that she wouldn't show her frustration to her aunt and father.

She made quick work of freshening up and hurried to the study. Her aunt, Beatrice Watson, must have heard her footsteps as she met her at the door.

"Elizabeth, it is good to see you as always." She enveloped her in a hug and whispered, "Thank you for coming on such short notice, dear,"

"You're welcome, Aunt Bea," Elizabeth whispered back.

Her aunt was an elegant middle-aged woman with sparkling blue eyes and blond hair always done up in the latest style, and she'd always been ahead of her time. Like Elizabeth's mother, she'd been raised to think for herself and make her own decisions—but would have, even had she not been encouraged to. Elizabeth knew this because she took after them both and her father had never encouraged her to be an independent woman. It wasn't a trait he admired.

She looked past her to her father, who'd crossed the room and quickly gathered her in his arms to give her a quick hug. His hair had more silver in it than it had the last time she'd seen him.

"Elizabeth, my dear, the older you get, the more you look like your mother. I've missed you."

"Thank you, Papa. That is quite a compliment. It's good to see you, too." And it was. She did miss him. But he traveled so much and she'd missed him back home, too. And now she loved her life in New York City and had no intention of going back to Boston to live.

"Dinner is ready, ma'am," Amanda announced.

Elizabeth's father offered both women an arm and escorted them into the dining room. After seating her aunt first and then her, her father took a seat across from her and adjacent to her aunt, who was at the head of the table.

"Charles, will you please say the blessing before Amanda serves us?" The maid stood just inside the door between the kitchen and the dining room and bowed her head.

"Of course. Our Father in Heaven, we come to thank You for our many blessings and we thank You for the food we're about to eat. Amen."

Short and to the point, as usual. But he did love the Lord, Elizabeth was sure of it. And he loved her—even though he rarely said it or knew how best to show it.

Amanda began to serve them and Elizabeth turned to her father. "Papa, what kind of business did you come to New York on?"

"Investment business, my dear. Nothing to bother your pretty head about at this point in your life."

Elizabeth exchanged a glance with her aunt. Would he always think women were to be seen and not heard in the matter of business?

"And hopefully you'll have a husband to worry about it before the time comes that you might need to."

There it was. The real reason he'd come to the city. He thought she should have been married several years ago and that was the reason he'd sent her to her aunt in the first place—well, that and the fact that he was upset with her for breaking her engagement to the man he'd handpicked, no matter that the man was only after *his* money.

"I want you to come home, Elizabeth. There's a young man I want you to meet."

"Papa, I'm sorry, but I'm not looking for a husband to take care of me. I like my life just as it is right now and I have no intention of moving back to Boston."

She watched as her father and her aunt exchanged glances and thought she saw her aunt give a little shake of her head as if telling him not to push. At least that was what Elizabeth hoped she was trying to tell him. Dear Aunt Bea, she'd come to her defense on more than one occasion.

Her father's face flushed and he took a sip of water before speaking again. "Elizabeth, I didn't ask you to move back. But I would like for you to come home for a visit soon."

"It is hard to get away from work, Papa."

"Surely you could come there for a weekend, same as I've come here."

"Maybe one of these days, Papa." Elizabeth was afraid to go back to Boston for a visit—afraid he wouldn't let her return. And yet, she was a grown woman, he couldn't keep her under lock and key forever.

"Perhaps we could go together, Elizabeth," her aunt offered.

Elizabeth flashed her a look of gratitude. If her aunt went with her, she'd make sure they both came back to the city. She nodded. "Perhaps we can plan something."

"Good. Let me know when and I'll make plans for entertaining the two of you when you come. Just don't wait too long." He glanced from one to the other, looked down and then added, "Please."

Elizabeth's heart softened toward him. She couldn't remember him ever saying *please* to her. She had a feeling her aunt had been coaching him, or maybe he'd actually changed since she moved to the city.

"We'll plan it and let you know the date, Charles," Aunt Bea said.

"Thank you. I'll look forward to your visit. I've several people I'd like you to meet—"

"Now, Papa—"

"Elizabeth, I didn't say marry, although there is one

young man I think you might actually like and I'd like you to meet him. Just meet him."

"It certainly won't hurt to meet an eligible young man, will it, Elizabeth?" Aunt Bea asked, looking at her, as if imploring her to agree and not cause a stir. Her father was here only for the night and Elizabeth supposed she should give in. After all, it was her aunt's home and she was the one who helped enable Elizabeth to live the independent life she loved. "I suppose it wouldn't, Aunt Bea."

But she certainly didn't have to look forward to it. Still, for the moment her words seemed to pacify her father and he went on to change the subject. She breathed a sigh of relief and joined in the conversation.

Just as dinner at Heaton House was finishing up the next evening, Kathleen O'Bryan, one of Elizabeth's dear friends and a fellow boarder, leaned toward Elizabeth and said, "I'd like to speak with you and John after dinner, if you have time. We could go to the back parlor if it's all right with you."

"Oh? Have you made some decisions about your wedding?" Kathleen and Luke Patterson had announced their engagement a few weeks earlier and Kathleen had asked Elizabeth to be her maid of honor and help her plan the wedding set for September.

Kathleen laughed and shook her head. "You know I wouldn't do that without your advice, Elizabeth. No. It's about a couple of buildings I ran across that are in deplorable condition." She leaned forward to bring John into the conversation. "I thought you and John might want to work together to find out who owns them, maybe write an article or two about them at some point."

John raised an eyebrow at Elizabeth. It appeared he wasn't any more enthused at Kathleen's suggestion than she was. Work together? He thought her writing was fluff and she thought he was just too full of himself.

Still, Elizabeth was curious to hear what Kathleen had to say. She was the liaison for the Ladies' Aide Society, in helping find families who were in need of the child-care homes they'd recently started.

"I'll be there," Elizabeth said. "But I can't answer for John."

"I'll be there, too. The boss seemed to like the articles about the child-care homes you and Luke suggested I do, Kathleen. And while he hasn't taken me off the high society affairs completely just yet, he's letting the new guy cover some of them."

"Oh, I know you're going to miss all of those, John," Luke said from the other side of Kathleen.

By the grin he flashed, Elizabeth could tell that just as she did, Luke knew how John felt about having to cover what he considered soft stories as opposed to the hard-hitting ones he chomped at the bit to do.

Mrs. Heaton pushed away from the table, signaling the end to dinner and John pulled Elizabeth's chair out for her, as Luke did the same for Kathleen. The other boarders headed for the big parlor while the two of them followed Luke and Kathleen to the smaller parlor at the end of the hall.

After they all had taken a seat around a small table in the middle of the room, Kathleen wasted no time in letting them know of the derelict properties she'd run across in the course of her job. She handed them pictures of the two buildings from the outside.

"I was about to take pictures of the hallways and

stairways in one of them when the landlord came out and told me to leave. He wouldn't give me any information about the owner of the building and with the work I do to try to help tenants get out, I didn't want to make things hard on any of them. But I know there are children living there and there's broken glass from some of the windows in the hallways," Kathleen said. "That's dangerous."

"We've reported it to the authorities, but whether that will help or not is anyone's guess," Luke said. "And Kathleen is in and out of that area so much, I don't want her in danger from what she sees and tells us."

"Don't worry about that, Luke," John said. "We won't tell where our information came from."

"I know you won't." Luke put a protective arm around Kathleen.

"I hope the articles you'll both write will bring the kind of attention that will make the owners clean up these places. You won't believe it until you see them for yourselves." Kathleen handed them the addresses of both buildings. "You will do it, won't you? With articles in both the *Tribune* and the *Delineator,* word will get out to more people and surely something will be done."

Elizabeth glanced at John. Working with him was the last thing she wanted to do—he had a way of irritating her on a good day. And he didn't look any happier than she felt at the prospect. But she couldn't tell Kathleen no. The woman had been through so much living in those tenements and now she was working hard to help others get out as she had. There was no way she could refuse to do what her friend asked. She nodded.

And she had no doubt that John would accept. It was

a chance to further his career—even if he had to have her tagging along.

"Want to check them out in the morning, Elizabeth?" John asked.

"Might as well. What time?"

"Let's go right after breakfast."

She nodded. "That's fine with me."

"Oh, thank you both!" Kathleen gave Elizabeth a hug. "I know your stories will make a difference."

"That's what we're hoping for," John said.

Elizabeth couldn't back out now. No matter how much she might want to.

Chapter Two

Elizabeth's alarm clock jarred her awake an hour earlier than usual for a Saturday and she fumbled to quiet it so as not to awaken the whole floor. After the meeting the night before, she, Kathleen and the other women boarders had stayed up much too late poring through magazines and patterns for wedding gowns, finally narrowing down Kathleen's favorites to a manageable number. Hopefully they'd trim down her choices more in the next few days.

She threw off the covers and hurried to freshen up in the bathroom she and Kathleen shared. After dressing in a plain shirtwaist and skirt for the trip to the tenements, she hurried down to breakfast, yawning as she entered the dining room. Julia Olsen, who worked at Ellis Island, was just leaving for work.

"See you at dinner," she said as she walked out of the room.

"Good morning, Elizabeth," Mrs. Heaton said. "You're down earlier than usual today."

"Good morning! Kathleen wants John and I to check

out some buildings this morning for possible articles and we're leaving right after breakfast."

"Oh, I'm glad. Something must be done to get those landlords to take care of those dilapidated buildings."

Elizabeth chose a muffin from the sideboard, along with a couple of pieces of bacon and some fluffy scrambled eggs before taking her seat at the table.

Saturdays were always more relaxed than workdays or Sundays when everyone was on their way to work or church. The boarders came down at different times and lingered at the table a little longer. This morning John entered just as she took her seat.

"Good morning," he said as he began to fill his plate. Ben and Matt entered behind him.

John slid into his seat beside her. "I'm surprised to see you up so early. I heard you women laughing when I went downstairs last night."

"We did have a good time. What did you and the men do?" Elizabeth asked.

"Oh, we played a few games, talked about the building Matt is working on and finally got bored with our own company and called it a night."

"I'm still not sure why all this secrecy about the wedding dress is necessary," Luke said from across the table.

"Missed Kathleen, did you?" Elizabeth asked.

Kathleen and Millicent Faircloud, one of the new boarders, entered the room just then and Elizabeth thought once more of how blessed she was to be living at Heaton House. As an only child with a father who was out of town often and only a housekeeper to look after her, she truly felt as if she were part of a big family living here.

"What's all this I'm hearing?" Kathleen asked. "If it makes you feel any better, Luke, I missed you, too."

That seemed to settle the man down and he smiled at his fiancée as she took the seat he pulled out for her.

Talk turned to the nice weather they were having and the Independence Day celebrations planned in the city the next month. As always there was much going on—parades, picnics and fireworks.

"There is much to choose from. But we really ought to go on a picnic while it's still fairly cool," Mrs. Heaton suggested. "Why don't we go this coming Saturday, if the weather holds up?"

"Oh, I love the sound of that," Millicent said. "I'd like to get photos of all of you at the park."

"It's about time we had some new ones made. But we need to include you and Matt in some. Maybe we can get a passerby to take a few."

"That'd be nice."

Everyone seemed excited about a trip to Central Park.

"It should be lovely this time of year. Just about everything has bloomed now," Mrs. Heaton said.

"If your garden is any indication, there will be roses everywhere," Elizabeth said.

"I think we should all take another trip to Coney Island and go swimming before long," Ben suggested. "That might be something to think about for Independence Day. And you know they set off fireworks on Manhattan Beach on that day, too."

"Most of the parks will have bands playing patriotic music, too. We'll just need to figure out what it is everyone most wants to do that day and do some planning," Mrs. Heaton said.

"That's a good idea. We'll have to see what we can work in," Luke said.

"Sounds good to me, too," John said. The clock in the foyer chimed the hour and he leaned near and nudged Elizabeth's shoulder. "You about ready to go check out those buildings?"

"Anytime you are."

"Let's go, then." He pushed back his chair and stood. "Let us know what you come up with for Independence Day."

Luke nodded from across the table. "We will."

"Where are you two off to so early?" Millicent asked.

"We've got some investigating to do," John answered.

"Oh, I see. Well, if you have any need for professional pictures to be taken…"

John had just scooted Elizabeth's chair out for her to stand and he turned to the other woman. "You know, Millicent, we may just call on you if we need to have photos taken. What do you think, Elizabeth?"

"I don't know. Photographs might help." Elizabeth didn't mention that she had a camera she could take. She wasn't really very good at photography and it *was* Millicent's career, and she was just starting out here in the city. Still, she felt John had put her on the spot and it irked her a little.

Millicent nodded and smiled. "I hope you can use me. I need the work and the exposure, you know."

"We do," John said. "But we couldn't pay you. That would only come if the *Tribune* or *Delineator* wanted to use them."

"I understand. I don't have a problem with that."

"I suppose you could tag along."

"Maybe we should take a look and make sure we have the right buildings before we waste Millicent's time," Elizabeth suggested.

Millicent's smile disappeared and she shrugged. "I'll be around this morning. I can meet you there if you need me."

Elizabeth sighed inwardly. What was wrong with her? If she didn't know better she'd think she was jealous. But she liked Millicent. She was very nice and she did need the work. If they did an article and used her pictures, she'd make money. "You know, on second thought, why don't you go get your camera and come on with us now?"

"Really?"

"Yes, but hurry," Elizabeth said. She didn't look at John for fear he'd see that she really didn't want the other girl to go with them. And she wasn't even sure why. She had little time to think about it, though, as Millicent was back downstairs in a flash, camera in hand.

"You know, I'm not sure taking your professional camera is a good idea," John said. "We really only need some snapshots and we don't want to alert the landlords to what we're doing right now."

"Oh, well, I can go get my Kodak. Will that work?"

"That will be fine."

Elizabeth sighed as the other woman rushed back upstairs.

"What's wrong? Don't you think a smaller camera will be better?" John asked.

"I do. But I have one. I could snap the pictures."

"Oh… I'm sorry, Elizabeth. I can tell Millicent we don't need her. I should have—"

"No—we can't do that. Not after telling her she could come. It will be fine. I'm just a little out of sorts this morning. I'm sorry."

"Maybe you didn't get enough sleep."

"Maybe not. At any rate, I shouldn't take my mood out on Millicent or anyone else."

"It's all right. We all wake up on the wrong side of the bed occasionally." But John couldn't remember when he'd seen Elizabeth in a bad mood of a morning. She was usually sunshine and light. Maybe it was lack of sleep, but he couldn't help but wonder if something had happened at her aunt's. She hadn't seemed quite the same since she got back.

He wanted to ask but had a feeling she wouldn't like his prying and he really couldn't blame her. Still… "If there's anything you want to talk about, I'd be glad to listen."

An odd look passed over Elizabeth's face and she opened her mouth—

"I'm back," Millicent interrupted the moment.

Elizabeth's mouth clamped shut and John felt let down. For a moment he was sure she was going to say something, but Millicent's arrival quickly put a stop to it before it could happen. Something was bothering Elizabeth and it wasn't just an out-of-sorts mood. But he wasn't sure what to do about it. And at the moment there was nothing he could do.

"Let's go, ladies." He motioned to the door and followed them outside. It was a beautiful early summer day, blue sky overhead with only a few puffs of white cloud. They took the trolley past Gramercy Park over to Second Avenue and then to Eighth Street. The tenements weren't pretty—especially compared to the neighborhood they lived in. All the buildings were pretty much the same, made of brick with stoops out front and most from six to seven stories high. But he knew the outside of them was deceiving—it was the inside that varied and most were in bad condition.

He didn't like taking Elizabeth and Millicent there, but the cause was important and he'd learned long ago that Elizabeth had no qualms about going into the area. It had been obvious she had empathy for the poor from the first time they'd come here together to help Kathleen move. Was she born with it, or did it come from something in her past?

He'd known her for three years now, yet she remained an enigma. He felt he knew her better with each passing day, but he also felt that what he *didn't* know about her far surpassed what he did. There was something about the woman that fascinated him and yet he was certain Elizabeth Anderson was far out of his reach. Not that it mattered. He'd learned his lesson about giving his heart to a woman the hard way and he had no intention of letting it happen again. Ever.

Still, he considered Elizabeth a friend and—

"Is this the address, John?" Elizabeth had stopped in front of one of the buildings.

"I think so." He pulled the paper Kathleen had written the address on out of his pocket. "Yes, this is one of them. I'll take a look."

The building looked much the same as the others on the block—until he entered. The foyer said it all. The paint was peeling, the lights were dim with dust and the smell made John want to gag. He backed out of the doorway and turned to the women.

"No need for you ladies to come in. It's no place for either of you."

"If you can stand it, surely we can, too," Elizabeth said. She and Millicent pushed their way around him to enter, and quickly grabbed their noses as they looked around.

"If the manager lets it look like this on the ground floor, what must it be like upstairs?" Elizabeth asked.

"If we want to know," John answered, "now would be the time to find out. No one has come out to see what we're up to yet. Are you up to it?"

Elizabeth gave a short nod while Millicent let go of her nose long enough to take a quick picture. Then they followed John up the stairs.

"If anyone asks, we can say we're looking for someone," he said in a low voice.

But they met no one in the halls. Everything was shut up, tight as a drum, the hallways dark from unwashed windows at the end of them, except where the broken windowpanes let light through, and only a dim lightbulb here and there. The stair railings were loose, just asking for an accident, and the trash in the hallways added to the odors that had them all holding their noses.

"Get a picture of that, Millicent." Elizabeth shuddered and pointed to a rat getting his fill of something in a sack in a dark corner. "I hate to think children live here."

Millicent let go of her nose and quickly took the picture. "Do we have enough?"

"For now," John said. "Come on. Let's get you both

out of here. I shouldn't have let you come inside in the first place."

"We had to know what it is Kathleen was talking about, John," Elizabeth said.

Just then a door cracked open. Millicent slid the camera into her bag and they all froze where they were.

Elizabeth held her breath and her heart seemed to stop beating as a big man backed out of the room. "You have one more day to pay your rent, Miss Hardin. If I don't have it by tomorrow, you're goin' to be out on the streets."

"I don't know where I'm going to get it—I don't get paid for another two days," a woman's voice said.

Elizabeth's heart went out to her. How awful it would be to have to live here—and to pay good money to do so!

"Then you'd best be packing now." The man turned and slammed the door behind him. He was big and foreboding as he realized strangers were in the hall.

"I don't recognize the lot of you—who are you and what are you lookin' for up here?"

John stepped forward. "Are you the landlord"

"I am. Mister Brown to you, and from the looks of ya, you aren't lookin' for an apartment. So just what is it you're up to in my building?"

"We're visiting."

"Who is it you're visitin'?"

Elizabeth hurried to the door he'd come out of. "Miss Hardin."

"You're friends of hers?"

Elizabeth had a feeling they were about to be. "We are."

"Well, if you are, ya might help her with the rent, as she's about to be thrown out on the street."

"And how much does she owe?" John asked.

He named a figure and John dug in his pocket as Elizabeth and Millicent opened their pocketbooks.

Together they quickly came up with the amount Miss Hardin owed and John handed it to the man. "We want a receipt for it so our friend has proof that she's paid up."

"I'll get you one. Come with me."

"You two go on in and let our friend know she doesn't have to move anywhere for now. I'll be back once I get the receipt."

John and the landlord started down stairs, the man saying, "If you're such good friends with Miss Hardin, why aren't you helpin' her get out of here?"

"If you're the landlord, why aren't you doing something to clean up this building?"

"That ain't any of your business, mister."

Dear Lord, please don't let anything happen to John, Elizabeth prayed as she hurried to knock on the door. "Miss Hardin?"

"Yes? Who is it?"

"We're the women who just helped pay your rent," Millicent said bluntly. "Please open the door."

The door cracked open and a young woman about their age peeked around the door. "Why would you pay my rent?"

"We don't like the landlord," Millicent said.

"Or how he talked to you," Elizabeth added. "And we wanted to help."

The young woman looked totally confused as tears rushed to her eyes and she opened the door to let them in. "I didn't know how I was going to do it. I have barely enough for food until payday. I was sick a week ago and couldn't work. I— My name is Lacy and I don't know how I can repay you."

"We aren't worried about that. We just didn't want you thrown out." Elizabeth dug in her pocketbook for one of Mrs. Heaton's cards. "If you have problems— ever need a place to stay for a while, come here. You'll be welcomed."

The young woman turned the card over in her hand. "Heaton House."

"Yes. It's where we live. And our landlady takes in temporary boarders from time to time."

There was a knock on the door and John said, "It's me, Elizabeth. I have the receipt."

"That's our friend, John Talbot. He got a receipt for you from the landlord."

Lacy opened the door and John handed her a piece of paper. "Keep that with you."

She looked at the paper. "I really don't know what to say."

"Thank you is enough," Elizabeth said. "And keep that receipt handy in case you need proof that your rent has been paid."

The woman nodded as Elizabeth and Millicent headed out the door. Just as they were about to leave, John turned to the woman. "You wouldn't happen to know who owns the building, do you?"

She shook her head. "No. The only person we ever see is Mr. Brown and then only when we pay the rent or he comes to collect. He's not here half the time. Can never find him when we need anything."

"Is it always in this condition?"

She sighed. "It is. I— Thank you again. I'll try to repay you one day."

"Keep safe and lock this door," John said.

"Yes, I will."

Elizabeth led the way back downstairs, wondering if the other two were as glad to get out of there as she was. She could hear the click of Millicent taking pictures along the way and hoped they would be good enough to use in the *Delineator* or the *Tribune.*

Once they were back outside, all three took deep, cleansing breaths—or they would be if the neighborhood had any clean air in it. It appeared that in spite of efforts to clean up the tenements, there was still much to be done.

"Do we want to find the next building?" Elizabeth asked.

"Maybe we should save that for another day?" Millicent suggested. "That was awful. I had no idea what it was like inside these buildings."

John looked from one to the other. "We can come another time. What do you think, Elizabeth?"

She nodded. She had no desire to go into another building as bad as this one today. "Yes, let's save it for another day."

It was a quiet walk to the trolley stop. Elizabeth didn't know about the others, but her heart was heavy at the conditions they'd seen and it made her admire Kathleen even more. "When I think of Kathleen and her family living in similar surroundings, my heart breaks all over again for her. I am so happy she and Luke have found each other."

"I knew she'd lived in the tenements, but I never

knew what kind of environment that meant until now," Millicent said.

"Her building wasn't quite as bad as the one we just saw, but the living conditions aren't good in any of them. Some of the landlords are better than others, though."

Millicent sighed and shook her head. "What a shame. I'm going to get off at Michael's office and develop these photos. Hopefully I got some you can use. I'll bring them back with me."

Mrs. Heaton's son, Michael, had cleared out a large storage closet near his office in the building he owned and was letting Millicent use it for a darkroom until she could afford to set up her business elsewhere.

"That'd be great, Millicent," John said.

"Yes, and thank you. You were a great help today." Elizabeth couldn't deny she had been.

The trolley stopped a block away from Michael's office and Millicent stepped into the aisle.

"Do you want us to wait for you?" Elizabeth asked.

"No need to. I'll see you both later." She gave a little wave and hurried down the aisle.

John had been sitting across the aisle, but he quickly moved to the empty seat beside Elizabeth, filling the seat up much more than Millicent had. Elizabeth caught her breath as his shoulder touched hers when he leaned near to say, "I think she did get some good shots. Hopefully we'll be able to use one or two for our articles."

"I hope so."

"Although I'd like to do a little more investigating before handing my article in. All we really have is the pictures, if they turn out, and a tenant who's being harassed by a bully of a landlord. And that's pretty normal for the tenements."

"Yes, sadly, it is." She thought about how John hadn't hesitated at paying Lacy's rent. "That was very nice of you to take up for Miss Hardin. And to offer to pay her rent."

John shrugged. "I hate seeing people bullied like that. Besides, you and Millicent helped with the rent, too. And it's a good thing. I didn't have the whole amount with me, but either way I was going to make sure Brown gave her a little more time."

John was so aloof at times it was easy to wonder if anything really touched him. But obviously, someone about to be evicted did. His quick action had warmed Elizabeth's heart. He'd always made it plain that his goal in life was to break a big story and to get promoted to lead reporter at the *Tribune*. But with his actions today she began to think there might be more to him than that. Was it possible John wasn't quite as full of himself as she'd always believed?

Chapter Three

It was after dinner before Elizabeth and John got a chance to look at the photographs Millicent had taken that morning. John had disappeared downstairs as soon as they arrived back at Heaton House, and Elizabeth and Kathleen decided to go window-shopping at the Ladies' Mile, trying to get a better idea of what kind of trousseau she wanted.

Going shopping with Kathleen made Elizabeth realize how much she'd taken for granted over the years. A.T. Stewart's Dry Goods, Macy's and Hearn's—all of those along the Mile were the kind of stores she'd always shopped in, but for Kathleen, it was new and an adventure.

Elizabeth had never had to check price tags to determine if she could afford something, and watching Kathleen do so now humbled her.

"I love this wrap, but oh, my, the price is quite dear." Kathleen touched the silk fabric as if it were a piece of gold.

Elizabeth had to fight the urge to tell her she'd buy it for her—Kathleen had a lot of pride and wouldn't appreciate it, especially now that she had a decent position. Instead, she thought she might give it to her as a wedding gift if she didn't find something she liked at a more reasonable price.

"Why don't we try Macy's? They might have something a little less expensive."

"Yes, let's go there. I do remember seeing something similar to this in there a while back," Kathleen said.

"I like going to Macy's. They do try to keep their prices down a bit. I always enjoy finding something I like at a better price." And she did. She'd found she could use more of her allowance to help others early on, if she shopped wisely and had money left over. Her father hadn't liked her spending her money on the needy, saying he gave enough to charities.

Now she and Kathleen proceeded to search the sales at Macy's, finding exactly what her friend wanted for less money in short order.

It'd begun to stress Elizabeth that her friends in the city didn't know that she could afford to buy anything that caught her fancy—didn't know she didn't have to work for a living. Even though she wasn't trying to hide the fact, she'd not made an effort to let them know she was wealthy in her own right from her grandmother's inheritance—not to mention what she stood to inherit from her father one day. But she didn't like living the life of the wealthy, other than being able to help at different charity functions.

When she'd moved to New York City, she hadn't wanted to be hired because she was the daughter of Charles Edward Reynolds of Boston and she'd been honest with her editor, who agreed to let Elizabeth use her mother's name for her articles. Mrs. Heaton and her son knew who she really was, but she'd asked them to keep it private. She'd wanted to be known as one of the boarders and didn't want to be treated differently because she didn't really have to work. She wanted to be one of them. Only now that she'd lived at Heaton House for several years, she wondered if she'd done the right thing.

She didn't know *how* to tell them she didn't need to work for a living. What would they think of her? Would they think she lied on purpose? Would they be disappointed in her? Think less of her? How would it affect her friendships with them? Much as she longed to quit feeling she was keeping secrets about herself, she was very afraid of the consequences of letting the people she cared about know she wasn't exactly who they thought she was.

"Are you upset about anything, Elizabeth?" Kathleen asked. "You seem a little down in spirit."

"Oh? I'm sorry. My mind was wandering."

"No need to be sorry. Perhaps you're tired. We did stay up very late last night and you were out and about early. Do you think Millicent got some good photos?"

"I hope so."

"I suppose we should be going back or we'll be late for dinner," Kathleen said. "Thank you for coming with me."

"You're welcome. Thank you for asking me to come. I think you're right, however, and we should be getting back."

When they saw the line for their trolley, they decided to ride the El instead. Hurrying up the steps of the nearest stop, they got in a shorter line, bought their ticket and boarded while people still waited in the trol-

ley line. They found a seat and looked out the windows
at the city.

"I love riding up over the streets," Kathleen said.

"So do I. It's a different view altogether."

They pointed out different sights to each other as
they rode along. "Look, you can see the building Matt
is working on from here. I don't know how those men
work so high up in the air."

"Neither do I," Elizabeth said. "But I love the way
the skyline is changing with the taller buildings."

They were at their stop in no time and walked the
rest of the way to Heaton House. The aroma drifting
through to the foyer told them Mrs. Heaton had planned
a great meal, but it was quiet downstairs as no one had
come down to the parlor yet. Happy they weren't too
late, Elizabeth and Kathleen rushed upstairs to their
rooms to change clothes.

They never dressed for dinner during the week—
Mrs. Heaton said it was just too much trouble for working people and it made it much easier on the boarders.
But on the weekends and special occasions they did
dress up and everyone seemed to enjoy it.

Elizabeth chose one of her favorite dinner gowns, a
sleeveless green silk with a sweetheart neckline. It felt
summery and cool and she felt pretty in it. She pinched
her cheeks in the mirror and pinned up an errant strand
of blond hair before leaving her room. She met up with
Millicent in the hall.

"Elizabeth! I'm glad you're back. I can't wait to show
you and John the photographs. I think they turned out
very well."

"I can't wait to see them. Perhaps after dinner—"

"What are you doing after dinner?" Kathleen asked,

coming up behind them and following them down the staircase.

"Millicent has the photos she took this morning and she's ready to show them to me and John."

"Oh, I'd love to see them, Millicent!"

"And you should," Elizabeth said. "This was your idea after all."

They entered the parlor, but John wasn't there. She felt a small stab of disappointment that he wasn't. Had he been called out on an assignment? And why did it matter? She had no idea why she should care.

However, just as dinner was announced and the boarders headed toward the dining room, footsteps were heard from the staircase leading down to the ground floor and he hurried to join them all in the hall.

"Sorry I'm late. I've been working on the article about the building we saw today."

"I thought you wanted to do more research before starting it," Elizabeth commented. Of course he would get a head start.

John shrugged. "I do, but I've already talked to my editor about it and he's eager to see the first one. Said there was a possibility of a series. He asked if I had pictures. Did you get them developed, Millicent?"

All thoughts that somehow she'd misjudged John earlier in the day went flying out the window. As always, it was all about him and his career. It was as if she hadn't even been along that morning.

"I did," Millicent said as she took her seat at the table. "Elizabeth suggested we look at them after dinner."

"Wonderful." John pulled out Elizabeth's seat as usual, but it wasn't until he'd sat down beside her that he acknowledged her at all. "Have you spoken with your editor yet, Elizabeth?"

"No, I haven't. I'll talk to him first thing on Monday, but I'm certain he'll want to do a series of articles, too." At least she hoped so. Something about John's attitude tonight made her feel competitive.

"I'm sure he will. But perhaps from a different perspective than what I'll be doing for the *Tribune*."

Elizabeth clamped her mouth shut before she made a scathing comment about his hard-hitting article on what Mrs. Vanderbilt had worn at the last social function he covered. Instead she tried to enjoy the meal and listen to the conversations going on around her.

"How is Rebecca doing?" Ben asked Mrs. Heaton.

Rebecca was Mrs. Heaton's daughter whom she'd been recently reunited with, having been missing for several years. Rebecca had a young daughter and was living with her brother, Michael, and his wife until after Kathleen and Luke were married.

"She's doing fine. She and Jenny, along with Michael and Violet, will be here for Sunday dinner as usual tomorrow."

Elizabeth smiled. Everyone loved having Rebecca's young daughter around. She livened things up around the dinner table.

"Did you and Elizabeth get any shopping done?" Luke asked Kathleen.

"I did purchase something, but we mostly window-shopped for ideas and fabrics. I have a better idea of what I want now, and where to look for things."

"And it's all still a secret I assume?"

"Most of it."

Luke sighed and shook his head. "Are you going to be locked away with more planning tonight?"

Kathleen smiled at him. "Not tonight."

"Good."

Elizabeth couldn't help but smile as she witnessed the look Luke gave her friend. It was obvious the two were deeply in love and she was very happy for them. Sometimes even a little envious, even though she had no intention of giving her heart to any man. After finding her fiancée didn't love her but only the money he'd have access to, how could she ever trust that any other man truly cared about her and not her inheritance? How could she trust that her heart wouldn't be broken again? She didn't believe it was possible to ever be able to trust that way again.

John leaned near and broke into her thoughts. "You're awfully quiet tonight. In fact, you haven't seemed yourself since our run-in the other day."

His concern surprised her and frustrated her all at the same time. The look in his eyes reminded her of what it'd felt like to be held by him that day she'd barreled into him and how it had taken her breath away. Something she'd been trying not to think about ever since. "I'm fine."

"You're sure? You seem a little—"

"I'm fine, John," she repeated. At least she would be if he didn't keep asking if she was. What was it about this man that had her catching her breath one minute and ready to bop him over the head the next?

"If you say so." He turned his attention to Millicent across the table from them. "I'm looking forward to seeing the photos you shot."

"Thank you. I should have made a set for each of you,

but I only developed one. I suppose you two will have to decide who gets what. I don't imagine your editors will want to publish the same ones anyway."

Elizabeth hadn't thought about it until now, but Millicent was right. "I'm sure you took enough that it won't be a problem."

"I hope so."

As some of the others began scooting their chairs out from the table, John said, "It appears dinner is over. Let's go see what you have."

"I'll run upstairs and get them," Millicent said.

"We'll be in the little parlor," Elizabeth said. "Come on back when you come down." She scooted her own chair out and stood before John had a chance to help her. If he thought he was going to get the best pictures, he was wrong. She might write fluff, but she knew what was needed to appeal to the women who read the *Delineator* and she was going to make sure she got it.

John and Elizabeth followed Kathleen and Luke to the back parlor and took seats around the small table. John pulled up an extra one for Millicent. They'd barely settled in their seats before she joined them.

She took a seat John pulled up for her and spread the photographs out on the table.

"Oh, Millicent, these are very good," John said.

They were very good. She'd caught shots that Elizabeth couldn't remember her taking. But John's high praise of her work when all he'd allow Elizabeth of her articles was that they were *nice* ruffled her feathers. And that it did annoyed her most of all. Not about to let on how she felt, she added her praise to the others.

"I can't see any way our editors aren't going to want to feature some of these photos."

John already had a grasp on several and Elizabeth decided right then and there that he wasn't going to take just any he wanted. She quickly picked several up and began to go through them.

"Hey, I haven't seen those yet," John said.

"And I didn't get a chance to look at the ones you're holding. I'll choose from these and you choose from those and we'll split up the rest."

"Oh, my, I hope I didn't whip up trouble when I asked for you both to do articles. I—"

"You haven't provoked anything, Kathleen," Luke said.

"I hope I haven't, either," Millicent added.

Elizabeth sighed. "You haven't stirred up anything, ladies."

"Elizabeth is right. I shouldn't have grabbed so many before she had a chance to look at them. I'm sorry."

Oh, now he'd made her look really bad-tempered. Well, maybe not. She seemed to have done that on her own and there was nothing to do now but apologize. "I'm sorry if I sounded miffed. Want to start over, John?"

He laid the photos on the table. "That's a good idea. But I will ask for this one, unless you have a real need for it."

The photo he held up was one Millicent had taken as they were walking up the stairs. It showed a broken stair rail and somehow included a shot of the broken window on the next floor and was a good example of the deplorable condition of the whole building.

"As long as I get the next pick."

"Thank you." John motioned to the photos. "You choose next."

She moved the photos around until she saw the one she especially wanted, the one she'd asked Millicent to take. She caught her breath as she looked at it. Not only had Millicent caught the rat in the pile of trash, there were eyes peeking out from the rubble. A whole family of rats probably lived there. She shuddered. "You are very talented, Millicent. I'll take this one."

John raised an eyebrow and grinned. "Perhaps I should have given you first choice."

Elizabeth smiled and shook her head. "I'd have chosen the same one. Your turn now."

From then on they played nice and each had a good selection of photographs to show their editors.

"I think you'll be hanging a sign out on your own business before too long, Millicent," Elizabeth said. "These are all very good and they show exactly what I hoped they would. Thank you."

"Thank you and John for allowing me to shoot these. I'm glad to be able to help garner attention to these places. Surely something will be done."

"That's what we're hoping for."

"Are we done for now?" John asked.

Elizabeth nodded. "I suppose so. I'll let you know which ones my editor wants to use, Millicent. I have no doubt that he'll want several."

"Thank you, Elizabeth. I guess I'll go join the others in the parlor. Sounds like they're having a sing-along."

The sound of piano music drifted down the hall. "It does sound like that," Luke said. "Want to join them, Kathleen?"

"I'd love to." She turned back to Elizabeth. "You coming?"

"Not tonight. I think I'll go up and take some notes on what I saw today and what Millicent's photographs have brought to mind. I'll see you all in the morning."

"What about you, John?" Luke asked.

"No, I think I'll go down and put the finishing touches on my article. Thank you for suggesting this, Kathleen. I think this may get me promoted one of these days."

And that's what it was all about for him. Making a name for himself, getting it splashed on the front page of the *Tribune*. Elizabeth headed out the door, photos in hand. If she wasn't so frustrated with him, she might feel sorry for him.

John felt unsettled as he went back to his room. He wasn't in the mood to sing around a piano tonight. He'd upset Elizabeth and felt bad about it. She had a right to be angry with him for grabbing the photos before she'd had a chance to look at them. But even though he'd apologized and she'd seemed to accept it, he could tell she still wasn't happy when she went upstairs.

And that wasn't like Elizabeth at all. She was usually the most even-tempered of all the boarders, so much so that he sometimes liked to "get a rise" out of her as Ben had put it the other day. Her hazel eyes would flash almost gold and her face would flush a lovely shade of pink that went clear to her light blond hairline.

But the last few days had been different—she'd seemed out of sorts ever since their collision the other day. He knew she'd been irritated about the last-minute summons to her aunt's; maybe there were family problems he knew nothing about. There was more he *didn't* know about Elizabeth than what he *did,* after all.

And it did him no good to surmise what might be wrong. As the fiasco with Melody had shown him, his instincts where women were concerned seemed to always be wrong and weren't to be trusted.

Instead of working on his article, he took a seat in the easy chair Mrs. Heaton had added to each of the men's rooms and leaned back his head. *Melody.* He didn't think of her often anymore, only as a memory to remind him that he never wanted to put his heart on the line again.

He'd thought he had it made down in Natchez, Mississippi. He was lead reporter of the *Natchez Daily,* and the owner's daughter had begun to flirt with him, asking him to go on a picnic with her and even inviting him to dinner on occasion. John had begun to believe he had a real chance with her and had actually dreamed of the family they might have one day, if he ever got up enough nerve to ask her to marry him. But then his dreams crashed around him.

A young new reporter was hired at the paper and began flirting with Melody. When John questioned her about it, she told John he was imagining things and not to worry, he was the one she cared about. But when John caught the two kissing in a darkened hallway, a fight ensued. Evidently the kiss wasn't all one-sided because Melody took up for the other man and blamed John for the fight.

Her father believed her, of course, and fired John then and there. Realizing that a terribly spoiled Melody had only led him on—whether out of boredom or cruelty, he didn't know—but feeling he'd been made a fool, he caught a train to take him as far away as he could get the very next morning.

From then on he decided never to fall prey to a woman's wiles again—and particularly wealthy young women who gave no thought to others' feelings. He might get lonely from time to time, but his heart was whole now and he intended to keep it that way, even if there were times when he longed for more.

He had a good life and couldn't complain. He enjoyed the family atmosphere living at Heaton House gave him and things at the paper were looking up. With his editor interested in a series of stories, he felt certain he was on the verge of getting the byline that would name him one of the best reporters in the city. And right now, that was all that really mattered.

Chapter Four

Normally Elizabeth would have stayed down and enjoyed the company of the other boarders, but she was still aggravated with John and didn't feel up to faking a good mood.

She went upstairs wondering why she was letting John get under her skin so much lately. Normally she was able to throw off her irritation at him, and sometimes even enjoyed the usually good-natured sparing back and forth between them.

As she readied for bed, she wondered why things seemed to be changing. In the past few months, since they'd started working together to bring attention to the needs in the tenements and their first articles had received good attention, the spark of friendly competition that had always existed between them seemed to be settling down. Until tonight, when it was obvious that John was intent on getting the photographs *he* wanted before she had a chance to look at them. She hoped this working together, as Kathleen wanted them to, wasn't going to turn that spark of competition into a flame.

She couldn't let that happen. It would affect all the

others at Heaton House, almost forcing them to choose sides, and she couldn't do that to them or Mrs. Heaton.

She felt even worse about her attitude in front of Kathleen, Millicent and Luke. She tied her wrap tight around her waist and sat down at her writing desk. She pulled her Bible close and held it to her chest as she whispered, "Dear Lord, please forgive me for acting the way I have today. Please help me not to get so irritated at John—and please help me to control my words and actions when I do. I don't know what it is about him that gets such a rise out of me, but please help me to laugh things off and not get so upset with him. I do want him to succeed at the *Tribune*. I want him to become a lead reporter. I just wish he weren't so…full of himself so often."

She sighed and shook her head as she continued praying. "I'm sorry, Lord. There I go being judgmental of him. Please forgive me. I don't want to be that way about anyone. I don't want to be irritated at him. I don't think he means to hurt my feelings or insult my work. At least I hope not. Please help me not to take his remarks so seriously, and not to show my temper when I do. Thank you for all my many blessings. Please help me to write these articles in such a way that they can help and, that in all I do, I bring glory to Your name. In Jesus's name, Amen."

She took a cleansing breath, pulled her notepad toward her and began looking over the photos Millicent had taken. Ideas on each photo began to bubble up and she wrote notes on each of them. She wanted to get the story to her editor as soon as possible in the coming week. John's article would be sure to come out first— the *Tribune* was a daily paper after all. But it was a good thing, because when the *Delineator* came out on the first of the month, her article would serve to reinforce the need for action on the part of the city to do something about the neglect. Together, their staggered articles could help, and that was what she concentrated on as she mulled over where she wanted to start and what she wanted to get across to her readers. And in such a way that it wouldn't be considered *fluff* by John.

John had worked into the night and was nearly late for church the next morning. He slipped into the pew next to Elizabeth just as the congregation started singing the first hymn and breathed a sigh of relief when she smiled at him and offered to share her hymnal.

She looked lovely, her blond hair piled up under a feathered hat that brought out the green in her hazel eyes. At least she didn't seem upset with him anymore and for that he thanked the Lord. She actually looked more relaxed than she had since she was summoned to her aunt's.

He wasn't sure why it bothered him so much when she was upset, but it did. He wanted to help but usually ended up being part of the problem when he said or did something stupid. He might as well face it. He was awkward around women. Didn't know what to say half the time. Maybe it was because he hadn't had a mother's influence growing up. At least that was what he told himself most of the time. Truth was, most of the time, his instincts where women were involved seemed nonexistent—or at the very least—wrong.

The sermon that morning was one on forgiveness and not judging each other. He prayed that Elizabeth had forgiven him for his selfish action of scooping up the photos he wanted before she had a chance to look at them the night before.

Deep down he wished he wasn't so quick to put himself first in situations and tried to tell himself that it was only because he'd been on his own too long and was used to looking out for himself. Without anyone to encourage him, to stand up for him—to just be there for him—at least until he came to Heaton House. He'd made real friends here, and yet he'd been let down so many times, he was a bit leery of trusting that those friendships were lifetime ones—no matter how much he wanted them to be.

He stood with the others for the final hymn and closing prayer, getting a whiff of Elizabeth's perfume as she stood beside him.

As the group filed out into the aisle, Elizabeth smiled at him again. "I thought you weren't going to make it this morning when I didn't see you at breakfast."

"I thought the same thing when I realized I hadn't set my alarm clock and was late waking up."

They met up with the others at the bottom of the steps and everyone began the walk back to Heaton House. He and Elizabeth fell into step behind Luke and Kathleen with Mrs. Heaton and her family taking the lead.

"Did you get much done on your article last night?" John asked.

"Actually I did get more done than I thought I would."

"Good. I'm about finished with mine. I wondered… do you think we might have better luck in talking to some of the landlords of the places Kathleen tells us about if we visited them during the week? Do you think your boss would let you do that?"

She seemed a bit surprised as she looked up at him.

Maybe she didn't want to work with him anymore after his photo grab the night before. "I promise, I'll let you get first choice of the next batch of pictures."

She smiled then and the tightness in his chest relaxed.

"I'll keep you to that promise, John. And I'm sure I can go during the week. I think you're right. We might have a better chance of getting information from some landlords during the week—at least they should be around. We can try it anyway. What day and time did you have in mind?"

He shrugged. "How about tomorrow just after lunchtime? In fact, I'll treat you to lunch and we can go from there. Surely we can catch a landlord in the early afternoon."

"Tomorrow should be fine. Where do you want to meet?"

"I'll come to your building and we'll go from there."

"Okay. I'll meet you in the foyer at noon."

That'd actually been easier than he thought it would be after last night. He had a feeling Elizabeth wasn't thrilled to be working with him, and there were times he felt the same way. But Kathleen expected them to do so and neither of them had much choice in the matter. Might as well make it as pleasant as possible.

They arrived at Heaton House to the smell of roast chicken, one of John's favorite meals. He loved Sunday dinner at Mrs. Heaton's. She often had her son, Michael, and his wife, Violet, over, and now with her daughter, Rebecca, and granddaughter, Jenny, added to the mix, John felt he and the other boarders were part of a large, loving family.

Everyone hurried to wash up, take off their hats and

in no time at all they'd gathered in the parlor in anticipation of Mrs. Heaton's announcement that dinner was ready.

Two more leaves and four more chairs had been added to the long table for the company. Michael and Violet sat adjacent to Mrs. Heaton on her left and Rebecca and her daughter sat across from them, leaving it easy for the boarders to figure out where their regular seats were. John pulled out Elizabeth's chair for her and slid it in before taking his own beside her.

"Will you say the blessing, Michael?" Mrs. Heaton asked.

"I'll be glad to, Mother. Please bow with me, everyone."

John bowed his head as his friend began.

"Dear Lord, we thank You for this day and for the people gathered around this table. We ask You to guide us to live each day in the way You would have us do and we ask You to bless this food. It's in Jesus's name we pray, Amen."

Several "Amens" were added from around the table before the clink of silverware against china competed with mingled conversation. John smiled and settled back to enjoy his favorite meal.

As Maida and Gretchen, twin sisters who worked for Mrs. Heaton, began serving, John's mouth began to water. Besides the roast chicken, there were mashed potatoes and two kinds of gravies, creamed onions and peas, carrots and crusty rolls—all favorites of his. It seemed everything served at Heaton House had become a favorite of his.

Elizabeth nudged his arm and nodded toward Jenny,

who was thoroughly enjoying her mashed potatoes. "Looks like everyone has a favorite tonight."

John grinned. The little girl had added another level of family feel to Heaton House. "She is enjoying herself, isn't she?"

He took the basket of rolls she handed to him and placed one on his plate before handing it off to Matthew Sterling, one of the newer boarders. He was a builder helping to put up one of the tallest buildings in the city.

"Thank you, John."

"You're welcome. How is work going on your building?"

He grinned. "It's getting taller every day."

"I don't know how you work up that high," Millicent said from across the table. "The very thought makes me queasy."

"Oh, I love it. The view is worth it. You can see the whole city from up there."

"I'd love to take photos from up there," Millicent said.

Matthew shook his head. "It's much too dangerous for women up there."

"Maybe you can go up in the elevator once it's finished, Millicent," Elizabeth said.

"I don't think it would be quite the same as getting shots with it in this stage," Millicent said.

"It wouldn't," Matt said.

John wondered if Matt was trying to irritate Millicent on purpose and then realized he often tried to get a rise out of Elizabeth in the same way. He hoped he didn't sound quite as sharp as Matt did. What was it about a woman that made a man want to ruffle her feathers? Maybe Matt didn't understand women any better than John did. Maybe it wasn't just him after all.

For now, he set about enjoying his meal and the conversations going on around him. Elizabeth and Kathleen were talking about wedding plans and he could hear Ben asking Rebecca if she was looking forward to living at Heaton House.

"I am. It will be good to get settled, although we've loved staying with Michael and Violet. However…" She broke off and looked at her brother.

As if planned, Michael stood and clinked his goblet with a spoon.

The table quickly quieted. "If I can have your attention, I have an announcement to make."

"Oh? What is it, son?" Mrs. Heaton asked.

Michael looked down at his wife and grasped the hand she held out to him. "Violet and I have an extra surprise for you. We're going to start a family. Our baby is due around Christmas."

Mrs. Heaton was on her feet in a flash as everyone clapped and congratulated Michael and Violet. With tears in her eyes, she hugged her daughter-in-law and son. "Oh, Michael, Violet, that is wonderful news."

"I almost gave it away, didn't I? I was about to say you'd have a full house soon," Rebecca said, a huge smile on her face. She leaned over and gave Jenny a hug. "You'll have a little cousin to play with before long, Jenny!"

Jenny clapped her hands as if she knew what her mother was talking about and Mrs. Heaton wiped her eyes and headed back to her seat to hug Rebecca and Jenny. "How blessed I am to be getting two grandchildren in less than a year. I don't know what to say except thank You, Lord."

The joy on her face had John clearing his throat as several of the women wiped their eyes. John wished he could excuse himself. All of this emotion was something he wasn't comfortable with. He was happy for everyone, especially Mrs. Heaton. She deserved all the happiness she was experiencing now. But the talk of weddings and starting families brought thoughts to mind he wanted to forget.

The next morning, Elizabeth watched her boss look over the photos she'd brought in and waited for his reaction to the ideas she'd told him about.

Mr. Dwyer laid the last photo on top of the others and looked over at her with a smile. "I'm very impressed with all this, Elizabeth. I like your ideas about doing a series of articles, too. In fact, I wish we were a daily publication so that we could get more information out about the condition of the tenements."

"I'm so glad you want a series. What about the photographs? Do you want to use any of them?"

"I do. I'd like to run a two-page spread, at least for this one. And I'd like you to continue to stress the need for the child-care homes in the city as you did in the first article we published about the tenements."

"I'll be more than happy to. I'll get the first draft to you this week."

Mr. Dwyer smiled. "I look forward to reading it."

For the rest of the morning, Elizabeth worked on the article and tried hard not to watch the clock. Excited as she was about her boss's response to her ideas, it was hard not to think about meeting John for lunch. She was ready and waiting for him in the foyer of the *Delineator*'s office building ten minutes early.

She looked at the clock just over the receptionist's desk. It was 11:55 a.m. now. John should be showing up anytime. Elizabeth still wasn't sure what to make of his suggestion that they go back to the tenements today. She was pretty sure he wasn't any happier about working with her than she was about working with him. At first. But now she couldn't deny that she was looking forward to spending more time with him, although she wasn't sure why. She'd like to do some more investigating, too, and at least this way, they would both have the same information to work with.

At exactly noon, John breezed through the doors and grinned when he spotted her.

"I knew you'd be ready. Out of all the women at Heaton House, you are the most punctual one."

"And you're right on time, too. I truly don't like to keep people waiting, but it was also taught to me that it was bad manners to do so from an early age."

"Well, I'm glad. Are you ready for lunch? I'm starving."

He crooked his arm for her to take and Elizabeth never thought much about it. He and the other men from Heaton House always did the same thing when escorting any of the women. It didn't mean anything. Only suddenly it had her remembering how it'd felt that day she'd barreled into him and he'd reached out to steady her in such a protective way. She gave a little shake to her head to clear her mind of the thought. "Where are we going?"

"There's a little café not far from here. I've eaten at it several times. It's got a good mix of men and women who come in to eat and I thought you might be more comfortable there than some of the places I usually eat lunch at. They mostly cater to reporters."

And obviously he didn't consider her a real reporter. Her stuff was fluff, after all. She felt her face begin to flush. "I see. And you don't think—"

"Elizabeth, don't even finish the thought." John stopped them in their tracks and turned her to look at him. "I didn't think either of us would want other reporters to overhear what we're working on. My boss is very enthused about doing a series of articles and, obviously, since you were able to meet me, your editor likes the idea, too."

Elizabeth felt a flush of embarrassment flood her cheeks. Why was it she always assumed he thought the worst of her? "You're right. Of course I don't want any other reporters overhearing us. And yes, Mr. Dwyer likes the idea very much. He even wishes we were a daily publication."

"That's wonderful. Did you bring your camera with you, by any chance?" John asked. "Just in case we need more pictures?"

"I did bring it. Mr. Dwyer wants to use the photos I brought in, so that will be some income for Millicent. He was quite complimentary about her talent. I thought you might have asked her to come along today, as well."

"She took so many good ones that I didn't think about needing any more right away. But I'm glad you brought your camera, just in case we run into anything we feel we need a photo of."

Elizabeth was glad she'd brought it, too. But she did feel bad that she hadn't made a point to ask if they should bring Millicent along, too—or that she hadn't mentioned it to the other girl on her own.

They took off again and walked the few blocks to the café John had in mind. It was busy this time of day, but they managed to find a table near the back of the room. A waitress hurried up to them, set water on their table and handed them a handwritten menu.

"The menu changes every day, but I've had most of what's here. The roast beef sandwiches are very good, if a little messy. And the turtle soup is great."

Elizabeth chose the soup and John decided on the sandwich. The waitress took their order and while they waited, John handed her a new address Kathleen had given him that morning.

"Maybe we can go to this one and the one we didn't get to the other day and see what we can find out. Kathleen says they are both in bad shape and the landlords are rarely there. Hopefully we can get some answers from the tenants without them being afraid of talking to us."

"I hope so. We need one or two who are willing to give us the truth about the conditions they're living in. I know it's not always easy for people to reveal what they know when they're afraid of the consequences if they are found out. But I don't know how we are going to be able to help any of them, if no one tells us who owns the buildings."

"We'll discover who does. It will just take longer if we don't get the information from someone on the premises. I'll have to go to city hall and do some research. It's long and tedious work and sometimes people have been paid to hide records. But we'll unearth the owner." John seemed determined and excited all at once.

"I hope so." She also hoped he'd share his findings with her. "I've never had to do that kind of research."

"And you don't have to now. I'll do it and let you know what I learn."

"Why, thank you, John."

"You sound surprised."

"Do I? I didn't mean to." Elizabeth breathed a sigh of relief that she was able to tell the truth, even though she did wonder if he really would share his findings with her. Then she felt bad for doubting that he would. He might not like working with her, and it might be his career he was thinking about, but he usually kept his word and she truly had no reason to doubt that he wouldn't do so now. "I imagine it's a lot of work."

John shrugged. "It can be. But sometimes the only way to find the truth is to dig for it and that's just part of a reporter's job."

Elizabeth's heart did a little twist as she once again regretted hiding her true identity from John and the other boarders. Was it time to tell them?

The waitress brought their order just then and Elizabeth was glad for the interruption. She wasn't ready to make that decision just yet. The thought of disappointing those she cared about was something she didn't want to face, but she knew the time was coming that she'd have to—just not today.

Chapter Five

John wondered at the look in Elizabeth's eyes just as the waitress brought their meal. Not for the first time, he had a feeling there was more to the woman sitting across from him than what he knew.

There was something about her that set her apart from everyone else, even as she was the same—working for a living and making a life for herself in this huge city.

But what about the aunt she visited so often? And what kind of life did Elizabeth live when she visited her? All he really knew about Elizabeth was what he saw at Heaton House. He did know that she was from Boston, but many young women from other places came to the city to work. That wasn't unusual.

"This turtle soup is delicious, John. Thanks for recommending it."

"I'm glad you like it."

She nodded. "It was a favorite of my mother's, too. I remember having it quite often before she passed away. Funny how some memories stay with you, isn't it?"

"It is. I don't have many of my mother, though. I

was only five when she passed. I don't remember special meals or anything like that. Just the warm feeling I have thinking about her reading to me, listening to my prayers and tucking me into bed at night."

"Oh, John, I'm so sorry you lost her so young."

"Thank you. There is a certain scent I connect with her, too"

"Oh? Some kind of toilet water? Lavender, maybe?"

He shook his head. "No. It's more like a combination of lilac and…now, don't laugh, but baking bread. Either one triggers what few memories I have."

The look in Elizabeth's eyes softened and she smiled, but she didn't laugh. "I love the scent of lilacs. We had several bushes around our house in Boston and Mother always filled vases with them in the spring."

"How old were you when your mother passed away?" John asked, and then regretted doing so as the expression in Elizabeth's eyes saddened.

"I was twelve."

"That had to be tough." He reached across the table and touched her hand. "I'm sorry. I didn't mean to bring up sad memories. I shouldn't have asked." As usual his timing was awful.

She pulled her hand back and shook her head. "No need to be sorry. I love remembering her. I just wished I had her longer, but you… I wish you'd had your mother longer, too."

It saddened John that they'd both suffered similar losses. At the same time, knowing that they'd both experienced the same kind of pain seemed to have created a bond of sorts—at least for him. Was it possible Elizabeth felt the same way?

* * *

By the time Elizabeth and John started back to Heaton House, they were both frustrated. Even on a Monday afternoon, the managers of both buildings they checked into were nowhere to be found and the tenants they were able to speak to didn't know who owned the buildings.

The conditions in both were every bit as bad—if not worse—than the building they saw on Saturday. Rickety staircases, no air ventilation, filth built up in the corners—one could see which tenants tried to keep their places clean—but there seemed to be no care of the area the landlord would be responsible for. Elizabeth took photos of it all, but was sure none of them would be the same quality of Millicent's.

When she mentioned as much to John, he shrugged. "It doesn't matter. I just realized we need to have proof of the condition of the buildings when we find the owners. If they don't do anything once they are notified, the city will need proof to go into action."

"That's true."

"I'm sure whatever you have will be fine. We just need to keep good records as to which buildings the photos come from, no matter who takes them."

"If you're going to do the research on who owns the buildings, I can at least keep a record of where the photos were taken."

John surprised her by agreeing readily. "Sounds like a good idea to me."

"I'm still having trouble with what some of the tenants told us about hardly ever seeing the managers except during the week the rent is due."

"I know. Even though they have apartments in the building, I wonder if they live somewhere else."

"Which means there is no one in charge, if a fire breaks out or something else awful happens," Elizabeth said, her heart heavy just thinking of the squalor the children lived in—playing in trash-filled streets, dark stairwells and hallways.

Her long sigh must have alerted John to her feelings as they got off the trolley and began walking down the clean streets of Gramercy Park. "I know. It's hard to accept that people have to live in those conditions."

"It's awful. It breaks my heart to see children trying to make the best of things."

"I don't think they know any better."

"To be born there and never leave— Oh, John! Hopefully our articles will do some good."

"I think they will."

"Oh, I do hope so." Seeing the surroundings so many lived in made her feel guilty for being born into a well-to-do family. She'd never had to worry about a roof over her head, much less the condition of it. Never had to worry about dust building up anywhere for that matter. And she'd never had to wonder about having enough to eat.

As they entered Heaton House and were greeted by the tantalizing aromas wafting in from the kitchen, tears sprung to Elizabeth's eyes remembering several children they'd seen who were much too thin. *Dear Lord, please help our articles serve to help those in the tenements. Please help us to find the owners of these buildings who have let them fall into such disrepair.*

"Are you all right, Elizabeth?" John asked, as she stood in the foyer, her head bowed.

"I'm fine. Just thinking how blessed we are to have Heaton House to come to at the end of a day."

He nodded. "Yes, we are. I—"

"Elizabeth and John, you're back. Did you find out anything about who owns the buildings?" Kathleen hurried down the stairs, eager expectation on her face.

"No," John said. "It seems that the landlords of the buildings of disrepair don't even want to live in them. The tenants see little to nothing of them unless they are collecting the rent. But don't worry. We're going to get to the bottom of it. We're going to find out who owns these buildings."

"I'm so glad I asked you two to help with this. I was getting more discouraged by the day. But I know that between all of us, we'll make a difference."

"I wish I had as much confidence in us as you do, Kathleen," Elizabeth replied.

Her friend put an arm around her shoulders. "I know it is difficult to see the bad conditions. But my family and I are proof that one doesn't have to live in the tenements forever. And we're going to do all we can to help those who can't leave right now have better living conditions while we help to show them they can get out, too."

"My admiration for you and Colleen grows each day, Kathleen," Elizabeth said. "And I'll do all I can to help."

"So will I," John added. "You've given us a challenge I don't think either of us will back down from."

"I'm glad to hear it. I know you'll both give it your best. Now let's go freshen up for that delicious dinner Mrs. Heaton has in store for us. And maybe we can get some wedding planning in this evening, if you have time, Elizabeth? I'd like to go over to Colleen's and get her input, too, if you don't mind."

"I'll make time, Kathleen. And I don't mind going to

Colleen's at all. I haven't seen her or those sweet nephews of yours in a while."

"Then that's what we'll do."

"And I'll leave all that planning to you two ladies. See you both at dinner." John grinned and took the staircase down to the ground floor while the two women headed up to their rooms.

Helping Kathleen plan her wedding sounded wonderfully refreshing after spending the afternoon in the tenements. And Elizabeth could think of no one she'd rather help right now than Kathleen.

As it was still light after dinner, Elizabeth and Kathleen took the short walk to Colleen's by themselves, with Luke promising to come get them if they weren't home before dark.

"Luke didn't seem too upset by not having your company tonight," Elizabeth said.

Kathleen chuckled. "Well, he has a new deadline and he wants to get his book edits finished before the wedding, so it should be a little easier to have a planning session now and again."

Luke made his living as a dime novelist, but because of Kathleen and what her family had endured in the tenements, he'd written a novel that he wanted to bring light to the problems there and at the same time give hope that others could make it out as Kathleen and her family had. It was to be on the shelves before Thanksgiving.

"I still can't believe we're getting married," Kathleen said. "I never thought I could be this much in love or this happy."

Elizabeth was truly happy for her friend, but she

was surprised by the sudden surge of longing to experience that kind of happiness for herself—even though she had no intention of letting herself fall in love again. She'd already experienced betrayal in her lifetime and she didn't intend to let it happen again.

"You deserve all the happiness you can get, Kathleen. You and Luke are perfect for each other." And they were. Neither of them could ever be accused of marrying for any reason other than love. But for Elizabeth—there was no real way to know if that was the case. It wasn't worth the heartache that came with finding out a man's interest was only in her wealth and not her.

"Thank you, Elizabeth. You deserve the same, you know. And it will happen one day. I'm sure of it."

Elizabeth only shrugged. She couldn't go into how she felt, as Kathleen didn't know who she really was—something that weighed on her mind more and more each day. This woman was her best friend. How would she feel if Elizabeth told her the truth? Would she feel betrayed?

"How is it working with John? I hope I haven't asked too much of you.… I know he can irritate you at times."

"So far it's okay. And it is for a good cause so we'll make it work."

"Thank you for agreeing to it, Elizabeth. I truly appreciate it."

"You're welcome. Now, let's talk about your wedding. Have you decided on the wedding dress you want?"

"I have narrowed it down to three. I wanted Colleen's opinion on them also. Violet has offered to make it for me, isn't that nice of her?"

"It is. She is a wonderful seamstress and I'm sure

Butterick is going to hate to lose her. Has she given notice, do you know?"

"I think so. But she's going to work a few more
months until they can find someone to replace her."

"Mrs. Heaton is thrilled. To have her daughter back
with a grandchild she didn't know she had, and a new
one on the way with Violet and Michael. I think I'm
happiest of all for her."

"So am I." Kathleen sighed. "I don't know what Colleen and I would have done without her help and yours
and the others at Heaton House."

"And it continues with you and Colleen. How is
she liking being in charge of a Ladies' Aide day-care
home?"

"She loves it. The boys love it. It's been a blessing
to be sure."

"And is Officer O'Malley still calling on her?"

"He is. After all she's been through it's hard for me
to believe she might trust another man with her heart,
but it appears she might be ready to."

Elizabeth wondered how she could, too—Colleen's
husband had tried to kill her after all! But she hoped she
would find happiness. "He seems to be a good man.".

"He does. And Luke says he'll treat her with care
and won't make a move until she's ready, but it won't
surprise me if he asks her to marry him soon."

All this talk of marriage and love had Elizabeth
wondering if she was going to make it through all the
wedding planning. It left her with conflicting feelings—
happy for her friends but longing for something she'd
never have. She'd have to get over it. She'd promised
Kathleen she'd help her in any way and she intended
to keep that promise, no matter how much it brought

long-buried dreams to life again. She sent up a silent prayer asking the Lord to give her peace about her future and she prayed to be able to concentrate on helping her friend.

But she was more than a little relieved to arrive at Colleen's. She'd let her boys stay up a little later so they could see their aunt Kathleen and their happiness at the change in their lives was contagious. So much so, that after they were put to bed and the women began their wedding planning, she found she could concentrate on Kathleen's happiness and trust hers to the Lord.

When Luke came to escort them home, Elizabeth was more than a little surprised to find John with him. She figured he was hard at work on a new article.

"Two escorts? What a pleasant surprise," Kathleen said, taking her fiancé's arm.

"It's such a nice night, we thought you two might like to stop at the Bailey's Soda Shop before going home," Luke said. "Sound good to you?"

"It does," Kathleen said.

"What about you, Elizabeth? Want to have a soda?" John asked. "You deserve one after this afternoon."

"Yes, I think I would."

"Good." He offered his arm to Elizabeth and she hesitated only a moment before taking it. She never used to think about taking his arm and wasn't sure why she did now, or why her pulse began to race when she did.

Luke and Kathleen had their heads close together, talking quietly as they took the lead.

"Wonder what those two are whispering about?" John leaned his head down and whispered in her ear, causing her pulse to speed up.

What was going on with her? This was John—a friend at most—and sometimes not. This was the man who thought her writing wasn't as important as his own. Who irritated her as often as he made her laugh. "Any number of things, I would imagine," she whispered back. "Did you get your article written?"

"Not all of it. I think we're going to do one a week to start with. Boss wants to see how it goes over. And since we have no names to investigate yet, that might be the best idea."

"I meant to give my film to Millicent and ask her to develop it for us. I'll ask her when we get back to Heaton House, or first thing in the morning."

"That will be fine. I'm sure she'll get to it as soon as she can."

"I just hope there's something worth developing in them." Elizabeth wasn't even going to pretend she was as good a photographer as Millicent.

"There will be."

She didn't know why he was being so…nice. Maybe, like her, he realized working together would be easier if they weren't always in competition with each other.

"What are you two whispering about back there?" Luke asked.

"Oh, this and that." John chuckled. "We just didn't want to disturb you two lovebirds' conversation."

Luke seemed to pull Kathleen a little closer and smiled down at her. "Nice of you to be so considerate."

They'd reached the crowded soda shop and were glad to find one empty table. "If it's this busy so early in the season, think what it's going to be like midsummer," John said, pulling out a chair for Elizabeth.

The men asked what they wanted and went to the counter to order.

"It was nice of the guys to think of this, wasn't it?" Kathleen asked, watching Luke and John make their way to the counter.

"It was."

"I'm glad John came along," Kathleen said.

Elizabeth wondered whose idea it was for him to come along. Not that it really mattered, but she thought it must have been Luke's.

"He doesn't always have a chance to do fun things— or hasn't up until lately. He's not covering the society doings as much as he used to, is he?" Kathleen asked.

"I don't think so." Which would be a good thing. Elizabeth always worried when she was with her aunt at one or another charity function that she might run into him and he'd find out who she really was. Although, lately she almost wished he would. It would force her to get things out in the open. If she weren't so afraid of losing the friendship of those closest to her, she would have made a point to try to run into him.

"Hopefully these articles he's doing about the tenements will help get him a better position at the *Tribune*."

"So do I." And she really did. She just didn't always like that it seemed to be all he thought about.

The men came back to the table just then and John set her chocolate soda down in front of her before taking his seat next to her. He'd bought the same for himself. Luke had bought a vanilla one for himself and a chocolate one for Kathleen.

As they all took the first sip from their straws, a collective sigh was heard around the table.

"Hmm, this is wonderful," Elizabeth said. "Thank you, Luke, for thinking of this."

"Actually it was John's idea," Luke said.

John shrugged. "I noticed it the other day and I've been thinking about it ever since. I'm glad you ladies agreed to come with us."

Lately the man never failed to surprise her. One minute he was focused only on work and the next he did something like this that made her wonder once again if there was more to him than she knew. And why was he just now showing that side?

John couldn't help but see the surprise on Elizabeth's face when she found out this outing was his idea. Why did she seem so surprised? Probably because he rarely found time to enjoy himself. Since coming to New York City, he'd been so busy trying to get to the same status he'd enjoyed in Natchez that he'd had little time to do anything else.

If he'd been able to give his editor as a reference, he more than likely wouldn't have had to start at what he considered the bottom. But he'd feared the man would have given him a bad reference and he wouldn't have found a job at all. At the time it'd seemed no reference was better than a bad one.

And maybe it hadn't all been for naught. At least he'd proved he was willing to cover anything—even the high society affairs of the city. He hated doing it, but he'd done his best at it and earned the respect of his superiors. Just today his boss had told him that he wouldn't have to write for the society page much longer. The new guy was getting the hang of it and John would soon be moving into a regular reporter's job.

From there it was up to him and his writing how far up he'd go. John was almost certain that the articles he'd be doing about the run-down buildings in the tenements would get his byline on the front page one day. That was the goal. But now that it was in sight, he wondered what he was doing sitting in an ice cream parlor with friends instead of back at Heaton House working on the next article.

But when Elizabeth got to the bottom of her soda and sipped the last bit through the straw, making an unladylike slurp, and then laughed at herself along with the others, he was very glad he was here and not hard at work.

Chapter Six

John's laugh was deep and rich and Elizabeth wished he did it more often. She didn't even mind being the cause of it.

But she couldn't resist saying, "Tickled your funny bone, did I?"

He chuckled and nodded. "I never thought to hear that sound coming from you."

She grinned. "I do love a good soda."

"Well, so do I." He took a last slurp of his soda as did Luke and Kathleen all at the same time and together the three of them managed to put hers to shame, causing much laughter at the surrounding tables.

The four of them were still laughing as they left the establishment. Elizabeth stumbled on an uneven patch in the sidewalk and John reached out to steady her, pulling her hand through his arm. It was a beautiful early summer evening, and she liked seeing lights on in the homes they passed on their way back to Gramercy Park and Heaton House.

"So, have you two decided where you'll live once you're married?" John asked.

"We've begun looking at a few places. It's going to be hard to leave Heaton House," Luke said.

"Yes, it will be. But we're not going to lose touch with everyone. We'll visit and have you all over," Kathleen said.

Somehow Elizabeth hadn't thought about them actually leaving Heaton House, and happy as she was for them, she hated the thought of not having Kathleen right next door to her. They'd become good friends from the very first and things wouldn't be the same with her gone.

She sighed deeply and John leaned his head near. "You're going to miss Kathleen, aren't you?"

"I am."

"I wonder who will take their places?"

"I don't know." Elizabeth didn't even want to think about it. She'd been close to Violet when she came and then she'd married Michael. But she considered Kathleen one of her dearest friends and she couldn't see anyone taking her place. It'd be lonely without her there.

"We've considered another boardinghouse that takes couples, but I think we'd like to have our own place," Luke said. "But it won't be far from Heaton House. It's been home to both of us and we hope to be asked to Sunday dinner once in a while."

"Oh, I'm sure you will be. Mrs. Heaton considers us all her family," Elizabeth suddenly felt better just saying the words. Even with her own daughter back in the fold, Mrs. Heaton cared about each and every one of her boarders. She'd be heartbroken if she didn't keep in touch with them.

There was no need to be anything but happy for Kathleen and Luke. Kathleen would still be her dearest friend and she'd see a lot of her, one way or another. No need to get all maudlin about her leaving.

"We do need to decide on something, soon, though. It's not all that long until the wedding, you know," Kathleen said. "And, well, I've never had to decorate a home of my own before. Elizabeth, you will help me with that, won't you? Luke keeps telling me I can fix it up the way I want, but—"

"You'll do fine," Elizabeth hurried to assure her. "But I will be glad to help you in any way I can."

"Good," Luke and Kathleen said at the same time and laughed at their timing.

"I don't want to be dragged from store to store," Luke said.

"I can understand that," John said.

"I truly will be happy with anything Kathleen chooses. Thank you for offering to help her, Elizabeth."

"Looks like we're going to be busy from here to your wedding, and after, Kathleen," Elizabeth said.

"Will you still have time to work on the tenement articles?" John asked.

"Oh, of course she will. I want her working on those," Kathleen said. "I'm not going to take all her time, John. Don't worry about that."

Elizabeth wasn't sure if he worried about her part or not, but she wanted him to know she wasn't going to back out. "Kathleen's right, John. There's no need to worry. I will manage things so I have time to work with you."

"Good. I'm glad to hear it."

John's words managed to surprise her. One minute she thought he wished he were working on his own and the next she thought he might not mind so much that they were working together. The man could make her laugh one minute and make her steam the next, but most of all, John had just confused her to no end.

The next evening, just as dinner was getting underway, Elizabeth was called to the telephone to find her aunt on the other end.

"Elizabeth, dear, I wanted to remind you about the Barclays' masquerade party for charity this coming Friday."

"Masquerade party?"

"Yes, dear. Remember, they want me to be the speaker and you promised to come with me and help take up the collections?"

Oh, yes, it had been in the planning for months, but Elizabeth had totally forgotten about it.

Normally Elizabeth was happy to help her aunt, but with how busy she was with the articles, she hated to take time off. Still, she had agreed. And besides, this was the aunt who had always been there for her and made the way easier with Papa. She couldn't try to get out of it.

"Of course, Aunt Bea. What time do I need to be there?"

"You can come here straight after work. I'll have your costume ready and waiting for you. I found a lovely one and I can't wait for you to see it. You'll stay the night, of course."

"Of course. But I need to be back here fairly early. We're all going on a picnic to Central Park."

"I'll make sure you get up early, then. I look forward to seeing you, dear."

"I look forward to seeing you, too, Aunt Bea." Elizabeth hung up the receiver and released a sigh. At least it was a masquerade party. She had no way of knowing if any reporters would be invited, but assumed they would. And it was possible that John could still be assigned to something like this. But she was becoming quite nervous about running into him. She'd seen him at several balls and functions her aunt insisted she attend. She'd always assumed that she could use working for the *Delineator* as an excuse to be there. And she did almost always write an article for the magazine. But if she were ever introduced as her aunt's niece in his hearing, she was afraid he'd unravel her secret.

If she knew he wouldn't think badly of her, she'd almost be encouraged to make it happen. She was so very tired of keeping who she really was a secret. Perhaps she should have sought the Lord's guidance before she decided to go by her mother's maiden name. In the darkened alcove, she bowed her head and silently prayed.

Dear Lord, please forgive me for not always seeking Your guidance. I went out on my own and made a decision without coming to You about it. And now, I'm living with the consequences of worrying if my friends will hate me once they know I've not been totally truthful with them since I came to Heaton House. I am so afraid they will feel betrayed in some way.… But I know the time is coming when I must tell them. Please let me know when the time is right and give me the right words to say. In Jesus's name, Amen.

She brushed a tear that ran down her cheek and took a deep breath. She needed to join the others or Mrs. Heaton would send someone after her.

She hurried to the dining room and slid into her chair beside John.

"Everything all right?" he asked quietly.

"Yes, of course. It was my aunt wanting me to come stay with her on Friday evening."

"But what about the picnic on Saturday?" Mrs. Heaton asked. "You will still be able to make it, won't you?"

"Yes, I'll be back in plenty of time. I wouldn't miss it."

"Good," Mrs. Heaton said.

"I've got to cover a society thing that night," John said. "I hope it isn't too late getting over with. But I'm looking forward to the picnic, too."

Elizabeth caught her breath. Was he covering the Barclay party she was going to? Oh, please, no. And she couldn't ask. Oh, she hoped her aunt had a good mask for her to wear.

"I'm glad everyone will be able to make it," Mrs. Heaton said. "Millicent has agreed to take pictures of all of us, but we'll need to get someone to take some that include her, too."

"That shouldn't be a problem," Millicent said. "There are always people around that are willing to take a few photos."

"That's true. But I want to hire you to take some family photos of me, Michael and Violet, and Rebecca and Jenny."

"Oh, Mrs. Heaton, I'll do that for free. After all, Michael has loaned me a room to develop in and I—" She clapped her hand over her mouth. "I totally forgot that I brought home the photos you took when you and John were out on Monday, Elizabeth! I'll go get them right now!"

She started to jump up, but Elizabeth waved her back to her chair. "No, don't worry about it, Millicent. You can get them after dinner. We can't do anything with them right now anyway. Sit back down and enjoy your meal."

"You got some really good shots," Millicent said.

"I know they aren't as good as yours, but hopefully they'll work to be able to prove what we saw," Elizabeth said.

"You're going to keep track of all that, right, Elizabeth?" John asked.

"I am." She'd already told him she would. Did he not trust her? "Unless you want to do it."

"No. I have— I'm glad you offered to."

Was he going to say he had enough to do? There was no way to know and Elizabeth told herself to quit being so suspicious of everything that came out of his mouth. What was wrong with her anyway? "It's the least I could do with you doing so much of the research."

"What is it you are going to research?" Luke asked.

"I'm going down to city hall to see if I can find out who owns some of these buildings as no one we've talked to so far seems to know."

"Maybe Michael could help in some way," Mrs. Heaton suggested.

"Oh, believe me, I've already talked to him and he's willing to. I just need to get some names for us to go on."

"I'm sure you all will find them out sooner or later," Kathleen encouraged them.

The front door opened just then and Julia breezed in, looking flushed and excited.

"I'm so sorry I'm late for dinner, Mrs. Heaton." She slipped into her chair across the table.

"Don't worry about it, dear. We kept a plate warm for you."

As if on cue, Gretchen came through from the kitchen and set a plate down in front of Julia.

"Oh, thank you. I think I may be too excited to eat, though."

"Why? What's happened, Julia?" Mrs. Heaton asked.

Her eyes fairly sparkled and Elizabeth leaned forward, as eager to hear what her friend was about to say as everyone else.

"Well, I-I'm sure you've noticed that I've received some correspondence from Oklahoma Territory."

It wasn't hard to notice something like that. All their mail was put on a table in the foyer and although it was sorted to each person, one could sometimes see the return address of the top letters.

"Well, as I sort them, I must admit to knowing. I didn't want to appear nosy by asking about them, though."

"Well, considering my news, I probably should have told you about them before now."

Everyone around the table grew quiet, waiting for Julia's news.

"Well, please do tell us what you are so excited about, dear," Mrs. Heaton said.

"Well, seeing so many come through Ellis Island, I've been inspired and have been thinking about going out West. There are a lot of opportunities in the territory. And well, when I mentioned as much to my superior at work today, I was offered a promotion to stay here."

"Why, that's wonderful news, Julia—if you are going to stay," Elizabeth said.

"Yes, it is," Millicent added. "But I imagine it will make it more difficult for you to leave. What are you going to do?"

"For now, I'm going to stay here. I'll have a raise in pay and that will allow me to save more money for when I decide where exactly I want to go."

"And give us some time to get used to the idea of you leaving," Mrs. Heaton said. "I'd hate to see you go, but I can understand wanting to head out West. I have a cousin who did just that years ago."

"Where did she go, Mrs. Heaton?" Elizabeth was surprised at the small twinge of envy she felt. Here she thought she was independent, but to move away from all that was familiar—

"She was part of the Oklahoma Land Run and settled out there."

"Oh, my. That is exciting. To be in on settling a new area. I don't think I'm quite that brave," Elizabeth said. "If I were, I might tag right along with Julia when she goes."

John didn't like the sound of Elizabeth's words. Surely she wouldn't up and take off for the Wild West!

"You wouldn't really, would you?" he whispered as everyone began to give Julia suggestions on where she might want to go.

She shook her head. "I'm not that brave. Besides, Heaton House is home to me. I can't imagine taking off and leaving everyone."

The odd tightness in John's chest lightened a bit. "I'm glad. I'm sure there is a lot happening out West, but it can't compare to what goes on in this city."

"I don't think so, either."

"I haven't heard from my cousin in a while," Mrs. Heaton was saying. "Perhaps I should write her and see how she likes it there and find out what it is like for you, Julia. It might be a place you'd like to go and you'd have at least one contact."

"That would be nice of you, Mrs. Heaton. I'd love to find out more. But I'm happy to be staying here for a while longer and thrilled that this promotion will make it possible for me to go out West one of these days. It gives me time to plan. So, please do write your cousin. I'm excited to see what she says about it all."

Talk around the table turned to places everyone had been. Luke had actually been all the way to Arizona and New Mexico and was planning on taking Kathleen out there to see it at some point.

By the time the meal ended, John had almost begun to think he'd like to go just to see what it was like one day. Almost. But with his career about to take of, he wasn't going anywhere.

He slid out Elizabeth's chair from the table and she stood. "Thank you, John. Do you want to see the photos Millicent developed?"

"I do."

"I'll run up and get them," Millicent said. "I'll be right back."

"Meet us in the back parlor, okay?"

The other girl gave a little nod as she hurried out of the room.

"Do you want to see more photos of what we looked at on Monday, Kathleen?"

"Of course."

She and Luke followed Elizabeth and him to the small back parlor but before any of them could take a seat, Millicent was back with a packet she handed to Elizabeth. "I'm going back to the big parlor—Julia is playing the piano and I don't want to miss that. See you all later."

She scurried out of the room fast as she could.

"I think we must have scared her away last time." Elizabeth looked sad as she took a seat at the table.

"It was my fault," John said. "I am sorry for that night."

Elizabeth took the seat he held out for her and rewarded him with a smile. "I am, too. I wasn't on my best behavior."

Luke chuckled as he pulled out a chair for Kathleen and took his seat. "You two almost scared me that evening. Play nice this time."

"We will," John said. "They are your photographs, Elizabeth. You take the first look."

She opened the packet and pulled out the photos. She'd taken more than John realized. She began to look at them and then handed him several and he, in turn, handed them to Kathleen, who handed them to Luke.

"These are quite good, Elizabeth. This is the second building we looked at on Monday, right?" The photo he held up was of a staircase missing several spindles, leaving an opening where a small child could easily fall through. And it also showed the dirt built up on the staircase and more cracked windows.

"It is. And thank you. They are better than I thought they were."

"They easily show what condition the buildings are in."

"I'll be sure to get them recorded as to which building they were of and the date the photos were taken."

Elizabeth was quite pleased with how they turned out. They weren't quite as good as Millicent's but they'd do the job. "If you want any, John, feel free to take them. You'll have articles out before I do"

"Thank you, Elizabeth. I would like this one and this one…and this one. Unless you want them."

They were the first two of children playing in the streets or sitting on the stoops. She'd taken several of them, so she'd have others to work with. She shook her head. "No, that's fine. I can use some of the others."

"Why, you two can get along after all, can't you?" Luke teased.

John glanced at Elizabeth and smiled. "We can."

"And we do," Elizabeth added. "Most of the time anyway."

They all laughed and headed toward the parlor. Julia was playing one of their favorites, "The Sidewalks of New York," and they joined the others around the piano to sing along.

John stood right behind Elizabeth and enjoyed the sound of her sweet alto and the way it blended with his tenor. The scent of whatever it was she washed her hair with wafted up as she swayed back and forth to the music. He should be working, but he'd do it later.

It was nice to spend an evening like this with friends. And it was one of the reasons he enjoyed living at Heaton House. These people were family to him. He'd miss Luke and Kathleen when they moved away, and Julia, too, for that matter. He counted on seeing the couple even after they moved out, but still things would be different. He wondered what boarders might take their place, but he knew Mrs. Heaton was selective in whom she rented to—only once or twice had she rented to someone who didn't get along with the others.

The group sang several other songs before breaking up and heading to their rooms.

"Thanks for the photos, Elizabeth."

"You're welcome."

"I'm going down to city hall tomorrow to see what I can find out about these buildings. I hope it doesn't take too long, but some of the guys have told me it could take weeks to find the current owners. I'll let you know how it's going."

"Thank you, John."

His chest suddenly tightened at the smile she gave him. "You're welcome. Good night."

"Good night."

He watched as she went upstairs with the other women. Working with her really hadn't been bad at all. In fact, he'd come to enjoy it. Perhaps too much for his own good.

Chapter Seven

Between matching the photos to the buildings they were taken from and helping Kathleen with her wedding plans, the week passed swiftly and it was Friday before Elizabeth knew it.

She headed straight to her aunt's apartment from work, hoping the evening would pass as fast as the week had. She would much have preferred spending the evening visiting with her aunt than going to a masquerade party. But it was for charity and she'd be able to go on the next day's outing with the others.

Amanda let her in and led her to her aunt's study where she had a pot of tea waiting.

"Elizabeth, dear, I'm so glad to see you," her aunt exclaimed, jumping up and coming to give her a hug. "Come have a spot of tea and then we'll have a bite to eat before we must get ready for this evening."

She led Elizabeth into the parlor and quickly poured her a cup.

"Thank you, Aunt Bea. It's good to see you, too." She took a seat on one end of the sofa, knowing her aunt would take the other.

"You'll love the costume I picked up for you. And I remembered to get a mask large enough to cover your beautiful face." At that she grimaced. "I wish you weren't so determined to hide at these kind of things."

"I've told you, Aunt Bea. One of the reporters that sometimes covers these events lives at Heaton House, and while I am regretting my decision to use Mother's maiden name instead of Papa's, I don't particularly want to be found out in the middle of a charity event."

And she didn't want it to be John who discovered she was Elizabeth Anderson Reynolds, heiress to the Charles Edward Reynolds of Boston, and not just Elizabeth Anderson.

"I do understand, dear. I wish I'd tried to talk you out of that idea at the time. But I didn't, so part of the blame must lie on my shoulders as well as yours."

"No, Aunt Bea, the blame rests with me. Everyone is so sweet at Heaton House, even had I let them know who I really was, I'm sure they would have accepted me sooner or later. But for them to find out now…" She shook her head.

"I'm sure they will still accept you, Elizabeth. If you've come to care for them, I'm sure they feel the same for you."

Tears sprung to Elizabeth's eyes and she jumped up and went to look out the window. "And that means they might feel I've betrayed their trust in me. Oh, Aunt Bea, aside from you and Papa, they are like family to me and I so hate to disappoint them."

"Elizabeth, dear, come sit back down."

Elizabeth did as asked and her aunt reached out to give her a hug. "I can see you're distressed. And I do think the only way you're going to get past it is to tell them."

Elizabeth released a large sigh and nodded. "I know. But I don't know when or how."

"Mrs. Heaton and her son know and—"

"But they knew from the first. And they won't tell anyone else. They wouldn't feel it was their place to."

"And it isn't. It's your place. But the timing should be the Lord's. He will let you know when the time is right, and give you the words to say to your friends. He knows your heart and His timing will be perfect. Just trust in Him."

Elizabeth nodded. "I do, Aunt Bea." And she did. She prayed each night that the Lord would guide her in what to do. She didn't for a minute think that He wanted her to keep her true identity secret, but she wasn't sure how to handle it all. So she would trust that He would let her know when and how and whom to tell first.

Until then she'd have to live with the consequences of keeping her secret. There were always consequences to not being totally truthful. Elizabeth wished she'd thought about them and asked the Lord to guide her before she—

"Supper is served, ma'am," Amanda announced.

"Come along, Elizabeth. Cook has prepared something light to hold us until later. Then I can't wait for you to see your costume. I think you're going to love it."

All Elizabeth cared about was that the mask would cover enough of her face that John wouldn't be able to tell it was her if he were there.

John dreaded these things with all that was in him. Masquerade parties were his absolute least favorite kind of event to cover, especially as he had to go in costume, too. The *Tribune* paid for the rental—otherwise he would not have accepted the assignment.

Tonight he was dressed as a steamboat captain and he had to admit he felt at home in the attire, in spite of the odd looks he garnered on the trolley. It brought back memories of steamboat trips between Natchez and New Orleans back when his dreams were down South and before—

The trolley came to a stop and jarred him out of his reverie.

It was his stop and he stepped off into one of the wealthier neighborhoods of the city, not far off Fifth Avenue. As he turned the corner and found the street he needed, he wished he'd taken a hack. At least it would have let him off at the doorstep and he wouldn't have had to endure so many curious stares. But as John got closer to the residence and he encountered others dressed in costume all headed in the same direction, he breathed a sigh of relief. He'd be sure to get a ride back to Heaton house.

He'd reluctantly brought a mask along and donned it just as he reached the Barclay mansion, but he would take it off later so that those who wanted to get their names in the paper would know him and seek him out instead of him having to guess whom it was he was talking to.

He showed the *Tribune*'s invitation to the butler and after the man had assured himself it was indeed genuine, he was given the nod to go on in. Most of the people there were familiar with him and the fact that he wrote for the society column. They would welcome him with more warmth than the butler had.

Of course, he realized that if it weren't for the fact that he was with the *Tribune,* they'd never give him a second of their time. To his way of thinking, there wasn't much difference between the very wealthy in the South where he'd been raised and those here in the North.

He moved with the others toward the ballroom, looking in the other rooms as they passed each one. Mrs. Heaton's home was decorated beautifully, with very nice furnishings, but this was another level altogether and one he wasn't comfortable in at all.

The ornate trim work, huge wall murals and lavish furnishings made him glad he was in costume. He didn't belong in this kind of setting and he'd be glad when the new guy got these assignments.

He made his way into the ballroom, which was already at near capacity. There were all manner of costumes, and with masks on many, it took him a while to spot the people he usually saw at this kind of event. Many of them would be leaving to go to their summer homes for the season before long. They did occasionally come back into the city for a special occasion, but for the most part they'd stay gone until late summer, early fall. He couldn't blame them. It could get awfully hot in the city and many of them had summer homes on the water where it'd be much cooler.

John turned and spotted whom he thought were the Astors on the other side of the room and… He took a second glance. There was a young woman dressed as a flower girl who caught his attention and when she looked his way, their glances collided and John had a feeling he'd met her before, even as her face was covered with a mask. There was something about her eyes.

He started her way, but she turned just then and went in another direction. In only a matter of seconds, he'd lost her in the crowd.

He shrugged. He'd probably seen her at any number of these events in the past few years. She could be the daughter of one of these couples.

He took his mask off and turned again and was surprised to see Mr. And Mrs. Barclay come up to him. They did not wear masks and it was a relief to be able to know whom he was talking to.

"Mr. Talbot, it is you, isn't it?"

"Yes, sir, it is."

"How good to see you here," Mr. Barclay said. "I read your article about the tenements in this morning's paper and thought it so excellent!"

"Why thank you, sir. I'm hoping to do more articles in the future."

"I'm sure you will. And I look forward to reading them. Something must be done about the conditions of those buildings."

"You did a wonderful job on your article about the Ladies' Aide child-care homes, too," Mrs. Barclay said. "We hope we'll get a good write-up on our party to raise money for them tonight."

"I'll do my best, Mrs. Barclay."

"I know you will. You've been covering the efforts to help in an admirable way. You go on and mingle around. We'll look forward to reading your next article."

"Thank you, ma'am." John inclined his head as the two walked off to greet other guests. They'd mentioned his article about the tenements. If he could get the people in this room to follow them, it could go a long way in furthering his career.

He smiled as he made his way around the room, hearing bits and pieces of conversation—sounded mostly like gossip to him—until the Barclays moved to a stage that had been set up and began to address their guests.

"Ladies and gentlemen, we want to get this party under way for the reason it was called. As you all know the Ladies' Aide Society is in need of donations to open more child-care homes in the city. These are helping those living in the tenements, giving the children a safe place to stay while their parents work to make a living and try to better themselves and their families," Mr. Barclay said.

He moved back and let his wife speak. "To explain more about it, we've asked Mrs. Beatrice Watson to speak about how these homes are making a difference."

A woman John had seen at several other charity events made her way to them and looked out onto the crowd.

"On the behalf of the Ladies' Aide Society, I thank you all for turning out for this event."

She spoke more, but John was familiar with the speech and he looked around the room, trying to see who he could recognize. Most had masks on, but some didn't. He'd be able to describe the costumes of many and do an overall article about the event—at least well enough to satisfy his editor and the Barclays. And maybe he could get out of there early enough to get his article written before he went to bed.

"And now, ladies and gentlemen, we have several young ladies who will be accepting your donations." Mrs. Watson had wasted no time getting to the reason for the party.

John turned to see her point out the young woman

on her right. It was the same one he'd thought familiar earlier. She looked out around the room and her gaze met his once more. Those eyes, even from this distance, made him surer than ever that he knew her or at the very least had met her before. But with that mask covering most of her face, there was no way to tell who she was, especially from a distance. He began to move a little closer to her through the crowd.

"Our Miss Flower Girl and—" she pointed to the young woman to her left "—Marie Antoinette will be mingling among you this evening. Please empty those pockets for our good cause."

With that, the flower girl broke eye contact with him and the two young women smiled, stepped into the crowd on opposite sides of the room, and began to mingle. The flower girl was on the other side of the room from John and he headed in that direction to see if he could recognize her voice as she spoke to the people giving donations. But each time he got close, she turned to another person trying to get her attention, or someone wanting to make sure their name got in the paper stopped him.

By the time they were called in for a late supper, he'd lost sight of her once again. After taking a quick glance around to see if he could spot the flower girl, he gave up trying to find her and decided to forgo the late supper. He'd eaten a good meal at Heaton House before he came and he'd spotted enough of those in society who would expect to see their names connected to giving to the cause of the Ladies' Aide Society. All he had to do now was get his article written and put the flower girl out of his mind. Surely, if he knew her, she would have come up to him, wouldn't she?

Elizabeth breathed a sigh of relief when she opened the door to Heaton House the next morning—even as she prayed that John hadn't recognized her from the night before. She'd caught him heading her way several times that evening, and it was only through quick thinking on her part and him getting stopped at the most opportune time that she'd managed to stay several steps ahead of him all evening. He'd certainly looked the part of a riverboat captain, tall and broad-shouldered, and very handsome. His broad-brimmed hat shadowed his face, giving him a slightly dangerous look, like a hero in one of Luke's dime novels. When she'd first noticed him looking at her, it'd taken her breath away.

And while she knew she needed to let her secret out, she hadn't wanted it to be in a public place and not before she knew what to say.

Surely he couldn't have recognized her from any distance—not with the full-face mask she'd made sure never to take off. Now she braced herself as she entered the dining room to join the others for breakfast.

"Elizabeth, you made it back and in plenty of time for our outing, too!" Kathleen exclaimed on her entrance.

Elizabeth smiled and took a quick glance in John's direction. The look he shot her made her pulse speed up. He seemed happy to see her, and with no hint that he'd recognized her the night before. She turned and expelled a huge sigh of relief as she took a plate from the sideboard and began to fill it. "My aunt likes to sleep in on Saturday, so I told her goodbye at bedtime and set my alarm. I didn't want to bother her cook for breakfast, but I'm glad I made it back in time to join you all."

"Did you have a nice visit with your aunt?" John asked as she slipped into the seat he'd gotten up to pull out for her.

"I did." Still no indication that he'd recognized her in any way the evening before. *Thank You, Lord.* "We had a very nice time catching up with each other. How was your evening?"

"Much the same as always at those kind of things. I think there was a good turnout, as usual and, Mrs. Heaton, you'll be glad to know that I heard they took in a great deal to help the Ladies' Aide Society with the child-care homes."

"That is wonderful news," Mrs. Heaton said from the head of the table. "We'll be able to open up another one very soon. The ones we have now are at capacity, as Kathleen knows. I think Colleen has all they can handle now."

"Oh, they'd take in more, if they needed to, Mrs. Heaton," Kathleen said. "But I'm glad that there are more in the planning stages and that people are still willing to help."

John leaned toward Elizabeth. "I think we can feel glad about that. It appears our articles have helped garner attention."

So, much as he hated covering the social scene, he'd decided to use it for something he did care about. And he did seem genuinely happy that the event had been a success. John seemed to be thinking of more than his career lately. Or maybe he always had and she hadn't noticed. And why was she noticing so much about him now?

"I'm trying to emphasize that the need for more homes still exists in the article I've written about the affair last night."

"I think that's a wonderful idea, John."

"So do I," Mrs. Heaton and Kathleen both said in unison.

"Thank you, ladies, I—"

"Granma!" Mrs. Heaton's granddaughter, Jenny, came rushing into the room, followed by her mother, Rebecca. "Did we get here in time for breakfast?"

"You did! Are you hungry?"

"I am! Mama said you'd have breakfast still, but I wasn't sure about that."

Mrs. Heaton pulled her granddaughter into her lap and kissed her on the cheek. "Jenny, love, even if we didn't have anything on the sideboard, I'd make sure you had breakfast."

"You would?"

"I would. It's what grandmothers do."

Elizabeth and John glanced at each other. Her heart went out to him and she wondered if he'd had a grandmother in his life. His mother died when he was so very young.

She couldn't remember either of her grandmothers. It'd been only her and her father, and of course Aunt Bea after her mother passed away. She swallowed hard, seeing Jenny cuddle up to her grandmother while her mother fixed her a plate. The look of love between the two was almost tangible. She was so glad the child had a grandmother in her life. She smiled across the table at Kathleen. Had it not been for her, the young girl might never have known she had a grandmother. But she did now, and what a blessing it was for them all.

Rebecca took her seat after fixing a plate of her own and her smile took in everyone at the table. "She barely slept a wink last night. It's not like she's never seen Central Park. I took her when I could. But she's so excited to be going with you all. She considers you part of her family now."

"Well, good. Because that's how we all feel about her," Ben said.

Tears sprung to Elizabeth's eyes. Jenny wasn't much different than anyone else around this table. Mrs. Heaton had somehow managed to make them all feel like family. Sort of. The exception might be the way she felt about John.

Lately there was something different about how Elizabeth felt about him, how her heart did a funny little twist and jump like it did last night when she saw him come into the room. Or how her pulse seemed to speed up when he smiled at her—like he was doing now. But she didn't want to analyze it right now and maybe not ever.

Feeling the color flood her cheeks, Elizabeth was glad when Michael and Violet arrived. Jenny looked up from the breakfast she was thoroughly enjoying and greeted them.

"Aunt Violet and Uncle Michael! Mama said you'd be going with us, but you weren't here and I didn't think you would come."

"We wouldn't miss a day at the park with you, Jenny!" her uncle said, giving her a kiss on the top of her head. The child exuded happiness—as did her mother, grandmother, aunt and uncle, although Rebecca was quieter about it all. There was a lot Elizabeth, and she assumed the others, didn't know about Rebecca.

Why she'd gone missing, what happened to her husband, and why she hadn't sought out her mother? But Elizabeth wasn't about to judge. Not when she had a secret of her own. Besides, it was none of her business. She was just glad the Heaton family had her back in their lives.

Chapter Eight

Soon as breakfast was over, the group hurried to get ready to go to Central Park while Mrs. Heaton went to the kitchen to make sure all the picnic food was ready. Colleen and her boys and Kathleen's sister and nephews arrived just as everyone was gathering downstairs.

The omnibus Mrs. Heaton had called for arrived right on time and they all piled in after making sure their lunch was onboard. The day was warm, but not too hot and it would be comfortable once they reached the park. The women had all chosen light skirts and shirtwaists; the men were in light-colored shirts, too.

John took a seat beside Elizabeth and began to roll his blue-and-white shirtsleeves up as he watched Kathleen's nephews, Collin and Brody, talking to Jenny. They were laughing and nodding and Jenny was giggling, her hand over her mouth. He couldn't help but wonder what they were talking about.

"I'm so happy Kathleen and her sister and the boys made it out of the tenements," Elizabeth said. "Look how happy they are now."

"It's a big change in them since the first time we saw

them, isn't it?" John finished rolling up his sleeves and turned to Elizabeth. "They don't have that heartbreakingly sad look anymore."

Elizabeth grinned. "No, they don't. Look how animated they are talking to Jenny. I think they like trying to impress her with their tales."

"It appears that way." John chuckled, seeing Collin spread his hands wide as he described something to the little girl. The young boy had her rapt attention. "Maybe I should take lessons from him."

"You, John? Is there someone you want to impress?"

She looked at him, her hazel eyes a shade greener than usual and the expression in them had his breath catching in his throat. Did she care? He gave a little shrug. "There might be. But I'm never sure what to say to women and my instincts where they are concerned are—"

"We're here!" Jenny exclaimed as the omnibus came to a stop at their favorite picnicking area. Everyone began gathering baskets and blankets and hurrying off the omnibus, leaving John to let out a huge sigh of relief that the conversation between he and Elizabeth had been put to a stop.

What was he thinking, confiding in her like that? He'd never told anyone what he'd just been about to tell her. Nor had he ever admitted—even to himself— that there was a woman he might want to impress. And while it surprised him that there was after the debacle with Melody, what really confused him was that the woman he'd most like to impress was the very one he had been speaking to. The one he knew deep down was way out of his league and only thought of him as a fellow boarder at Heaton House. Who didn't seem to want to work with him, just as he'd felt about her… until recently.

He felt a bit consternated by the revelation and fell quiet as they all began to spread out blankets and set the baskets of food under the shade of the trees to keep cool until they had lunch.

First up, the children wanted to fly the kites Luke had brought for them and John hurried to join him, Michael and Ben, in trying to get the bright-colored kites to sail up into the blue sky. He was glad of a reprieve from his thoughts.

The women cheered them all on until it was time to set out the picnic lunch. Then they called the men and children over to eat. As usual, Mrs. Heaton had provided quite a spread, with fried chicken, fresh bread and baked beans. There were two kinds of pies and John's favorite, a huge chocolate cake.

Once they fixed their plates, everyone spread out on the blankets and John found himself sitting by Elizabeth once again. There was something about the woman that he'd always been drawn to. She was one of the kindest and most caring of the women at Heaton House. Oh, they sparred from time to time—usually brought on by him putting his foot in his mouth—and mostly about their work. But she'd always been nice to him as she was with everyone else.

Still, he felt there was more to Elizabeth Anderson than any of them knew. He didn't know what it was about her that made him feel that way, but she had an air about her that made him think of the people he covered for the paper…high society. And yet, she worked for a living like the rest of the boarders. She never acted in any way superior to anyone and went out of her way to help anyone who needed a hand. Still, there was—

"The children had such a good time flying those kites." She looked over at him, her eyes now a muted green and brown under the shade of the tree. She looked very pretty in her pink-and-white-striped skirt and pink blouse.

"So did we men." He chuckled and looked at her from under the rim of his bowler. "I think one of the best parts of having children around is that we get to feel and act like kids again."

She gave a soft laugh and nodded. "You all looked as if you were having as much fun as they were. I love Central Park. Everyone in the city is able to enjoy it, including the poor. And remember? It's where we first met up with Kathleen and her family—although it wasn't under the best of circumstances with her awful brother-in-law threatening her and her sister. Luke had come to their aide and Mrs. Heaton had given Kathleen one of her cards in case she ever needed a place to stay."

"I remember."

But then her expression sobered as she glanced at the family group next to them. "Those children over there have the same haunted look in their eyes as some of those in the pictures I took in the tenements. They remind me of what Kathleen's nephews looked like when we first saw them."

He looked at the group and saw the children she was speaking about. She was right. John cleared his throat, seeing that heartrending look on their faces. One had to wonder what their home life was like. "I do hate that children have to live in such conditions as we've seen lately. That so many live in some of the buildings we've been into. It's more than a shame. It's a travesty."

"I know. I feel the same way," Elizabeth said. "I do hope the Ladies' Aide Society can keep opening child-care homes. Just think of how many families they will help!"

His gaze traveled over Elizabeth's face as she spoke with such feeling, finally settling on her full lips as she stopped speaking and smiled at him. His heart began to hammer against his chest as he wondered what it would be like to kiss her.

Elizabeth suddenly jumped to her feet. Her face seemed flushed as she asked, "Would you like a piece of cake? I'm going to get one for me."

"I… Yes, please."

He watched her hurry over to where the food was laid out and released a deep breath. Had she read his mind just then? She'd seemed to catch her breath as he'd looked at her. What would she have done had he leaned over at that moment and pressed his lips to hers? Would she have responded?

What was he thinking? It was broad daylight and they were in a public place! Besides, he wasn't her kind and he knew it deep down. Whatever it was he felt, he'd best keep reminding himself of that fact.

Elizabeth took several deep breaths, trying to calm her rapidly beating heart. What was wrong with her? It was just that the way he'd just looked at her had her thinking all manner of things and for a moment she'd thought he might kiss her.

Wishful thinking on her part? No! Surely not. She and John had been around each other for several years now and she'd never thought much about his personal life—well, not that much—and never in connection to herself.

For the most part, she'd excused his absences from dinner or outings she and the others went on because of work. And no one had ever mentioned anything about him seeing a woman or having any interest in any of the women at Heaton House. So what was the identity of the woman he might be interested in? And why did it upset her to think that there was one? For it had given her pause when he'd said there might be one earlier. And if he was interested in someone, why had he looked at her the way he had just now?

As if… She shook her head. She'd never thought about kissing John, at least not until now. And she had no business thinking about it at all. She couldn't become attracted to John Talbot, or any other man, for that matter. She could never trust that they wouldn't care more about her inheritance than her, just as Richard had.

But John didn't know about any of that. Didn't know she'd been engaged. Didn't know who she really was. Did he? No. He couldn't. But what would he think when he found out? Elizabeth took a deep breath and released it. She wasn't going to think about that now, either.

They were friends and that's all they'd ever be. That was all they ever *could* be. She never wanted to care that much about anyone again only to find out it wasn't her they were interested in, but the money. Suddenly she felt a little queasy.

She cut one large slice of cake instead of two and headed back over to where John was sitting. "Here you are." She handed him his cake, but didn't sit down. "I need to go speak to Kathleen."

He looked a little puzzled, but said only, "Oh? Well, thank you for getting the cake."

"You're welcome." She turned and walked off, suddenly feeling as if she were deserting him. Whatever was wrong with her? Just because she'd had a glimpse of a different John than the one she'd always thought of, the one who was only concerned about his future and what was good for him, didn't mean she had to go all mushy where he was concerned. She couldn't. She wouldn't.

Elizabeth managed to stay away from John for the rest of the afternoon, flitting from one group to another. Along with the other women, she watched the men play ball from under the shade trees while the children napped.

Then Mrs. Heaton and Violet, who was feeling sleepy herself, offered to watch the children while the rest of the women went for a stroll or canoeing.

"I'll stay, too, Mother," Rebecca said. "It feels nice here in the shade."

Elizabeth, Kathleen, Colleen, Millicent and Julia all decided they didn't have the energy to go rowing and decided to stroll in the gardens for a bit, making sure not to go too far.

"It is a beautiful day," Millicent said as they walked along a path filled with rosebushes. "Let me take a photo of you all."

"We need you in here, too," Elizabeth said. "Let's get someone to take one of all of us."

They quickly found a young man willing to let Millicent instruct him on how to use her camera and he took several shots of the women. With little effort, they persuaded him to come back to the picnic area and take photos of the whole group so that Millicent could be included.

When they got back it was to find that the men had given up their game to help the children try out their kites again. But everyone quickly gathered under the tree while the young man took several photos of the whole group. Mrs. Heaton updated group photos for Heaton House when new people came in and Millicent and Matt were the newest boarders.

Elizabeth found herself next to Millicent and in front of John as they all scrambled together for the photo shoot.

"Move in a little closer," the young man said, trying to get them all in the shot.

Everyone pressed together and Elizabeth found herself so close to John she couldn't tell if it was her heart or his she felt pounding. Could it be both? She tried to concentrate on smiling for the photo and hoped it didn't show how flustered she felt.

But once the young man got the shots they wanted and was rewarded with the last slice of cake, Millicent took over and snapped photos of Mrs. Heaton and her family.

Seeing them all together—Mrs. Heaton, Michael, Violet, Rebecca and Jenny—and noting the joy on their faces that they were finally together again brought a tear to Elizabeth's eyes and she quickly hurried over to help the other women repack the picnic items and fold up the quilts they'd used. Millicent continued to snap first one and then another photo of everyone while they were gathering things up. And right before they left, she took photos of Kathleen's family—her soon-to-be husband, sister and nephews. To see their happiness, too, brought a sudden longing along with fresh tears to Elizabeth's eyes and she raised a hand to brush them away.

"You all right?" John asked from behind her.

Surprised, Elizabeth turned too quickly and lost her balance. John reached out to steady her.

"I'm sorry. I didn't mean to startle you. I just saw you wipe your eyes and—"

"I'm fine." Or would be if she could get her racing pulse to slow down. "I was just moved, seeing the Heaton family reunited, and Kathleen and her family so joyful after all they've been through."

John nodded, but still held her upper arms. "It had the same effect on me."

She nodded and pulled away from his gentle hold. She wasn't used to this John. The one that seemed to really care. She looked up at him and could see flecks of gold in his blue-green eyes, but it was the expression in them that had her feeling all fluttery on the inside. This had to stop. She took a step back. "I'm fine," she repeated.

The blue in his eyes deepened and for a moment his expression had her wanting to step back into his arms.

"The omnibus is here to pick us up," Mrs. Heaton called. John turned and took hold of a couple of baskets and headed out toward the omnibus. Elizabeth fell into step beside Millicent and Julia, but her heart felt heavy when she got on the bus and saw that John was sitting on the other side between Ben and Luke. Was he upset with her?

Mrs. Heaton asked Colleen and her boys, along with her own children, back to Heaton House for supper, but they declined.

"Jenny is worn out, Mama," Rebecca said, looking

down at the child leaning against her. "We'll pass this time."

"So are Collin and Brody," Colleen added. "I don't think they'll have any trouble sleeping tonight. Thank you so much for asking us to share your day."

"It was our pleasure," Mrs. Heaton said. They stopped to let Colleen and her boys off at their home, then the rest of the Heatons at Michael and Violet's, and then they headed back to Heaton House. It'd been a long, tiring day by the time they arrived and the aroma wafting in from the kitchen reminded them all it'd been a while since they'd eaten.

They all hurried to freshen up, but Kathleen stopped her in the hall when they came out of their rooms to head back downstairs. "You were awfully quiet on the way home. I saw you and John together before we boarded the bus, but then you didn't sit together on the way home. Are you upset with him?"

Was she? She had no reason to be. He'd been nice and considerate of her all day. "No, of course not. I think that's just how it happened. He got on the bus before I did."

"Oh, I see," Kathleen said with a dubious look.

"Did we look angry?" Elizabeth answered.

"No." Kathleen shrugged and grinned. "I'm reading things into nothing, as Luke says I do sometimes. I just wanted to make sure everything was all right between the two of you."

They continued downstairs, but Elizabeth wondered what had brought on Kathleen's question. Maybe Kathleen was trying to play matchmaker? She was so happy with Luke, maybe she wanted everyone else to be in love, too.

Well, that wasn't going to happen. Elizabeth had no intentions of falling in love with anyone. Not again. She wasn't going to put herself through all that pain ever again.

John tried to shrug off his bad mood as he shaved before heading up to dinner. He had no real reason to be upset, but he had the feeling that Elizabeth was trying to distance herself from him this afternoon and he didn't know why. He didn't think he'd said anything to upset her. But he supposed it was possible that he had. Of course it was possible.

And yet, she'd been fine while they'd picnicked together, even being very complimentary of his plan to incorporate the child-care homes in his articles about the tenements. For a moment there he'd even thought… He paused, razor in hand. He'd thought about kissing her. Had to catch himself before he'd bent his head and done just that. And now he thought about it, that was when she began to be standoffish.

He slowly wiped off his shaving cream. Had Elizabeth known what he was thinking? It was about that time she'd jumped up to go get more cake and then she'd spent the rest of the afternoon with the women. But there was nothing odd about that. He'd spent his time with the men.

He slapped bay rum on his face before putting on a fresh shirt and collar. But she'd still seemed distant when he'd walked up and surprised her. And what was he doing trying to figure Elizabeth out? He'd never been able to figure any woman out.

John looked in the mirror and sighed. His thoughts went back to the moment he'd realized he had wanted to kiss her. Still did, for that matter. He was more than a little attracted to her. There was no denying it. But he wasn't going to do anything about it. His track record with women had proven one thing to him and that was never to give his heart to another. And he couldn't let the attraction he felt for Elizabeth grow or he'd be in danger of doing just that.

But he wasn't willing to give up the friendship they'd managed to form—not if he didn't have to. He'd never confided in many people in his lifetime and today— well, he'd found himself wanting to open up to Elizabeth in a way he'd never opened up to anyone else.

He headed back upstairs wondering if it was possible to have Elizabeth's friendship and keep from falling in love with her. *Dear Lord, please let that be possible.* He'd have to keep his distance. Not let himself think about her in any way other than as a fellow boarder and friend.

He arrived upstairs just as Mrs. Heaton was calling everyone to the table. He pulled out Elizabeth's chair for her, slid it toward the table as he always did—nothing more than using his manners at the dinner table. No one could think he was being any more than gentlemanly.

He slid into his seat beside her and as she turned to him, he caught the scent of her hair as he had that afternoon, which made him remember wanting to kiss her and—

Who was he kidding about only thinking of her as a friend? Something had changed today and if he wasn't careful everyone at this table would realize it.

Chapter Nine

Over the next week, Elizabeth and John's relationship seemed near normal. Maybe that was because they were both busy with their jobs and Elizabeth and Kathleen had spent several evenings at Violet and Michael's having fittings for Kathleen's wedding dress. Still, she hadn't been completely able to keep her heart from giving a little jump start when he came into a room and smiled at her. Then she'd wonder if he had meant to kiss her that day in the park. Wondered what it would have been like if he had.

It also helped that it was baseball season and the men had taken to going to the New York Giants games when they were in town. This Saturday, they were playing the Brooklyn Bridegrooms at the Polo Field while she, Kathleen and Mrs. Heaton went to Violet's. Michael had gone to the game with them, so it was a women-only gathering and it seemed to be a relief to the others, as well. Living in a boardinghouse with both men and women boarders was wonderful—but occasionally made it difficult to have a talk-fest for any length of time. The men never liked it much when they tried to.

They were upstairs in a room Violet called her sewing room, but that for the time being also doubled as a small sitting room. "I am so glad that the men had something they wanted to do today," Violet said, slipping a pin into what would be a shoulder seam of Kathleen's dress. "Michael has been hovering over me ever since we found out I was expecting."

"He loves you, dear," Mrs. Heaton said.

"Oh, I know, Mother Heaton. And I'm so very blessed that he is the kind of man he is, but at times he can be a bit overprotective." Violet smiled. "Of course, that comes from protecting me in the past, but still—"

"I know that feeling." Kathleen laughed and lifted an arm as Violet pinned the bodice in place. "Luke is worse now about my having to go into the tenements for my work than he was at the beginning."

Elizabeth's heart seemed to do a little twist in her chest. Was she envious of her friends? At one time she'd dreamed of having a man love her like the men in their lives loved them. And at one time, she'd thought it possible. She'd looked forward to her wedding just as Kathleen was doing now.

Oh, she'd been upset with her father for making a match for her, but she'd eventually fallen for Richard on her own. Only to later find out she'd been right to be leery of any matchmaking at all. Richard had set out to get control of her money while being in love with another woman. What an actor he'd been! She'd found out at their engagement party, when she caught him and the other woman in a very compromising position.

Her dreams had come crashing down around her that night. And while she was thankful she'd found out what kind of man Richard really was before they'd said their vows, she was horribly disillusioned by it all. So much so that she still felt there wasn't a man out there she could, or would, trust with her heart. No matter what her heart seemed to want when she thought of John.

"You are both very blessed," Rebecca said. "Not all men are like my brother and Luke."

Elizabeth didn't know what Rebecca had gone through, but she had a feeling the woman had also been deeply hurt in the past. "You're right, Rebecca. Men that good don't come along all that often."

"I pray you both find men like Michael and Luke," Mrs. Heaton said. "There still are a few good ones out there, some even living at Heaton House."

She was right. John and Ben seemed to be good men. So did Matt, although he hadn't been there that long. But how could one be sure? Really, truly sure? She didn't think it was possible after what she'd gone through. But that didn't keep her from thinking about John and wondering how the game was going and if he and the others were having a good time. Was he thinking about—

Violet's maid came into the room with a tea tray laden with treats and Elizabeth welcomed the intrusion into her thoughts.

"Will you pour, Mother Heaton?" Violet asked.

"I'd be glad to. Too bad you've already put Jenny down for a nap, Rebecca, dear. She does like tea."

Her daughter chuckled. "Yes, she does, Mama. But she also needs her sleep or she turns into a very grouchy little girl."

"I understand." Her mother smiled over at her. "She takes after you a bit and brings me so many good memories of when you were young."

"Are you saying I was a grumpy child, Mama?" Rebecca raised an eyebrow and grinned at her mother.

"From time to time, but not very often." Mrs. Heaton handed her daughter a cup of tea. "And you've always liked tea. Another trait she picked up from you and one I totally approve of."

"Well, the way this little one has begun to kick, I think it's going to be a rowdy little boy." Violet smoothed a hand over her growing middle and smiled.

Elizabeth could tell that she would be happy no matter if she had a girl or boy. She glowed with happiness. So did Kathleen for that matter. She sighed inwardly as she took a cup of tea from Mrs. Heaton. What would it be like to be looking forward to marrying the man you loved and then to start a family with him?

Violet stood back and looked at the gown she'd pinned on Kathleen. "I think that's it for today."

"It's beautiful, Violet," Elizabeth said. "You are going to be a lovely bride, Kathleen."

"Only with the help of all of you. I could never have afforded to buy a dress like this and I can't thank you enough for making it for me, Violet."

"We're all loving helping out, Kathleen. And what good is a talent the Lord gives us if we can't use it to help someone?"

"Still, thank you."

"You're welcome. Now, let's get you out of this gown so we can dive into these treats. I'm starving as usual. Michael tells me it's because I'm eating for two and I certainly hope he's right and that it stops once I have the baby."

She helped Kathleen slip out of the gown, from behind a screen she'd set up in the corner, then hung it up while Kathleen changed back into her skirt and shirt-waist.

For the next half hour they talked and laughed, discussing the upcoming wedding, Rebecca's future move and the new member of the family that'd soon be there.

When it was time to leave, Violet called for a hack to pick them up—amid claims that they'd walk back to Heaton House.

"No, you won't. It's much too hot out there this time of day. You'll wilt."

Mrs. Heaton laughed. "Now, Violet, you know that none of us are wilting kind of women. We'll be fine."

"You're right, of course. Still, it is getting warm out and Michael would have a fit if he thought I let you all walk. No need to upset your son, Mother Heaton."

"Michael never gets upset with you, Violet. But we'll give in and take the ride. No need to upset the mother of my next grandchild." She kissed her daughter-in-law on the cheek.

By then the hack was there and the three women waved to Violet as it took off. Within minutes they were opening the door to a very quiet home. Elizabeth wondered if the men were back from their game. If so, she supposed everyone was getting ready for dinner.

Mrs. Heaton had already disappeared in the direction of the kitchen when the door opened once more and John, Luke and Ben entered. They seemed to be in excellent moods.

"Your team must have won today," Elizabeth said.

John grinned at her. "It did! The Giants beat those Bridegrooms six to three. It was nice to see them win."

Luke sidled up to Kathleen. "I kind of feel bad they

beat the Bridegrooms, seeing as how I'm going to be a real one in a few months."

"Oh, he's just trying to get on your good side, Kathleen," John said. "Those grooms beat us the last two games. He cheered as loud as we did at this game."

But the way Kathleen was looking at her fiancé, Elizabeth was certain her friend took no notice of John's teasing. She was also sure the two wouldn't mind a moment alone.

Even John seemed to get the message as the couple moved a few steps away and began speaking in low voices. He cleared his throat. "I guess I'll go down and freshen up for dinner. You coming, Ben?"

"I'm right behind you,' Ben said.

Elizabeth was already on the stairs leading to the second story. "See you in a bit."

Her heart gave another little twist even as she smiled. She did long for someone to love her the way Luke loved Kathleen. She couldn't lie to herself about that. But neither could she take that chance again. It hurt way too much to repeat.

She released a deep breath. So…she'd be happy for her friends and put her deepest dream to the back of her mind as she did quite often of late. Especially since John Talbot had begun to wiggle his way into those dreams.

John hurried downstairs to freshen up and change clothes. It was Saturday, after all, and while he was glad Mrs. Heaton didn't ask for them to dress for dinner during the week, he knew she liked them to on the weekends. Still, her version of dressing for dinner was a little more casual than others would have asked of them and for that he was thankful. It'd been a good afternoon spent with Luke, Michael and Ben. Matt had to work that day or he would most likely have been with them. He liked the friendship he and the other men in the house shared and enjoyed spending time together.

They'd all looked forward to returning home— especially Michael. He'd worried about Violet all afternoon. And Luke couldn't wait to get back to see Kathleen—that'd been obvious in the foyer. John had to tamp down a sudden rush of...jealousy? Envy? What was the right word? He was very happy that Michael and Violet, and Luke and Kathleen, had finally realized how much they cared about each other. He'd watched their relationship develop living here and he knew it wasn't really jealousy he felt. But perhaps it was envy that he didn't have a relationship like theirs.

And yet, he'd been the one to decide not to give his heart to another and he still stood by that decision. Still, there were times like now that he did long to have someone who cared for him the way Violet loved Michael and Kathleen loved Luke. His thoughts flashed to Elizabeth.

She'd looked quite fetching just now in a green-and-white dress, a small green hat with feathers atop her head that brought out the green in her hazel eyes. Truth be told, he'd thought of her off and on all afternoon. He was sure she'd enjoy watching a game of baseball. He'd have to ask if she'd like to go. Maybe the whole group would enjoy going to a game. If not a group then perhaps just he and Elizabeth.

What was he thinking? Spending more free time with Elizabeth wasn't a good idea. Yet he'd thought of little else all since the Saturday at the park when he'd nearly kissed her. And if he had? What would she have done? Kissed him back? Or slapped him? He couldn't imagine her kissing him back in the middle of the day with all their friends there to witness it. But he could certainly imagine kissing *her*.

He'd even dreamed about it. And on more than one occasion. Well, he'd always awakened just before his lips touched hers, but still, it was hard not to think about when it was also what you dreamed about.

John looked into the mirror as he parted his hair and combed it to the side. He tried to get his thoughts off Elizabeth. Tomorrow he had another article about the tenement coming out in the *Tribune*. His editor had been quite complimentary about it and he hoped it was received well by the readership. Mostly, he hoped it pleased Elizabeth. And there she was again. John put his collar on and shook his head before leaving his room.

He had to stop thinking so much about the woman. Because even if he let himself care deeply for her, she'd given no indication at all that she could care for him in the same way.

He heard the telephone ring as he walked down the hall to go back upstairs. His footsteps slowed when he heard Elizabeth's voice say, "Oh, Aunt Bea. He's not coming here so soon, is he?" There was a pause and then he heard, "I can't…but I—" A pause, a sigh and then, "You're right. It will be better than traveling there. Yes, ma'am. Yes. I love you, too. Good night."

He reached the top step as Elizabeth left the alcove under the second-floor staircase. She looked distracted.

Elizabeth looked up and only then did she see John. The expression in her eyes was stormy and her brows were knit together.

"Are you upset, Elizabeth?"

* * *

John. How much had he heard of her conversation
with her aunt? Enough to know it'd upset her. The concern in his eyes touched her and she managed a smile.

"No bad news, I hope?"

"Dinner is ready," Mrs. Heaton announced from the
foyer, saving her from answering. It wasn't horrible
news, but it wasn't good.

John offered his arm and she took it as they joined
the others coming from the parlor. She would be fine.
But right now she was totally frustrated. She couldn't
believe her father was coming to town over the Independence Day weekend and on top of spoiling all her plans
for the holiday, he was bringing that man he wanted
her to meet.

And yet, her aunt was right. It would save her from
having to go to Boston and it was only for a few days.
But still, over the holiday weekend? She slipped into
the chair John held out for her and said, "Thank you,"
as he pushed it closer to the table.

He took his own seat and leaned near and whispered,
"Are you all right? You look upset."

"I am. But thank you for your concern." She didn't
want to go into detail about the conversation right now.
And there was only so much she could tell if she wasn't
ready to explain who she was, who her father was and—

"John, would you say the blessing, please?"

"Certainly. Please pray with me." John bowed his
head and Elizabeth did the same.

"Dear Lord, we thank You for this day, for all our
many blessings. For Heaton House and Mrs. Heaton
who provides us with a true home. We ask that You be
with us in all our decision-making and we ask You to
bless this food. In Jesus's name, Amen."

Did he know how she was struggling with the decision to tell everyone here who she was? No, of course not. He couldn't know that. Still, she was thankful for the prayer—it reminded her to take her frustrations and struggles to the Lord and she'd sent up her own prayer along with John's.

As the dishes were being passed around the table, the discussion revolved around baseball, weddings and the upcoming holiday.

"It was a great day for a ball game. You ladies would have enjoyed it, too," Ben said.

"Not as much as seeing how my wedding dress is coming along," Kathleen said.

"And how is it coming along? Any chance we could move the wedding date up?" Luke asked.

"Now, Luke. Kathleen deserves the kind of wedding all little girls dream of and you said we could give her that," Mrs. Heaton reminded him.

"I did and you're right." He turned to look at Kathleen. "Still, I wish the days would pass faster."

John grinned at Elizabeth. "Those two are something, aren't they?"

Elizabeth glanced at the couple, love for each other so obvious one would have to be blind not to see it. "Yes, they're very much in love."

The platter of roast beef came his way and he held it for Elizabeth to help herself to it. "They are."

"Independence Day is two weeks from today. We need to start talking about what we want to do," Mrs. Heaton said. "Does anyone have plans already?"

"I may have to work that day," Julia said. "Several of my coworkers have asked for that weekend off."

"Oh, no," Millicent said. "Couldn't you ask for time off, too?"

Julia shrugged "They thought of it before I did. But I only work during the day, so if you all go to watch the fireworks, I can probably join you for that."

"I got to thinking that maybe going to Coney Island might not be that great an idea for that day," Ben said. "It's bound to be extra crowded. So maybe a picnic and then fireworks later?"

"I like that idea," Mrs. Heaton said. "I'm not sure I'll do the fireworks, but I'd love a picnic. I'll check with Michael, Violet and Rebecca."

"That idea sounds good to me." John turned to Elizabeth. "What about you?"

She sighed and shook her head. "It sounds wonderful to me. But I'm not going to be able to join everyone."

"Oh? Why not?"

Was he disappointed? The expression in his eyes seemed to say he might be.

"My aunt telephoned me earlier to let me know my father is coming to town, and of course they want me to come stay with them that weekend."

"Why, we'll miss you, Elizabeth, but I'm sure you'll have a nice time with your family," Mrs. Heaton said from the end of the table. "I imagine you're looking forward to it."

How did she say she was when she wasn't? "I might if my father wasn't trying to make a match for me. He's bringing someone he wants me to meet and he knows I don't want him to." She caught her breath. The words had tumbled out of her mouth before she knew it and now she had the attention of everyone at the table.

"Oh, my." Mrs. Heaton's brow furrowed.

"A match for you?" John raised an eyebrow. "Seriously?" He didn't look pleased at all, which gave Elizabeth some comfort.

"I didn't think that was done anymore—at least not in our circles—only among the rich, but even then I'm not sure it happens to everyone," Millicent said. "I certainly don't want my family trying to set me up with anyone."

"It used to be done in Ireland," Kathleen said, "but—"

"Don't worry, everyone," Elizabeth rushed to assure them. She'd already said too much, but perhaps it would be easier if she let out some of her past a little at a time instead of just dumping who she really was on them all at once. "My father still holds to old ideas in many ways. He was very against my coming to New York City, but has finally accepted it—with the help of my aunt. But he's been after me to come home so that I could meet this person and as my aunt said, 'Better to have him come here for only a weekend than spend a week or more there.'"

"Yes, yes. I can understand your agreeing to that. I just never realized…" Mrs. Heaton shook her head as her voice trailed off.

At least they all seemed sympathetic to her plight. John looked almost angry. Could she dare hope he cared?

John clenched his jaw to keep from speaking his mind, took a deep breath and forced himself to relax. He'd been looking forward to spending Independence Day with the group. And if he were truthful with himself, it was Elizabeth he'd been hoping to spend the day with—good idea or not. And now he had to admit he was disappointed.

Elizabeth did seem saddened she wouldn't be able to join them. And she seemed truly upset about the matchmaking business. No need to make her feel worse by asking the questions he wanted answers to.

Why would her father think he needed to make a match for her? Elizabeth was a beautiful, wonderful woman.

Was he broke and needing to bring money into the family or did he just want her married? She'd never talked about her life back home. Not many did, now that he thought about it. He hadn't talked about his past life, either, until lately. They both had shared that their mothers had passed away, but not much else. Still, that'd been a start. Perhaps one day she'd open up more.

"We'll miss you, Elizabeth, but I hope you have a good time." Kathleen brought his thoughts back to the present. "And who knows? Your father might bring you the man of your dreams."

John's chest tightened at those words. He didn't want Elizabeth to find the man of her dreams. *He* wanted to be the man of her dreams. John inhaled deeply. What was he thinking? He wasn't any woman's dream and he knew that from experience.

"I don't think so," Elizabeth said. "He's tried before and it didn't work out. And I'm not happy about him trying again."

Now she really had him curious. What had happened? Most probably she didn't want to talk about it any more than he wanted to talk about his romantic disappointments. At least she wasn't looking forward to meeting this man her father had in mind. But what if he turned out to be someone she thought attractive and what if—

John gave himself an inward shake. It wasn't any of his business anyway. He certainly had no claim on

Elizabeth and no right to voice his opinion, much as he might want to.

"And your father knows all of this?" Mrs. Heaton asked.

"He does, if only he listened to me on the subject. Please don't get me wrong," Elizabeth said. "I do love my father. But after my mother passed away, he seemed to—" She stopped and shook her head. "I'll not bother everyone with family differences of opinion. I'm sure many of you know what that is like."

"Oh, yes, I do," Millicent said. "I felt smothered back home."

"Times have certainly changed and are still changing since I was a young woman," Mrs. Heaton said. "Some things for the better and some not."

"Well, I hope you all have a wonderful time Independence Day. At least I'll be at my aunt's and it will be better than going home to Boston."

John had to agree with Elizabeth. It'd only be for a few days and then she would be back at Heaton House.

"Where is it your aunt lives?" Millicent asked.

"On the other side of the city," Elizabeth answered.

So. Even after opening up the way she had tonight, she still wasn't willing to give out her aunt's address. Nor should she feel she had to, he supposed. There were all kinds of reasons not to, but the more he found out about Elizabeth, the more he wanted to know. And the more certain he was that there was much more to her than any of them knew.

Chapter Ten

At breakfast the next morning, all the talk was centered on John's second article about the deplorable tenements. It wasn't on the front page of the *Tribune,* but was near there, and he thought he'd done a pretty good job with it. He'd tried to give a vivid picture of the tenements' conditions and several of the photos Millicent and Elizabeth had taken were included. He'd made a point to reinforce the need for more child-care homes by writing about the children, how they lived and the looks on some of their faces as they passed on the streets.

Elizabeth looked up from the paper. "This is the best article you've ever written, John. I know it's going to go over very well."

His chest seemed to expand at her words. "Thank you, Elizabeth. Your opinion means a lot to me." More than she'd ever know.

"Elizabeth is right," Luke said from across the table. "It's an excellent article and one that should get some response from the city leaders."

"I hope you're right, Luke."

"So do I," Mrs. Heaton said. "I know the Ladies'

Aide Society will be quite pleased with your article, John. I'm very proud of you."

John could feel the color flood his face at the compliments he was receiving, as if he were still a schoolboy. But the people in this house and especially Mrs. Heaton's good opinion warmed his heart. "Thank you. I hope my articles will result in the buildings being better taken care of and that they help bring in some good donations for more homes."

And he did. Of course, he truly hoped the articles would serve to advance his career, too. More and more he felt as if that was on the verge of happening. Would he finally feel he could get on with the rest of his life if it did?

"We'd better get going if we're going to make it to church this morning," Elizabeth reminded them, forcing thoughts he was better off not thinking to the background.

Everyone pushed back their chairs and the women hurried up to grab their Bibles, purses and hats.

John and the other men took their hats from the rack in the foyer. He picked up the Bible he'd brought up and had put on the side table before going in to breakfast, and waited along with the other men until the ladies returned.

It was a beautiful day out, not too warm for late June, so they decided to walk the few blocks to church. Still unsettled about the matchmaking business her father was up to, John fell into step with Elizabeth.

"We're going to miss you over Independence Day weekend."

"I'll miss everyone as well. But I should probably

be relieved that Papa decided to come here instead of insisting I go to Boston."

"Yes, well, that is a good thing." He certainly didn't want her gone any longer than necessary. But the woman worked for a living and was making her own way, why did her father seem to want to marry her off?

John took a deep breath. *Put yourself in his place, man. He has this lovely daughter living in this city, away from home—*

Perhaps Elizabeth's father just wanted someone to take care of her so that she didn't have to work. Maybe he was ill and wanted to make sure things were settled for her before anything happened to him. Or maybe he was just a cantankerous, controlling man.

"All I know is that I'll be glad for the weekend to get here and get over with."

He couldn't have said it better himself.

"I'd much rather—"

She stopped midsentence and he had a feeling she didn't want to be disloyal to her father by saying she'd rather spend the holiday with them. He could understand that.

"Perhaps we can all do something special next weekend—kind of an early celebration."

He was rewarded by a huge smile. "That would be wonderful, John."

"Maybe we could go to Coney Island. It won't be near as busy as it will be during the holiday weekend," Ben said from behind them.

John had forgotten his friend was there, hearing everything they said. "That might work. But I was thinking we could take in a ball game. The Giants are playing the Bridegrooms again. Then maybe we could go out to dinner that evening. What do you think, Elizabeth?"

"Either of those ideas sounds good to me," Elizabeth said. "Maybe we should put it to a vote and see what everyone else thinks when we get back to Heaton House."

John nodded. "We can do that." He'd go along with her suggestion—up to a point. It would be for her after all. She was always willing to go along with what everyone else wanted, but this time she should do the choosing. "Long as you let us know what it is you really want to do."

All Elizabeth really wanted to do was spend time with John, but she wasn't about to say so. Didn't want to admit it even to herself…except she just had. They reached the church and John lightly gripped her elbow as they entered and followed Luke and Kathleen down the aisle. Did he know his touch sent her pulse to racing? Oh, she hoped not.

Mrs. Heaton slipped into the pew to sit beside her children and grandchild. Luke and Kathleen took the pew behind, and Elizabeth and John took seats beside them. Millicent sat next to Elizabeth, and Matt sat down beside her, leaving Ben to take the last seat on the pew, motioning to them all to move a little nearer to one another to make room for him.

As Elizabeth's arm came into contact with John's, a current of electricity shot all the way to her fingertips. She jumped and caught her breath as she and John exchanged glances. Had he felt the same thing?

This new emotion she felt for John was different from anything she'd ever experienced. On one hand they were friends. Had been for several years now. But her reaction to his nearness wasn't what she felt for other male friends and it was totally different from how she'd felt about him several months ago. Elizabeth didn't know when, or why, things had changed, but there was no denying they had.

All she knew was she liked John more each day, liked being around him, loved his smile, especially when it was directed toward her. That smile of his could make her feel as if a thousand butterflies had been let loose in her stomach. And that's exactly what she had to fight against—liking him too much, and feeling more than friendship for him. She couldn't seem to control the racing pulse, or the shots of electricity, but she must fight her growing attraction and reactions to him. She'd vowed never to give her heart to another man and she meant to keep it.

As the service began and they stood for a song, Elizabeth took a deep breath and raised her voice to sing along with the others. She tried to force her attention away from the man next her and focus it on the Lord.

Mrs. Heaton's family joined them for Sunday dinner and their presence made the table feel complete. Violet had stayed in the room Kathleen was in now, before she and Michael married, and while she lived there, Elizabeth and Violet had become good friends. Elizabeth had missed her greatly until Kathleen had been brought to Heaton House. Now she'd have to go through all that again, once Kathleen and Luke married and moved out.

But she knew their friendship would remain and she'd still see them often. That was one of the blessings about living here. The family feel Mrs. Heaton had infused her home with.

After the blessing had been said, John brought up the ideas for the next Saturday. "Elizabeth suggested we take a vote, but since she won't be able to spend Independence Day with us, I thought we should just let her choose."

"That's right, she should get to choose," Kathleen agreed. "What is it to be, Elizabeth? Swimming or baseball?"

Elizabeth really didn't have a preference, although as warm as it'd been lately, getting in a swim did sound nice. But she could see how John and the other men's eyes lit up at the prospect of going to a ball game and sharing their knowledge of the game with the women.

"Well, I've never actually been to a baseball game before, so why don't we do that?"

She had to smile at the men's reaction, especially John's. His smile was huge as he leaned over and whispered, "Are you sure?"

"I am."

"Better now than later in the summer," Violet said. "The heat could get worse and it's not too bad right now. Besides, going swimming later will feel even better— although I won't be joining you for that. I could sit and watch your antics, however. That would be fun."

Elizabeth hadn't thought about how Violet wouldn't be able to swim in her condition. And sitting at a ball game might be uncomfortable, too. "Will the ball game be too much for you? If it will, we could—"

"I think I'll be fine, Elizabeth."

"If it gets to be too much, I can take her home," Michael said, concern showing in his expression. Evidently he hadn't thought about the warmer weather possibly effecting Violet until just now, either.

"We should pray that next Saturday is a nice cool day. If not, we'll go another time."

"You'll go and I'll go another time," Violet said. "No need in ruining everyone's fun."

"It wouldn't be as much fun without you," Elizabeth said.

"No, and neither will Independence Day be without you. But sometimes we don't have a choice."

"So true. And we might as well make it easier by accepting that fact." Elizabeth certainly didn't feel she had any choice about the holiday weekend this year. But she'd decided she was going to make the best of it. Her father was showing more interest in her and she didn't have to do anything more than be polite to the young man he wanted her to meet.

John didn't much like the turn in the conversation between Elizabeth and Violet. Especially the part about making the best of what one had no choice in. Did that mean Elizabeth would give this man her father wanted her to meet a chance?

His chest tightened at the very thought that she might become interested in someone. She'd not had a beau that he knew of since she'd moved to Heaton House. Like the rest of the boarders, she mostly spent her free time with other boarders.

"John?" Elizabeth nudged his arm, bringing his thoughts back to the present. "Want a roll?"

He looked down to see the basket she held out to him. "Oh, yes, thank you." He took a roll and handed the basket off to the next person.

"I thought so. Those are your favorite. You seemed lost in thought."

"I was. I'm looking forward to Saturday. I hope you'll enjoy the game. I'll explain it to you as best I can."

"Thank you. I'm looking forward to it, too. But you'll need to do a lot of explaining. I don't know much about baseball."

He couldn't help but wonder why her father had never taken her to a baseball game. Surely the man liked the sport. He'd never met one who didn't. "It will be my pleasure."

"And what he gets wrong, I'll make sure you understand, Elizabeth," Ben said from across the table. "Rebecca tells me she knows all about the game, so there'll be no need to explain it to her."

"Well, Michael played back home," Rebecca said with a smile. "It's hard to have a big brother and not know about baseball."

"Rebecca is actually a pretty good pitcher." Michael chuckled. "Except for that time she hit me in the head. Thanks for the memory, sis."

His sister chuckled. "I hadn't thought of that in a long time, Michael. I am sorry I aimed so high that time."

John wondered what it would have been like to have a sibling. He often thought he was missing out by being an only child. Did Elizabeth feel the same way?

She turned to him just then as if she read his thoughts. "I love seeing those two together. I'm so glad they are all reunited. Seeing them interact sometimes makes me wish I had a brother or sister."

"I know that feeling."

"Sometimes—" They both chuckled as they said the same thing at the same time.

"You first."

"Well, I sometimes wonder if Papa would quit concentrating on trying to run my life if I had a brother or sister. But I shouldn't really complain and I feel bad about doing so. I mean…I do have a parent still living. I'm sorry, John. I shouldn't be so thoughtless."

She thought she'd offended him. John shook his head and smiled at her. "No need to be sorry. You have to deal with—" He clamped his mouth shut. What was he thinking? Here he was about to insult her father. She may be frustrated with the man, but it was doubtful she'd want anyone else saying anything bad about him.

"What do I have to deal with?"

He shook his head and opened his mouth to try to get out of an awkward moment and was more than a little relieved when Millicent spoke from across the table.

"Oh, now I'm getting homesick for my brother. You've reminded me how nice he is and how I miss being able to have him around to give me advice—even though I totally resented that he expected me to take it."

That made everyone at the table laugh and John's awkward moment passed. Would he ever learn to think before speaking?

Elizabeth let herself into Heaton House the next afternoon, wondering if it would stay nice until Saturday. She truly hoped the weather was good that day; she didn't want it to be hard for Violet in any way.

Next month promised to be warmer and she could understand why so many left the city for the summer to spend time along the coast. It sounded wonderful to her and she knew her aunt would like to go. But her life was here at Heaton House, as a regular person, and if she sometimes missed some of the advantages of living the life of a wealthy young woman, she reminded herself of all she didn't like about that kind of lifestyle. Even at the beach, the wealthy had strict rules to follow. One had to change clothes for every activity during the day, then dress up for dinner each night. It was a day filled with flitting from one place to another, and then back to change again, day in and day out.

No. She didn't want to live that way again. Not even for a holiday at the seaside. Besides, she'd feel guilty for enjoying a stay at the beach when her friends were stuck in the city.

She didn't like spending her time trying to live up to rules that truly had nothing to do with living. Most of the people her father associated with were most concerned with making money and keeping it, with impressing those who were richer only to make their place in society stronger. At least it seemed that way to her.

Oh, not everyone was like that. Her aunt was very concerned about the less fortunate, but then she hadn't always been wealthy, nor did she use her wealth to impress others. And if not for her, Elizabeth would still be longing to escape the life she'd lived in Boston.

Dear Aunt Bea. She should visit her more often. Or even invite her to Heaton House. She'd love it. And if Elizabeth let everyone know who she really was, there would be no need to keep her aunt's identity secret, either. She was ashamed that she'd put her own desire to be able to live a private life before what would benefit those she loved. She was going to have to let everyone know her true identity soon. If only she knew how to do it. If only she knew how they would all react to the news.

And who should she tell first? Kathleen or John?

Kathleen had become her best friend. And John… Well, they both had to be told.

But when should she do it? Before Independence Day or after? How would the people who meant so much to her take the news? Would they turn on her? She prayed not, but only the Lord knew.

Dear Lord, please help me to have the courage to tell everyone, and please help me to know when, and how, and who to tell first. I know I've asked this before, but please help me to be quiet and listen and know what You would have me do.

Almost immediately, she felt awash with peace about it all. She'd have the answers to her prayer, but the timing would be the Lord's. There was no need to rush. If she left it all in His hands, He would let her know. And His will would be done. Oh, why hadn't she done that in the first place?

John couldn't remember a better day at work. His editor was very happy with the feedback he'd gotten on John's Sunday article.

"Not everyone was thrilled with it, mind you," he'd said, sitting at his desk with John across from him. "There were a few who voiced dissatisfaction, but I know why. And no amounts of anonymous threats are going to make me stop printing your articles. In fact, I'd like to put two out a week. They still won't be on the front page, but I'd like to print one on Sunday and one on Wednesday if you can handle it. It'll mean a small raise. Are you up to it?"

Was he up to it? He'd been ready for this for years. "Yes, sir, I am. But these threats? What is the reason for them?"

"John, I suspect there are those in the city who don't care how they make their money as long as they continue to acquire it. But they aren't as motivated to take care of their investments. They'd rather just sell their property for less than they paid for it, knowing they've made their investment over and over again in the time they've owned those buildings."

"Do you know who—"

"No. And that's what the threats are about. Obviously, they don't want to be found out. But I think its time they are. You ready to do some digging?"

"I am. I've already begun, actually."

"It may take a while, but you'll find the owners, I'm sure of it."

"Might I ask what kind of threats you've received?"

His editor shrugged. "Mostly that they'll pull their advertising. I don't think they'll carry through with them. Of course, they might, but then I'll have an idea of who they are and we'll be closer to finding out what buildings they own."

"Surely they'd know that?"

"One would think. Anyway, go full steam ahead on those articles. I do need you to cover one more charity event and then Fredrick is going to take over that column for you so you have time to work on these kinds of articles."

"When is the charity event?"

"It's this weekend at the home of Cornelius Vanderbilt II. They want to get one more event in before they go to The Breakers for the summer. And he's mentioned he'd like to meet you." He handed him the particulars on a piece of paper.

John took the note and tried not to show his surprise.

"That's quite an honor. I've covered several events at the Vanderbilts', but Cornelius always seemed much too busy to notice me." Cornelius Vanderbilt II was one of the hardest-working in his family and from all accounts, he was kind and always willing to give to a good cause.

John stood to take his leave. "Thank you for giving me a chance to do this series of stories, sir."

"I see promise in you, John. Don't disappoint me."

"I'll certainly try not to, sir." The two shook hands and John waited until he walked out of the room, down the stairs and out the door of the *Tribune* before grinning from ear to ear. His articles might not be on the front page yet, but he had his own byline and if all went well, he felt sure he'd make it. If he could crack this story—get the names of people who owned those buildings—he'd make the front page.

It was all he could do to keep from letting out a loud whoop and kicking his heels together.

He had a lot of work to do and he'd stay with it until he found who owned those deplorable buildings. If threats were being made there was no telling who was involved. His boss wanted more articles and he had a ball game with Elizabeth to look forward to at the end of the week. He couldn't even complain about having to cover the Vanderbilt function.

He couldn't wait to tell everyone who'd encouraged him about the article—especially Elizabeth. It was her idea to include the need for more child-care homes in his articles, and he was sure that helped garner even more interest in the stories. He wanted her to be the first to know. He pulled his watch out of his pocket. It was four-thirty. If he hurried, he could catch Elizabeth as she left the *Delineator*'s offices and they could ride the trolley home together.

Chapter Eleven

Elizabeth was more than a little surprised to see John just outside her office building. He was standing near the front door watching people leave. She couldn't imagine why he was there. She rushed up to him. "John, what are you doing here? Is something wrong?"

He smiled and shook his head. "No. Everything is fine, Elizabeth. I just, well, I was in the area and hoped we could catch a ride home together."

Something must be up. He looked happier than she'd ever seen him. "Of course we can."

They fell into step together and arrived at the trolley stop just as it was pulling up. They gave the driver their tokens and found an empty seat midway back. Elizabeth slipped in and scooted over toward the window while John slipped in beside her.

"What brought you near the *Delineator* today? Are you following a news story over this way?"

His blue eyes studied her as if he were thinking about what to say. "No, I came specifically to meet up with you. I have some news to share and I wanted you to be the first to know."

"Did you find out who owns the buildings we've seen?" He looked so excited she figured it must be that.

"No. But I intend to." There was another smile hovering around his lips. Something was definitely going on.

"Then what is it?" she said half-exasperatedly. Then he looked into her eyes and let loose the smile that sent her pulse charging through her veins like a racehorse at the starting shot.

"I have some news. My boss wants two articles a week. No front page yet, but he says he sees promise in me."

"Oh, John, that's not some news, it is wonderful news!" And it was. It looked as if he'd soon have his byline on the front page. She couldn't help but be happy for him.

He let out a huge sigh. "I couldn't wait until tonight to tell you, Elizabeth. You've been very encouraging and I wanted you to be the first to know."

Her heart seemed to melt inside her chest at his words. All this time, it never really dawned on her that her opinion meant that much to him.

"Thank you for telling me first, John. I'm very happy for you. You've wanted this for a long time—more than anything else." Or so she'd thought. Now that it was within his grasp, would it satisfy him? Was that all he really wanted in life?

His brow furrowed for a moment before he smiled again. "Thank you, Elizabeth. I—"

The trolley stopped to take on more people and John got up to let an expectant woman take his seat. Elizabeth smiled at her and then up at John. He really was considerate. Had she somehow missed that about him during all the sparring they used to do? They didn't bandy words over their work that much anymore. Was that because they'd been working together or because they'd gotten to know more about each other? Or was it because she'd come to care for him as more than someone to bandy words with? As more than a friend?

Elizabeth was happy for him. John could see it in her eyes and hear it in her voice. But his heart was heavy, for her words had opened his eyes to how she and others must think of him—that the only thing he was interested in, the only thing he cared about, was becoming a lead reporter with his articles on the front page of the *Tribune*.

And that was true, at least until lately. Oh, he still wanted it very badly. But it wasn't all he thought about any longer. No. The woman conversing with the lady he'd given up his seat for had been taking up a lot of his thinking these days. When he counted the dreams he'd been having, he'd have to say she'd overtaken most of his thoughts and he knew his feelings for her were growing. But the risk of caring about her more than he already did put too much on the line. He was way more attracted to her than any other woman he had known. In fact, he feared his feelings for Elizabeth already far surpassed what he'd felt for Melody.

And if that were true, he felt he was headed for heart-break. Elizabeth was way out of his league. It didn't matter if she lived at Heaton House and worked for a living. Deep down he was sure he didn't have a chance with her. But how did he keep his feelings for her from deepening? How did he stop the dreams?

John had wondered whether or not to announce his news at dinner. Now that he realized everyone thought moving up at the paper was all he cared about, he was a little hesitant to mention it.

But once dinner was under way, Elizabeth nudged him. "Aren't you going to tell everyone your news?"

"What news? What are you keeping from us, John?" Mrs. Heaton asked from the end of the table.

"Yes, John, what news do you have to share?" Ben asked.

"Oh, it's not all that big."

"It is, too," Elizabeth insisted. "Tell them. Or I'll do it for you."

He couldn't help but grin at the glint in her eye. She meant what she said.

"I was called into my editor's office today and, well, he wants two articles a week on the tenements. They won't be on the front page, but near there and he gave the impression that might be possible one day."

His news was met with congratulations from everyone around the table.

"Why, John, that's wonderful. And of course it is possible!" Mrs. Heaton exclaimed. "I wish I'd known earlier, I would have made you a celebration dinner. But I'll plan it for tomorrow night."

"Oh, Mrs. Heaton, there's no need for you to go to the trouble."

"John Talbot, you know I love any reason to celebrate with my boarders. We'll have your favorites tomorrow night."

"Thank you, Mrs. Heaton, I'll be looking forward to it."

"And we could all take a walk after dinner tonight for ice cream," Luke suggested.

"I like that idea, don't you, John?" Elizabeth grinned at him, sending his heart hammering inside his chest.

If she wanted ice cream, he was happy to go along. "That sounds great. But it's my treat. I got a raise, too."

"Now that's the kind of news to celebrate," Ben said. "Count me in for ice cream."

John laughed. "Will do." He'd never expected the raise, but he was very pleased with it. And everyone had been so supportive, he was happy to be able to show them how much he appreciated them.

It was still warm out when they all headed out the door, so getting ice cream sounded better than ever. John fell into step with Elizabeth, as he'd become accustomed to doing.

She looked up at him and smiled. "It's nice that you are able to take more time to go on outings with us all. Are you totally finished with covering high society goings-on?" She hoped so. He'd missed many of the group outings because of his assignments.

"Almost. My boss said I only had one more society event to do. I can't tell you how glad I was to hear that. I've never been comfortable covering those kinds of things. Charity events are one thing, but the balls and all that kind of thing that are held to impress others gets to be too much at times."

"I know. I'm thankful that most of what I cover for the *Delineator* are the charity events. I've never been comfortable with all the hoopla of the other, either."

"Really?" Her words surprised him. Elizabeth worked for a women's magazine and he'd always assumed that most women had a great interest in all the social goings-on in the city. Besides, there was that something about her that made him think she'd be comfortable in that setting.

"Really. Much of the daily goings-on of the wealthy seem meaningless to me. Oh, I don't mean they don't do good things. They certainly do. And this city benefits greatly from their generosity. But—"

"Come on, you two," Luke said once they arrived at the soda shop. "We're ready for ice cream and John's paying."

"We'd better get in there," Elizabeth said. "No telling what you'll have to pay for if you don't."

John chuckled. He would much rather have heard what Elizabeth was about to say, but he'd offered to treat everyone and he needed to be the host. He took hold of her elbow and steered her inside. "I don't think it will be that bad. What are you wanting?"

"Hmm, I think I'd like a chocolate sundae."

"Sounds good to me, too." He walked up to the counter. "Two chocolate sundaes and whatever the rest of this group wants. Let me know what it comes to."

The man behind the cash register grinned. "You can be sure I will, sir."

They all gathered around a large round table and were soon enjoying their sweet confections. Too many conversations were going on at one time and John did what he usually did when that happened. He sat back and listened.

The women were talking about Kathleen and Luke's upcoming wedding, while the men were talking about the upcoming baseball outing. Although, every once in a while he'd catch Luke looking at his bride-to-be with such love and indulgence, John almost felt envious that his friend had a loving relationship. Deep down, John longed for the same thing, and for the first time in a very long time, he wondered if it'd ever be truly possible for him.

"You're a lucky man, Luke."

His friend turned his attention away from Kathleen and grinned. "Oh, I know. I'm blessed beyond my wildest dreams. I hope the same will happen for you one day, too, my friend."

"I'm not holding my breath." But he wished for the same thing. John pulled his thoughts up short. What was he thinking? He'd made up his mind long ago that he wasn't going to fall in love again. Wasn't going to let himself care that way about a woman again.

Elizabeth laughed at something Kathleen said and his gaze riveted to her. My, she was lovely. She made him wish all kinds of things and he was beginning to wonder if he had any control over his feelings at all when it came to her. They seemed to deepen each and every day.

He shook his head. Longing for something didn't mean it could or would happen. His past experience had taught him that and he'd best not forget it. She must have felt his eyes on her for she turned and looked directly at him. Her smile lingered in her eyes, which deepened in color as their gazes met and held. His chest tightened. Remembering all that'd he'd vowed he would never do again was one thing. But keeping that vow was going to be much easier said than done.

Elizabeth's breath caught as she saw John looking at her with something in his eyes she'd never seen before. Whatever it was, the expression in them turned her heart to pure mush. What was happening to her?

What was happening to him? He seemed to be changing right before her eyes, or was it her who was undergoing some kind of change? She forced her gaze from his and tried to turn her attention back to what Kathleen was saying but her thoughts were all over the place.

She'd never seen John enjoying himself with the group as much as he seemed to tonight. It was as if he were more relaxed, more attuned to what was going on around him. Not long ago, even when he'd joined them on an outing or in the parlor to play games or sing around the piano, he seemed to distance himself a bit. And she realized that's what was different now.

He seemed to be part of the group instead of looking in on it. It was almost as if he'd been an observer before, which could have been just the way most reporters reacted, but now he was joining in and letting himself enjoy spending time with everyone instead of holding himself aloof.

He seemed more interested in the things going on around him than just his work. He had been excited about the raise and the promotion, but it wasn't all he was talking about. Maybe now that he seemed to be moving in the direction he wanted in his profession, he felt he could live his life more fully. She looked over at him once again and felt her face flush with warmth when his eyes met hers. He smiled and she took a shaky breath before smiling in return.

That man's smile seemed to be more powerful by the hour. How was she going to fight this attraction she felt for him when he smiled at her like that?

The walk back home was a leisurely one, with everyone spacing out enough to carry on a conversation.

Elizabeth and John were the last to leave the ice cream parlor, as he wanted to give the waiter a tip.

By the time they left, only Kathleen and Luke were visible, walking slowly, surely so they would have more time alone to talk. "Should we catch up with them and play chaperon or let them be?"

The couple were obviously only aware of each other, walking close with their heads turned to each other. "I think we can chaperon from a distance," Elizabeth said.

"I'm sure they'll appreciate it." He couldn't say he was disappointed in Elizabeth's answer. It gave him more time with her. They matched their pace to the couple in front, being sure to give them space enough to speak privately.

"Kathleen told me about another building we should check out. I have the address in my reticule. I'll give it to you when we get back to Heaton House."

"What did she say about it?"

"She said it was even more deplorable than the others. That some of the tenants had complained that they couldn't open their windows to get any fresh air."

"That's not good at all. It's been plenty warm lately and bound to get warmer in the next few months."

"I know. Maybe we should check it out."

"Could you go tomorrow?" John asked. He'd come to like having her along.

"I would. I could probably leave around lunchtime again, if that's agreeable to you."

"That would be fine. I'll meet you like I did last time."

"I can meet you, John. I hate for you to have to go out of your way, when I can just as easily meet you wherever you say."

He knew times were changing for women—they came and went to work, to shop and to visit friends. "It's not a problem for me. I'll pick you up."

"But—"

"I'm going to be over that way, Elizabeth." And he was. He was going to be there to pick her up. "I'll be waiting like today."

She gave him a suspicious look and then smiled and shook her head as if she read right through him. "All right. At noon, right?"

"Yes." He was glad she remembered the time. "We'll have some lunch and then go see the building."

"I'll bring my camera, unless you want to ask Millicent to come along?"

He shook his head. "I think we can handle this on our own, don't you?"

"I think so, yes." He could see her smile in the street lamp they passed under.

"When does your first article come out for the *Delineator?*"

"Should be in the July issue. I'm as excited as you've been about yours. I truly hope our articles help bring attention to the fact that the tenements need constant scrutiny by our city leaders. And that we can help bring more money in for the child-care homes."

"Yes, so do I." It felt good to say the words. It felt good to feel strongly about what he was writing about instead of feeling it was all just...fluff. He chuckled at the realization that he'd been writing the very same thing he'd told Elizabeth she wrote—didn't matter if he thought he'd touched on a few more serious topics than she had—as in what the gentlemen talked about. It was still pretty much fluff.

"What's so funny?"

"You might not think it is."

"No?"

"Well, I hope you do, but…" He told her what he'd been thinking and the realization that he'd been writing the same kind of articles she wrote. Then he held his breath, waiting for her reaction. It wasn't what he was expecting.

"You mean, you never meant my actual writing was fluff—but only the subject matter?"

"Why, yes, of course. What did you think I meant?"

At that she began to giggle.

"Did you think I was insulting your writing?" Surely not.

Her giggling stopped and she nodded. "Why, ye_s_, I did."

He stopped in the middle of the walk and turned her toward him. "Oh, Elizabeth, you're a very good writer. I'm sorry you took it that way. I never meant to hurt your feelings or make you feel bad in any way. I just never truly realized that you could have said the very same thing about what I was writing until just now. Please forgive me."

"Oh, John. You've done nothing to forgive. It's me who should be asking your forgiveness for not realiz-ing—"

"How could you? I am sorry, Elizabeth. I should have realized—"

"John!" Luke called. "You two coming?"

It was only then that John realized they were nearly home. "Yes, we're coming. You two can go on in."

"You sure? I'd hate to leave you unchaperoned." Luke

laughed and pulled Kathleen along with him. "Don't tarry, you hear? Otherwise we'll have to come get you."

"We'll be right there." John took Elizabeth's elbow and steered her down the walk. "And here we thought we were chaperoning them."

"So much for jumping to conclusions—like I did." Elizabeth began to laugh.

John joined her and then the laughter diminished as they gazed into each other's eyes. "Elizabeth, I am sorry if I hurt your feelings with my remarks."

"I—"

John stilled her words with his fingertips while his gaze took in her face and then settled on her lips.

He heard her quick intake of breath and realized he was holding his own. John's heart began to beat rapidly as he realized he wanted to pull her closer, wanted to kiss her.

He reached out and tilted her face to his. His thumb gently caressed her soft skin as he lowered his head and heard her quick intake of breath just before his lips grazed hers, lightly and then more firmly.

For a moment, he thought she responded but then she pulled away and hurried up the steps. "We'd better get inside before Luke makes good on his threat to come look for us."

John followed Elizabeth into Heaton House and into the parlor where Julia was playing the piano. What had he just done? What was he thinking? More important— what was Elizabeth thinking?

Elizabeth's pulse was racing in time to the music and she hoped she didn't look as dazed as she felt. What had just happened? He had kissed her, hadn't he? It'd been so brief…and she'd wanted it to last longer. But had she imagined it? No. Her lips still tingled from the touch of John's kiss, brief though it had been.

She couldn't, wouldn't, let herself read too much into it. He'd kissed her as an apology for how she'd taken his talk of her writing. He was just trying to make amends for that. That's all it was. All it could be.

Even if she let herself care more about him, once he found out who she really was, things would change. He'd think she'd—

The music ended and she looked around. Had she been singing along with the rest or just standing there with her thoughts swirling about her? No one was looking at her oddly that she could see and she dare not look at John to see if he was. Her face flushed warm just thinking about him. But she couldn't let on how much his kiss had affected her. That her insides were all fluttery just thinking about how his lips had felt on hers.

Julia started playing another song and Elizabeth forced herself to sing along, to act as if nothing out of the ordinary had happened. If her world had suddenly turned topsy-turvy, there was no need for anyone to know.

Chapter Twelve

As the clock inched nearer to noon the next day, Elizabeth wondered if John would be waiting for her in the foyer of the *Delineator* building. She'd forgotten to give him the slip of paper with the building's address the night before, choosing to take the coward's way out and hurry upstairs after the last song was sung.

It wasn't like her at all, but then again, she'd never had quite this predicament to deal with, either. Fearing she'd see only regret that he'd kissed her in John's eyes, she hadn't looked at him. And she didn't want to give him a chance to voice any apology, either.

Instead, she'd hurried into the bathroom and got ready for bed, knowing she had time before Luke and Kathleen said their good-nights downstairs. If Kathleen wondered why she wasn't up to talking over the evening, as was their custom, she wouldn't know it until the next day. And by then, hopefully she'd have her feelings under control…if that were possible.

She'd gone to her knees in prayer, asking the Lord to help her sort them out. She wasn't even sure what she was feeling the most. Embarrassment that she'd begun to press her lips to John's before she had sense enough to pull back? Or regret that she had pulled back?

Elizabeth caught her breath at that thought, for it seemed to be the strongest at the moment. Or was she simply confused about it all? What had she been thinking to let him get that close in the first place?

She hadn't been thinking. She'd only been feeling. And that was something Elizabeth hadn't let herself do about a man in a very long time. And she couldn't afford to let herself feel anything more for John than just friendship. Not now, not ever, for she was sure he'd regret kissing her once he found out she wasn't who he thought she was.

Elizabeth sighed and forced herself to get back to work, looking over the photos she might work into her next article for the magazine.

She picked up a photo of the children who'd been sitting on the stoop of one of the buildings in the tenements. They so reminded her of Kathleen's nephews the first time she'd seen them in the park. That look of anguish that so many children in the tenements had. It broke her heart. She laid it aside to use. If it and others like it didn't garner support for those in the tenements, nothing would.

She chose another of the horrible condition the buildings were in. Trash everywhere, probably rats hiding inside the piles. She shivered. Then she chose another photo she'd taken the day she and John went by themselves—John again! She couldn't let herself keep thinking about how his lips felt on hers or how much she'd wanted to kiss him.

Perhaps it was a good thing she'd be going to her aunt's for a few days. Maybe she needed some distance from John, some time to put the changes in their relationship into perspective.

The lunch bell rang and she gathered up her parasol and reticule and headed downstairs. Would he be there? Or perhaps he didn't want to face her? He might not if he regretted the momentary kiss. Oh, she didn't want him to apologize. *Please, Lord, don't let him feel contrite about it or tell me he's sorry he kissed me.*

She reached the foyer and glanced over at the spot where he'd stood the afternoon before. He was there, but his back was turned to her and he hadn't seen her yet. She let out a deep breath trying to prepare herself for seeing him face-to-face once more.

John looked at the large clock on the wall. Elizabeth should be coming down the stairs anytime now. She hadn't come down to breakfast before he'd left for work and— What if she didn't meet him as planned? His pulse slowed and his chest tightened.

He couldn't blame her if she didn't. What had possessed him to kiss her? Not that he regretted it—he didn't. Couldn't bring himself to. Her lips had been soft and sweet and he'd wanted to keep kissing her. Then she'd pulled away and he had no idea if she was upset with him or not. She hadn't looked at him for the rest of the night and had hurried upstairs so fast he didn't have a chance to say good-night to her.

He feared her opinion of him might have fallen and that was the last thing he wanted. But he didn't know what to do about it. Did he apologize or act as if nothing out of the ordinary had happened last night? And could he pull it off if he did? Because kissing her, even for that brief few moments, had been anything but ordinary for him.

He didn't know what had come over him but as he'd stood looking down at her last evening, he'd felt inexplicably drawn to her. Felt compelled to let her know he truly was sorry for making her feel her writing wasn't important.

A man jostled him coming through the door and John realized he'd been pacing back and forth in front of it. He looked at the clock once more then turned and looked up to find Elizabeth coming down the stairs.

John searched her face and their gazes caught and held. He smiled and she smiled back, easing the tightness in his chest. He hurried to meet her at the bottom of the staircase.

"Did I keep you waiting?" she asked.

No mention of the night before. He wasn't sure if that was good or not, but at least she didn't tell him he had no business kissing her. "No. You are right on time. Do you have the address?"

"I do. I'm sorry I forgot to give it to you last night." She reached into her reticule, pulled out a slip of paper and handed it to him.

He'd forgotten it, too, until this morning. His mind hadn't been on anything but her last night. "It's no problem. We have it."

"Kathleen said it's about a block or so down and across the street from the last one we checked out."

"We'll find it. Are you hungry? I didn't see you at breakfast this morning." Which was one of the reasons why he'd wondered if she'd meet him at all today.

"Actually I am hungry. I was running behind this morning."

Still no mention of the night before and he released a sigh of relief. *Thank You, Lord.* He certainly wasn't going to bring up last night if she didn't. He didn't know how she felt about the kiss and thought it might be safer not to find out. He wasn't sure he wanted to know.

"Let's go get you something to eat, then." He held out his arm and she took it without hesitation. He steered her out the door and down the street to a new café he'd been told about. Both men and women frequented it, and he felt she'd be comfortable there.

As they ordered and then ate their lunch there was no mention of the kiss and he didn't know whether to be relieved or disappointed. And if he didn't bring it up would she be relieved or disappointed?

Elizabeth seemed the same as always, but that didn't mean she wasn't upset with him. It only meant she hadn't let him know if she was. Obviously he couldn't read her well or he would have known she thought his referring to her writing as fluff was a reflection of her actual writing style.

He didn't know what to say or how to act right now and he was afraid if he alluded to the kiss at all, he'd be making a mistake. But then, he felt sure he'd make a mistake either way. He'd never been in a situation quite like this before. He'd never kissed someone so spontaneously as he had Elizabeth last night. And he hadn't thought about the consequence…what it might mean for their friendship. He prayed he hadn't harmed that relationship.

"John, is something bothering you? You seem miles away."

The look of concern in her eyes reassured him that

she cared about him at least a little. "I'm sorry. I'm fine. I was just woolgathering."

"I've been doing a lot of that lately. Maybe it's the heat?"

He chuckled and nodded. "It could be." But in his case he was sure it only had to do with her and how pretty she looked today and especially how— No, he couldn't let his thoughts go back to that kiss. "I suppose we'd better go check out the building."

"Yes. I did bring my camera with me but I hope there's nothing really terrible to take a photograph of."

He stood and went around the table to pull her chair out for her. "So do I. Did Kathleen tell you what we should look for? I didn't see her this morning either."

"Just that it was appalling. Oh, and she said we should look up a Mrs. Oliver. She said she'd show us what she could. She's on the fourth floor, apartment 4B."

They walked out onto the street and to the next corner where they caught the trolley that would take them over to the tenements.

Children were playing in the streets and vendors were hawking their wares, ever watchful of the police that might shut them down. There was no telling where some of them got the things they sold, but Elizabeth suspected much of it was stolen for the prices they asked were not a lot.

But the people here couldn't afford much. Like Kathleen's family, it sometimes took everyone working to be able to pay rent and put food on the table. It was hard to see people who worked so hard living in these kinds of conditions and she had to keep reminding herself that it was possible for them to get out, to have a better life eventually. Kathleen and her sister had. She let out a sigh.

"I know seeing all this is hard. You don't have to go with me if you'd rather not."

"No. I'll be fine. But thank you, John. I don't imagine it's any easier for you to see people living the way some of these people have to."

"You're right. What's hardest of all is going back to Heaton House knowing how blessed I am." John couldn't believe he'd just said that. He barely even realized he felt that way. What was it about Elizabeth that had him telling her things he'd never shared with anyone? Had him wanting to share his thoughts with her?

"I feel the same way. John, there's something I…"

He waited for her to finish what she was about to say, but she sighed and shook her head.

"Never mind. Let's think of the bright side of things. Our article will help get the city leaders' attention on the run-down buildings. And changes will happen. Probably slower than we want, but they will happen if we don't give up."

"We won't." Her words made him feel as if they were a team, wanting the same things and always there for each other. But history showed he couldn't trust his feelings or his instincts where women were concerned. Could things be any different with Elizabeth?

The building was every bit as damaged as Kathleen had described. The manager wasn't there, which came as no surprise to them. In these kinds of buildings they rarely were. There was trash in the stairwells, dirt in every corner of the stairs and hallways. Lightbulbs were burned out here and there along the halls and Elizabeth shivered at the very thought of anyone having to go in and out at night.

They made their way up to the fourth floor, found Mrs. Oliver's apartment and knocked on the door. "Who's there?"

"It's Elizabeth Anderson and John Talbot, Mrs. Oliver. Kathleen O'Bryan sent us and said you'd be expecting us."

"Hold on." It took a few moments before they could hear several locks being unlocked, and the door creaked open just enough for Mrs. Oliver to peek out and see who was there. They must have passed her inspection for she opened the door wider. "Yes, you fit her description. Come in, come in."

Elizabeth breathed a sigh of relief to see that this woman's small apartment was as clean as she could get it. Still, it wasn't in good shape.

"Sit down. Would you like some tea?"

"Oh, no, thank you. We just ate." The woman motioned for them to take a seat on the sofa and Elizabeth sat down in one corner of it. John sat down beside her, and Mrs. Oliver sat in what Elizabeth felt sure the woman considered *her* chair, as it had a ball of yarn and what looked like a mitten she'd been knitting.

"Did Miss O'Bryan explain why we wanted to speak with you, Mrs. Oliver?" John asked.

"She did. Said you two were writing articles trying to get something done about the condition of buildings like this one."

"We are," John assured her.

"Well, I hope it works. I don't have much hope that the manager here will do anything, but perhaps in some of the other buildings…"

Get 2 Books FREE!

Harlequin Reader Service,
a leading publisher of inspirational fiction, presents

Love Inspired **HISTORICAL**

A series of historical love stories that will lift your spirits and warm your soul!

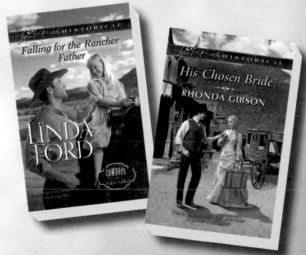

FREE BOOKS! Use the reply card inside to get two free books by outstanding inspirational authors!

FREE GIFTS! You'll also get two exciting surprise gifts, absolutely free!

GET 2 BOOKS

WE'D LIKE TO SEND YOU TWO FREE books from the series you are enjoying now. Your two books have a combined cover price of over $10, but are yours to keep absolutely FREE! We'll even send you two wonderful surprise gifts. You can't lose!

Each of your FREE books is filled with joy, faith and traditional values as men and women open their hearts to each other and join together on a spiritual journey.

HOW TO GET YOUR
2 FREE BOOKS AND 2 FREE GIFTS

1. Return the reply card today, and we'll send you two novels, absolutely free! We'll even pay the postage!
2. Accepting free books places you under no obligation to buy anything, ever. The two books have combined cover prices of over $10, but they're yours to keep, free!
3. We hope that after receiving your free books you'll want to remain a subscriber, but the choice is yours—to continue or cancel, any time at all!

EXTRA BONUS

You'll also get two free mystery gifts!
(worth about $10)

FREE!

Return this card today to get **2 FREE BOOKS and 2 FREE GIFTS!**

YES! Please send me 2 FREE novels, and 2 FREE mystery gifts as well. I understand I am under no obligation to purchase anything, as explained on the back of this insert.

102/302 IDL GGDS

Please Print

FIRST NAME	LAST NAME

ADDRESS

APT.#	CITY

STATE/PROV.	ZIP/POSTAL CODE

EMAIL

◄ Detach card and mail today. No stamp needed. ▼

Visit us at
www.ReaderService.com

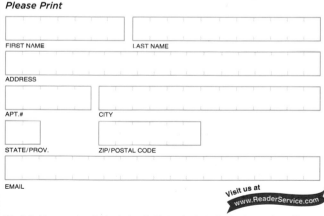

LIH-914-2F-13

"She said something about windows not opening," John prompted.

The woman nodded. "I can't get mine to budge. Go see for yourself. I think most of the windows in this building are like mine."

John got up and went to the window looking out onto the street. He tried to open it and inspected it from all angles. "It looks as if it's been painted shut. Can you remember ever being able to open it?"

The woman shook her head. "Not since I've been here."

"Elizabeth, let's get a photo of this, if we may, Mrs. Oliver?" He looked inquiringly at the woman.

"It's fine with me."

Elizabeth took several shots of the window and the thick paint all around it.

John reached in his pocket and took out a folding knife, one like Elizabeth's father carried. He scored the thick paint along the windowsill once and tried to open the window again. It gave a little but still didn't open. He scored around it once more, and Elizabeth could see him putting more pressure on the knife. Then he went around it one more time.

He tried the window again and this time it opened, not all the way, but enough to feel a slight breeze.

Mrs. Oliver jumped up from her seat and hurried over to the window. "Oh, thank you, young man! Could you do the same to the one in the bedroom?"

"I'll be glad to. Perhaps you could answer some questions for Miss Anderson while I do?"

"Certainly. What can I tell you, young lady?"

Elizabeth pulled a pad and pencil from her reticule.

"Do you know who the owner of the building is? His name or where he could be reached?"

The older woman shook her head. "I'm sorry. I wish I could but I have no idea. The manager's name is Smith, or at least that's what he says to call him. He's only here around the first of the month to collect the rent, although he's supposed to live on the premises. We're supposed to slip requests under the door of his apartment on the first floor, but a lot of good that does us. They never get answered."

"I'm sorry. Do you live alone or is there family?"

"My husband died on the way over from England. My daughter and I live here. She works at the laundry and I take in mending. We've been here two years now and well...one day we hope to get out of here."

"I'm sorry for your loss," Elizabeth said. "And it is possible to get out of here. Miss O'Bryan and her sister did. Did she tell you?"

"She did. It gave me hope." The older woman smiled and Elizabeth wished she could get her and her daughter out now.

John came back into the room and headed to the small kitchen where he proceeded to work on the small window over the sink. He must have gotten the hang of it because it took only a few minutes for him to break the dried paint seal and get it open. Then he went back to the first window and worked on it until he could open it all the way.

"Oh, I can't thank you enough, Mr. Talbot." Mrs. Oliver got up and went to the open window. She took several deep breaths. The noise below wafted up to the fourth floor, but she didn't seem to mind, looking down on the street and then in both directions. "I can't say it's the freshest air I've ever smelled but at least it isn't stagnant like the inside of this building. And it might at least give us a nice breeze to make sleeping easier in this heat."

"I hope so. And you can choose whether it's open or closed now," Elizabeth added.

The woman chuckled. "It's nice to feel I still have a choice on some things in life. Now sit, both of you, and ask away. I'll tell you all I can about this building. I only wish I knew who owned it."

"We're going to do all we can to find out who the building belongs to, I can promise you that, Mrs. Oliver," John said.

The older woman spent the better part of the afternoon answering their questions and even taking them to several other apartments and getting the tenants to answer more. John helped open several more windows while they were there and by the time he and Elizabeth left the building, they had enough information for several articles.

"If this doesn't help get the city leaders' attention, I'm not sure anything can," Elizabeth said once they got on the trolley to take them back to Heaton House.

"Oh, we're going to get their attention. You took some good shots today. I doubt that Millicent could have done any better," John said.

"Thank you, John. But it wasn't hard. Those two children playing in the hall captured my heart."

"Mine, too. They didn't seem to realize that they should have somewhere better to play."

"It was as if they just accepted the conditions they live in. But, of course, it's all they know." She turned her head to look out the window, trying to will away the tears that suddenly threatened to fall. "I wanted to pick them up and bring them with us."

"I know. I did, too. It made me more determined than ever to find the owners of these places. First thing tomorrow I'm going to start digging. And if I can't find out anything, I'm going to ask Michael to help. The owners of these buildings can't get away with this."

Elizabeth's heart swelled with admiration for him. She'd never seen him so passionate about anything, and she had no doubt he meant what he said. He wanted to help these people as much as she did—only she'd never realized it until now.

As soon as they arrived back at Heaton House, Elizabeth gave her film to Millicent and she promised to have it developed the next day.

"We'll pay you for developing them, of course," John said.

Millicent shook her head. "No need. After seeing how awful the tenements look, I'd like to contribute something to the cause. Besides, I know you don't always know when you might need a photographer and I've been keeping fairly busy lately. The shots you used for the paper really helped. I've had several requests for photo shoots and have made enough on those to tide me over for a while."

"I'm glad," Elizabeth said.

John hoped she didn't feel guilty for taking the photographs herself. But she did and whispered as much to him right before dinner as they met up in the parlor.

He shook his head. "You have nothing to feel bad about. Millicent was right. It's hard to know when we might need photographs, and to my way of thinking we'd be wasting her time to ask her to be available and then not be able to use her."

"Really?"

"Of course."

Elizabeth released a sigh. "Thank you. I was feeling horrid for not asking her to go with us. But you're right. I'd feel just as bad if she'd gone and we hadn't needed her. I do hope the photos turn out."

"They will." He was getting to know Elizabeth better every day, but it surprised him to hear the vulnerability in her voice. This was a side of her he'd never seen. He'd always thought of her as one of the most self-confident women he knew. But perhaps he'd gotten self-confident and independent confused. That she was an independent woman was evident. But that didn't mean that she wasn't vulnerable at times.

Realizing that made him want to be there for her, to assure her, protect her, do whatever he could to encourage her…just as she'd been doing for him.

"Thank you for your confidence in my photography skills, John. But I know I'm just an amateur."

"That may be so. But you're a talented one. I don't think there's anything you couldn't do if you set your mind to it, Elizabeth."

"Why, John Talbot, how can you say you don't know how to talk to women? That's the nicest thing anyone has ever said to me."

And that was the nicest thing she'd ever said to him.

"Dinner is served," Mrs. Heaton called from the foyer.

John crooked his arm and smiled down at Elizabeth.

She took his arm and they headed to the dining room. Was it possible he'd learned a few things in the years he'd been at Heaton House? Oh, he hoped so.

Chapter Thirteen

On Wednesday another of John's articles came out in the *Tribune,* and Elizabeth arrived home with a copy of the *Delineator* that featured her piece. Mrs. Heaton declared it reason to celebrate and hurried to the kitchen.

John was called to the phone just before dinner and was pleased to hear Michael's voice on the other end of the line.

"Congratulations, my friend. I'm very impressed with your article."

"Thank you, Michael. I hope it helps."

"It certainly can't hurt. Violet let me read Elizabeth's write-up and she did a great job, too."

"Yes, she did. She gets right to the heart of the matter, doesn't she?" He'd been more than impressed with her piece. "If any of the city leaders' wives read her story, I have no doubt that they'll be looking into things very soon."

"Neither do I. Listen, Violet and I were wondering if you, Elizabeth, Kathleen and Luke might want to come over after dinner and let us in on everything. We feel a bit out of it all not living there and being able to keep up-to-date with what's going on."

"Why, I'm sure they'll be glad to come by. If not, I'll let you know, but I can't imagine them not being up to an outing." He knew he'd be glad to go, especially if it meant spending more time with Elizabeth. He was dreading the upcoming holiday more each day knowing she'd be gone.

"Good. We'll expect you if we hear no different." Michael ended the call and John hurried to the parlor to let the others know of his request.

"I'd love to go see them," Elizabeth said.

"So would I," Kathleen added. "After all, they had a lot to do with getting me and my family out of the tenements and have helped so much with getting the child-care homes started."

"We should have realized they'd want to keep up with things," Elizabeth said.

"Well, we can do that from now on," John said. He felt bad for not keeping his friends up-to-date on what was going on. He just figured they had enough going on in their lives what with Rebecca and Jenny living with them and Violet expecting their first child. But none of that was an excuse for not keeping them abreast of what was going on. "And they needn't feel left out. I'll ask Michael to see what he can find out about these owners. Won't hurt to have a professional investigator on this."

Mrs. Heaton called them in to dinner and was quite pleased they were going over to see her children. "I do think they feel left out from time to time. They'll love getting caught up on everything and being asked to help where they can."

She brought out a three-layer chocolate cake—a favorite of both John and Elizabeth—to celebrate their articles coming out on the same day.

"Thank you so much, Mrs. Heaton. This does make it a celebration," Elizabeth said.

"Thank you. And don't feel you have to tarry. I know you'd all like to be on your way. Why don't I just send half of this with you and you all can celebrate with them?"

"We'd be delighted," Elizabeth said. "The least we can do with them feeling left out is share our celebration cake with them."

"That's a wonderful idea," John said. "Thank you for thinking of it. Would you like to go with us?"

"I would. But I think I'll let you all go and give them my love. I have several things I need to catch up on in the office. I'll have some wrapped up for you to take as soon as you are ready to go." She served cake to the boarders who'd be staying and then hurried to the kitchen with the rest of the cake.

Elizabeth and Kathleen hurried upstairs to freshen up and John took charge of the basket Mrs. Heaton brought back to the dining room.

"You all have a nice time, and enjoy your cake."

"Thank you, Mrs. Heaton, we will." He knew he'd enjoy the cake. And with Elizabeth along, how could he not have a nice time?

It was a beautiful evening to enjoy a walk and Elizabeth found herself wishing Michael and Violet lived a little farther. But when they opened the door and greeted them she was very happy they'd gone to see them.

"Come in, come in," Violet said.

"Mother called to let us know you were bringing

dessert. Thanks for letting us in on your celebration." Michael motioned them inside.

"Can't think of anyone else we'd rather celebrate with," John said, handing the basket to Violet.

"Let's go to the dining room and I'll serve this up right away. We let Hilda off for the evening."

The men didn't need a second invitation as they filed into the room right away. Elizabeth and Kathleen went to the kitchen to help Violet. Her kitchen was smaller than the one at Heaton House but quite nice.

Violet put her to work getting cups and saucers, and putting cream and sugar on a tray to take in, and Kathleen helped by taking the dessert plates with the cake she'd sliced into the dining room. Rebecca came down from putting Jenny to bed and joined them in the kitchen.

"Oh, I would have loved to have seen Jenny," Elizabeth said.

"I know. But she'd be so excited, I'd never get her to sleep," Rebecca said. "We'll come over soon and visit."

"We're going to miss them when they move to Heaton House," Violet said. "The house will seem much too quiet."

"Not for long," Rebecca said. "You'll have your very own little noisemaker in the house."

"I can't wait," Violet said, leading the way into the dining room.

Once they were all settled around the table, talk was all about the articles John and Elizabeth had written and how proud they all were of them.

"They are both excellent," Michael said. "I feel sure they are going to make a difference."

"Oh, I know they will," Kathleen said. "I'm ever so

thankful John and Elizabeth agreed to work together on this."

"We're the ones who should be thankful," Elizabeth said. "Without you we wouldn't have any stories. You see these places first and let us know which ones are in the worst shape."

"I thought the building Colleen and I lived in was bad, but oh, compared to some I've seen..." Kathleen shuddered and shook her head.

John told them he'd be doing two articles a week for the foreseeable future and that there'd already been some threats of taking away advertising. "I've started going through property records, but it could take a while to find out who actually owns these buildings now."

"It certainly could," Michael said. "And much as I hate so say it, the owners could be people normally considered to be upstanding citizens. Though, I'm sure not all of them know about the neglect. As you know, some people invest their money with others and then in turn they invest in properties without always checking everything out."

"Yes," John agreed. "That's what makes it so hard to get to real owners."

"I do wonder about the threats to the *Tribune,* though," Michael said. "Do you think you could get a list of the advertisers? It might lead to something you could use."

"I'll sure try. I was going to ask if you might want to do some investigative work for the cause."

"I'd be glad to," Michael said. "Then I'd feel I'm doing my part for the cause."

"I've a feeling I'm going to need all the help I can

get locating some of these owners. I truly appreciate your offer to help, Michael," John said.

"Good."

"Well," Violet said. "If we have all that settled, I want to take Kathleen and Elizabeth upstairs for a few minutes to show them some fashion plates I've found that Kathleen might like for her trousseau."

"Go right ahead. We'll be in the parlor." Michael stood and led the men back to their parlor while Elizabeth and Kathleen followed Violet up the staircase.

"I'm sure they'll be gone for more than a few minutes, so let's not get our hopes up they'll be joining us anytime soon," Michael said, once the men had settled in the parlor.

"Not when they get to talking wedding talk," Luke said. "This planning takes up a lot more of Kathleen's time than I thought it would. I should have insisted on eloping."

"Getting anxious, Luke?" Michael asked.

"Probably about as much as you did before your wedding."

Michael laughed. "Well, I can assure you of one thing. It will be worth it when you see her come down the aisle on your wedding day."

John listened to their banter and chuckled along with them, but he honestly couldn't relate to how either of them felt and he felt a bit envious that he couldn't. Michael and Violet were very happy; no one in their company could question that for a moment. And John had no doubt that Luke and Kathleen would be just as happy. He could no longer deny that he longed for the same thing. A wife he loved to share his life with, to begin a family with.

And despite his vow never to give his heart to anyone again, he was having trouble keeping it. In fact it was entirely possible that he might have broken that vow already. The way Elizabeth took up his thoughts, he was—

"You're awfully quiet over there, John. Getting tired of all this wedding talk?"

"No. I'm glad to see my two best friends happy."

"You could be, too, you know."

John laughed and shook his head.

"I've seen the way you look at Elizabeth," Michael said.

John's heart pounded ferociously against his ribs.

"Yes, so have I," Luke added.

If they could see how he felt, how much chance did he have of keeping his feelings to himself around Elizabeth? He forced a chuckle and shook his head. "I... Elizabeth wouldn't... Never mind. Besides, my instincts where women are concerned aren't very good. I always end up saying the wrong thing."

"Well, join our club, man. We all end up saying or doing the wrong thing a lot of the time, if not most of the time. Who can understand the mind of a woman? You're no different from the rest of us," Luke said.

"Even so. Elizabeth is way out of my league."

"What makes you think so?" Michael asked.

He shrugged. "A feeling I've had since the day I met her."

"She works for a living like the rest of us," Luke said. "And I've seen her looking at you the same way you look at her, too."

"You have?" John shrugged. "She'd never—"

"John." Michael laughed. "You have a lot to learn about love. It doesn't have a thing to do with being 'out of one's league.' It has nothing to do with where one comes from, what social standing one is in, how rich or how poor. It doesn't even have to do with having like personalities. It only has to do with how two people feel about each other. Whether they hate the thought of being apart, and don't want to live one more day without being together as man and wife. It's missing her when she isn't with you, even if she's only in another room. It's—" He broke off and shrugged and chuckled. "Hard to explain."

"Very true," Luke added. "It's wanting to protect the person you love with everything in you, wanting their happiness before your own and—"

John raised his hand and nodded toward the foyer. His ears had been taking in everything his friends said, but also listening for the return of the women. The sounds on the stairs let him know the women were on their way back down.

"I'm sure looking forward to that ball game this Saturday," Luke said, understanding what his motions were all about. "I think it's going to be a good one."

John's hearing had been right on as the women entered the room.

"Did you miss us?" Violet asked, crossing the room to her husband.

"No doubt about it, we did," Michael responded.

"We missed you, too," his wife responded.

Luke stood and hurried to Kathleen's side. "I think we'll be taking off. Colleen telephoned earlier and asked Kathleen if we could stop by for a few minutes."

That meant he and Elizabeth would be alone on the walk home. John's gaze met and caught Elizabeth's and he wished…for so much more than he dared. All this talk with Michael and Luke hadn't helped him shore up his determination to keep his distance from this woman. Instead they'd made him want to take one more chance. His friends had stirred up a hope he feared reality would dash out.

Still, when Elizabeth smiled at him, he let that hope take over and smiled back. *Dear Lord, help me please. My feelings for this woman are growing with each passing day. But I'm afraid if I act on them, I'll suffer more than a broken heart. This time I could lose a very dear friend. Please help me to know what to do. And what not to do, especially on this walk home.*

"I suppose we should be on our way back, too, if you're ready, Elizabeth?" John said.

"Yes, I suppose we should." She turned to Michael and Violet. "Thank you so much for having us over. We do miss you at Heaton House."

"We'll have to do this more often," Michael said. "I'm glad we have the ball game to look forward to this weekend."

"So am I," John said.

They all said their goodbyes, and once on the street Luke and Kathleen headed in the opposite direction, waving goodbye. "We'll see you back at Heaton House."

John glanced at Elizabeth and crooked his arm. She smiled and slipped her hand through, resting it on his sleeve.

"It's a nice night out, isn't it?" he asked.

"It is. I'm glad it's cooled a bit since we came over.

Maybe Mrs. Oliver will get a breeze in her apartment this evening."

"I hope so," John said. "It was nice visiting with Michael and Violet, wasn't it?"

"It was. I've missed her since they married. And now I'll have to get used to a new boarder next door when Kathleen leaves."

"Yes. But so far we've been lucky to keep in touch and still be friends with those who've moved on. And you know it will be the same with Luke and Kathleen."

"That's true." Elizabeth's chest lightened at his words.

"And at least it's never boring at Heaton House."

"You're right about that. Thank you for making me feel better, John. I must admit I was feeling a little down."

"You're welcome. I do understand, you know. Though it's not quite the same and we men don't…"

"Don't what?"

"Well, we don't…" What had he gotten himself into? Again, he wasn't sure what to say without it sounding as if he were putting women down.

"You men don't share quite as much as we women do?" She chuckled and smiled up at him. "Don't have quite the same kind of gabfests?"

He laughed. She'd made it easy for him. "Not quite."

"What did you talk about while we were upstairs?"

"Oh, this and that." He wondered what she'd say if she knew they'd talked about her? "We're all looking forward to the baseball game with you ladies."

"Oh, I am, too. But I wasn't joking. I don't know much about the game, you know."

"I'll be glad to explain it to you."

"That's what I'm counting on."

"I wish you could be with us on the Fourth of July." He didn't like the thought of her not being there. But more, he hated that her father was bringing someone he'd like her to think of as husband material. And what if she liked the man?

"So do I. But it's only for the weekend."

"That's true." But much could happen in a short time. Would she have that other man on her mind when she came home? Best to quit thinking or talking about it. "I think I'll go back to the building with the windows painted shut and show the other tenants how to open them tomorrow. I've been worrying about it. I don't know how they're able to sleep at night."

Elizabeth stopped in her tracks and actually hugged his arm. "Oh, John. Thank you! I've been worrying about that very same thing. Why don't you get Luke to go with you? I'm sure he'd be glad to. His hours are pretty much his own, you know."

"That's a great idea, Elizabeth. I'll ask him when he gets back tonight. You don't remember any mention of windows being hard to open at any of the other buildings we checked out, do you?"

"No. But ever since we found out Mrs. Oliver's were, I've wondered how many others might be."

"Well, we'll do what we can and maybe ask Kathleen to check into that in the buildings she visits."

Elizabeth released a huge sigh. "I feel ever so much better now. I know I'll sleep well tonight. You're a good man, John Talbot."

Her words sent his heart to swelling so big he was afraid it might burst. He looked down into her eyes and his gaze traveled over her face. Her eyes shined in the lamplight at the corner they'd halted at. He had to fight the urge to take her in his arms and kiss her soundly. He let out a deep breath and said, "Elizabeth Anderson, that's the nicest thing anyone has ever said to me."

"Well, it's true." She gave a little jerk to his arm and took off a step, forcing him to come along with her. She chuckled. "But don't you dare let it go to your head."

They both laughed as they walked the half block to Heaton House.

Chapter Fourteen

The next night at dinner, John and Luke reported that they'd opened the windows in five apartments and showed others how to do it in ten more.

"It's a start," John said.

"At least we know some tenants will be able to get some air in their apartments at night. And we can check with more now that we know it's a problem." Elizabeth smiled at him. She wondered how she could ever have thought him full of himself. He was one of the most caring people she'd met and he couldn't have become that way overnight. No, she'd made a snap judgment about him and let it stick far longer than she should have.

She'd wanted to throw her arms around his neck and hug him the night before when he'd said he was going back to open some of those windows. And when he'd gazed down at her after she'd told him what a nice man he was, she'd hoped he might kiss her again. Then she'd become afraid he would and that was when she'd jerked on his arm. She couldn't let him kiss her again. They had to remain only friends. She couldn't afford to let her feelings for him grow any stronger.

"I'll be sure to find out what I can about the buildings I go into," Kathleen said. "It's a shame so many of them aren't taken care of—and when they have been painted, it's such a shoddy job that the tenants can't open their windows."

"I know," Elizabeth said. "It makes me sad and angry all at the same time. I hope we find out who owns these awful buildings soon."

"We will. Having Michael looking into it will help, too. He's got connections I don't have," John said.

"I'm sure you already have more connections than you think just from covering events for the society page. Many of those people will remember your name and how you wrote about them—you've always found something nice to say, much as it might have pained you to do so. They won't forget," Elizabeth assured him. As soon as the words left her mouth she wondered what she was thinking. Would he suspect that she knew those people better than she let on? But then she was rewarded with a smile that had her pulse racing to keep up with her heartbeat.

"Thank you. In fact, you may be right about that. At the last charity function I covered, the host came up to me and mentioned that he'd enjoyed my first article."

"Well, then, see? Through your covering all those society events, you've met a lot of influential people and you'll have all the connections you need when you need them most one day," Elizabeth said.

"That is, if I don't make some of them angry with my coverage on the tenements. The paper has already gotten threats of advertising being pulled. I hope it doesn't happen and my editor says we're going on with the stories, but I'd hate for him to change his mind."

"We'll be praying he doesn't. And whoever they are, they are just trying to get their way. Wouldn't it make them look suspicious to pull advertising? Why would they possibly want to call attention to themselves if they own one of those buildings?" Mrs. Heaton asked from the head of the table.

"That's what we're thinking, Mrs. Heaton."

"Well, I'm very proud of you and Elizabeth for getting stories out there and of Kathleen for all the work she does in the tenements. I feel we are doing all we can to make things better for those living in such deplorable conditions."

A thought suddenly came to Elizabeth and her heart twisted deep in her chest. "Are you in any danger from writing these articles, John?"

Mrs. Heaton gasped. "I hadn't thought of that."

"Neither had I until now," Elizabeth said. But now that she had, she needed an answer.

"I suppose anything is possible. But I don't believe I am. Please don't worry about me. I think the worst anyone would do is put so much pressure on the paper that they would stop the articles. But my editor is more enthused than ever about them, so I'm not really worried about that right now and I don't want you to worry, either."

Her thoughts flitting all over the place about the possibility of John being in danger, Elizabeth managed to send up a prayer. She was determined to trust the Lord to keep John safe.

John could see the concern in Elizabeth's eyes. She truly cared about what happened to him—even if only as a friend. But knowing she cared enough that she would turn pale at the thought of anything happening to him, made his heart swell with joy...and made him long for more.

He'd thought of the conversation at Michael's the night before over and over again. Could he and Luke be right? Did Elizabeth have a special look for him? And had she noticed the way he looked at her, as Luke had? One thing was for certain—he was still as unsure of himself where Elizabeth was concerned as he'd ever been. He wanted to believe, wanted to hope—

"Are either of you covering the Vanderbilts' charity event tomorrow night?"

"I am," he and Elizabeth both said at the same time and then chuckled.

"I believe it might be my last time for these things from what my editor said." John glanced at Elizabeth. "Want to go together?"

Elizabeth seemed a bit surprised by his invitation and he couldn't tell what she was thinking. Everyone at the table quieted as if waiting for her answer, too, and John found himself holding his breath.

"I— Well, yes, why not?" She smiled at him.

"Good. We can split up when we get there and cover the room and then compare notes afterward."

"That's a good idea. And then we might be able to get out of there earlier than normal."

John grinned. "That's what I was thinking."

As dinner came to an end and everyone began heading into the parlor, Elizabeth could only wonder what she'd been thinking to agree to going to the Vanderbilts' with John on Friday. What if someone mentioned her in connection with her aunt? What if John found out she was one of "them" while there? *Oh, please, Lord, help me here. Should I have said no? Should I back out?*

Deep down she knew the answer to both those questions was no. It was time to let those she cared about know her secret, especially as she'd let so much out the other night about her father. But she didn't want to just blurt it out. She felt she owed Kathleen and John the courtesy of telling them privately.

But John had excused himself and gone downstairs to work, so telling him would have to wait. However, she had no excuse where Kathleen was concerned. They spoke nearly every night when they went upstairs to bed, told each other things they didn't tell anyone else. Except that Kathleen had been more honest about her past than Elizabeth had. Would she still be her friend once she knew?

Just the thought of what she and John and the others might think of her was enough to set her to trembling on the inside. Trying not to think about it, she forced herself to play charades with the others until it was time to go upstairs. But thankfully, Luke excused himself early to go work on his latest dime novel and Kathleen slipped into the foyer to tell him good-night. When she came back in, her cheeks were flushed and her eyes sparkling.

"You look awfully happy," Elizabeth said to her. *And here I am going to spoil that mood in a bit.*

"Well, you look awfully pale. You aren't sick, are you?" Kathleen asked.

"No. I'm fine." For now, at least. She wasn't sure how she'd feel once she told her best friend what she'd been keeping from her for months. Or, in John's case—for several years. *Oh, why didn't I come to You about all of this in the beginning, Lord?* Well, not doing so had its consequences and she'd have to live with them, no matter what.

"No. That's not exactly true. I need to speak with you."

"Let's go up, then. I can tell something is wrong and I want to know what."

Millicent and Julia decided to head upstairs at the same time and they all told each other good-night at the top of the stairs. Kathleen followed Elizabeth into her room and shut the door. "Oh, I'm relieved that they didn't want to chat. Now, tell me what is bothering you."

"Let's sit down." Elizabeth led the way to the settee in front of the fireplace and they both took a seat. But Elizabeth found she couldn't sit still. She jumped up and began to pace. How was she going to go about this?

"Elizabeth, you have me concerned. Whatever is wrong?"

"It's me. I've been wrong. I haven't been totally truthful with you or John and some of the others. And now I know I must tell you about it. But I'm afraid to tell you in fear that you won't want to be my friend any longer."

"Oh, Elizabeth. Come sit down. You have nothing to fear. You've been there for me from the day I was brought to Heaton House. You're my best friend and I can't imagine you telling me anything that would change that. I know you—"

"No. You don't. Not really, anyway. Oh, you know *me,* but you don't know who I really am."

"Well, come sit and tell me." Kathleen patted the spot on the settee that Elizabeth had vacated.

Elizabeth released a long sigh and took her seat once

more. "My real name is Elizabeth Anderson Reynolds and my father is Charles Edward Reynolds of Boston. I know that probably doesn't mean much to you, but he is very wealthy and well...so am I."

"Why, Elizabeth, there is certainly nothing wrong with being wealthy. Why would you think—"

"The money isn't important to me except for what I can do to help others. But my father never saw it that way and I had to fight for my independence to be able to do what I felt was right. And then...well, I didn't want the other boarders here to look at me as anything but one of them. But I worry about everyone finding out and feeling I've deceived them and—"

Kathleen reached over and gave Elizabeth a hug. "Oh, sweet friend, I think I do understand. At least as much as I can, coming from such a different background. And you have nothing to apologize to me for. I have things in my background that I'd rather not have everyone know about, either."

Compassion for Kathleen flooded Elizabeth. It wouldn't be easy to tell people that your brother-in-law beat you and then later tried to kill your sister. Would have, if the police hadn't shown up and shot him in the nick of time. All that and living in the tenements, striving to get ahead.

She sighed in relief that she could still call this wonderful woman her best friend. "Thank you so much, Kathleen. I hope the others are as understanding as you. I'm afraid John might..."

"John will be fine. He cares about you, Elizabeth. He's not going to hate you."

"No. But he and the others might feel I've betrayed them and—"

"Elizabeth, you are still the same person I've always known. You just have more money than the rest of us. From your conversation the other night, it was apparent that you wanted to be independent and on your own. I don't think there is any need for everyone to know every little thing about a person they are friends with. You've shown what kind of person you are over and over again to me and to the others. But what made you feel you had to tell me all this now?"

"It was getting too hard to avoid. I'd like my aunt to get to know you all and I'd like everyone to get to know her. I want to quit worrying that someone might let others know exactly who I am before I have a chance to tell them."

Kathleen nodded. "I can understand that reasoning. But I don't believe you have anything to worry about."

"Mrs. Heaton and Michael know and they were kind and understood my reasons. But while it might have made sense at the time, I acted hastily in my decision not to let others know, too. I didn't ask the Lord to guide me and wait for him to show me what to do."

Kathleen nodded. "We all act hastily at times. I know I have."

"Oh, Kathleen. You're the best friend I've ever had. I can't tell you how much better I feel getting this out. Now I just have to find the right time to tell the others."

And pray that they accepted her as Kathleen had. Would they? Could they?

Elizabeth had hoped to get a chance to speak to John before the charity event, but he didn't come in until dinnertime and she knew she'd have to wait—and pray that nothing came up at the Vanderbilts' before she had a chance to tell him. His response was the one she was most worried about. They'd come to know each other so much better since they'd been working on the articles together, and just as she'd opened up to him more, she felt he'd done the same thing with her.

She was finding it hard enough to tamp down her growing feelings for him and she didn't want to even contemplate losing the fragile friendship that had developed between them.

She hurried to dress after dinner, choosing a gown that was nice enough for the event as a reporter. No one would expect her to be dressed as well as the hosts or the guests. And if she were, there might be questions. She'd rather not deal with any of those until after she talked to John.

Her better gowns were at her aunt's anyway, and Aunt Bea had mentioned that she wouldn't be attending this event. She felt the Vanderbilts were still a bit out of her league, and while she saw them at events others held, she wasn't on their guest list.

Elizabeth wouldn't be attending the event except for covering it for the *Delineator*. But she had to admit she was looking forward to going with John—even if spending the evening in his company had let those butterflies loose to flutter inside her stomach once again.

She put on an aqua gown trimmed in cream-colored lace and dabbed on her favorite scent. She picked up her wrap and reticule and made sure it contained her pad and pencil before heading downstairs.

John was waiting for her in the foyer and he looked quite grand in his tux and tails. He gave her a leisurely perusal and she could feel warmth creep up her neck to her cheeks.

"You look quite lovely tonight, Elizabeth."

"Thank you. You look very nice yourself." An understatement, to be sure. His shoulders seemed even broader in dress clothes and her heart thudded against her chest as he held out his arm to her and they went outside.

"No trolley for us tonight. I've ordered a hack to pick us up."

"That's so nice of you. We might have been the center of attention if we rode the trolley, or the El and had to walk to the Vanderbilts' portico."

"I'm sure *you* will be anyway. I might have to fight off anyone who stares too long."

His words made her feel special and protected, and flirted with. He flashed her a smile as he helped her into the waiting hack and then took his own seat beside her.

"If we get finished in time, perhaps we can take a ride through Central Park on the way home."

"I'd love it. I can't remember the last time I've done that." It must have been with a group for she'd had no suitors, and Mrs. Heaton was very strict about her girls being out after dark without an escort.

"With both of us taking notes and comparing them, I'm certain we'll get out early. And we'll have more information than we would have otherwise. I quite like working with you, Elizabeth."

"We do make a good team, don't we?"

"We do."

His voice had turned husky and her heartbeat seemed to stop for a moment at the realization that they did indeed work well together and that John thought so, too.

The expression in his eyes had her pulse racing once

again and she was reminded of that one brief kiss they'd shared. Not that it took much to remind her. A glance from John, a smile, just his presence seemed to be able to bring that thought to mind quite easily.

The hack pulled up to the Vanderbilt mansion and she gave herself a little shake. Thinking about kisses was not what she should be doing. They were here for their work and nothing more. Her thoughts seemed to get more carried away each time she was with John.

Just because he thought they made a good team and liked working with her didn't mean anything more than what he'd said. She had to quit reading so much into his words. Or maybe it wasn't what he said but what she longed for. *Oh, please Lord, help me to concentrate on the reason we are here tonight.*

John helped her out of the hack at the entrance and they strolled to the front door, as several other guests were doing. After giving the doorman their credentials, he checked them against a list he had in front of him and let them in to the main hall, directing them to the ballroom where the benefit would be held.

The sheer size of the hall took Elizabeth's breath away. Carved caryatids supported the marble mantelpiece, and she knew many of the paintings had to have come from Europe. The standing candelabras lent a warm glow to the hall and brought out the rich colors in the rugs.

"Whoa," John whispered. "I'd heard it was something to see, but I wasn't expecting this."

"No, neither was I." It put most other homes she'd been in to shame, and made her feel as if her worries about her family's wealth were almost laughable. "I can't imagine living in something like this. I don't even know how to describe it."

John chuckled. "Neither do I. And we're both writers. One could get lost for days in here."

They stopped at the doorway of the ballroom, which was even more magnificent than the hall, and John stood tall and straightened his tie. "I always feel a little intimidated coming into this kind of wealth."

"This mansion would intimidate anyone coming into it for the first time. But you have no reason to feel that way. Many of these people inherited their wealth through no effort of their own. You are making your own way and, who knows, one day you might own your own paper."

John laughed outright. "Now, that's a thought I like. Actually it is a dream of mine, but I don't lie awake worrying about it."

"It could happen, you know."

"Elizabeth, you are the most encouraging person I know. Thank you for boosting my confidence when I most need it. Which side of the room do you want to take?"

Elizabeth gazed out onto the crowd, trying to gage which side might be the safest to mingle in. But she recognized only a few faces and those people only knew her as a writer for the *Delineator*. "Either side is fine with me."

"Then I'll go to the right and you take the left. When we meet in the center, we'll decide if we have enough information to share and if so, we'll make an exit."

He grinned at her and all she could think of was getting finished early enough so that they could have some time together. After all the talk about wealth, tonight might be the time to open up to John. If so, she prayed he'd take her news as graciously as Kathleen had. "Let's go."

Chapter Fifteen

Elizabeth gave him a smile and took off, leaving John wondering if he were imagining the shadow that'd suddenly appeared behind her eyes. She always seemed self-assured, but was it possible she felt as out of place here as he did? He should have tried to boost her confidence as she had his.

Her words *had* bolstered him, and as he began to make his way around the crowd of people, he reminded himself that Elizabeth seemed to be proud that he was making his own way. If she felt that way, perhaps he should act as optimistic that he might own his own paper one day as she was. Or at the very least, that he was confident his editor wanted more stories from him and that he was working himself up at the *Tribune*. And doing his best at reporting on these events—even though it wasn't the kind of thing he wanted to do, hadn't hurt.

This particular event was a charity auction of some of the Vanderbilts' paintings and John was exceedingly glad that he was there to cover it and not as someone expected to place a bid. He was sure it would take more than he made in several months or even a year to put up an opening bid.

He did recognize many people from covering other events and most greeted him as if he were one of them, but he knew it was only because they wanted their names in his article.

As the first item came up, he watched as the bidding started, and then accelerated, when two prominent men of wealth were left to try to outbid each other. That they were competitors couldn't have been more obvious, but finally one gave it up and shrugged to his companions, letting the other man have the artwork at a price John couldn't even fathom paying.

At least tonight was to benefit the poor and these people did do a lot of giving. Still, their pockets seemed lined with gold, and he knew they spent money even more lavishly on their own families and their wants and desires. And that they spent in order to impress each other. In their bidding, their attire and the carriages they arrived in—it was all about outdoing each other.

Everyone mingled and helped themselves to refreshments in between biddings. John circulated among them, listening for anything that might be news worthy. Mostly he heard how many of them would be leaving for their summer homes for the season. The Vanderbilts were very genial when they spotted him.

"I'm enjoying the articles you've been writing, Mr. Talbot," Cornelius Vanderbilt II said. "You're doing a very good job."

"Thank you, sir. I'm hoping to do more." John was a little surprised at how easy it was to talk to them. Mrs. Vanderbilt told him they'd be going to The Breakers for the rest of the season. He'd heard much about their summer place and would have liked the chance to compare the two houses. Could people really afford more than one home like this? And why would they want to?

He couldn't really even imagine the kind of life they lived. As he went from one cluster of people to another, he overheard conversations about the newest designers in Europe and how much one woman had paid to have her drawing room redone. Another had no problem mentioning the amount she'd paid for the gown she had on.

Forget bidding on the art, the dress alone would set one back a mighty penny. And then…another man was talking about the trip he and his wife were taking to Europe. They'd be gone until the fall. Perhaps he had business dealings there. Many of these people had relatives still living in those countries, so there was that. At least that's what he assumed. It might be nice to be so wealthy one could gallivant all over the world, but when one had places like this, why wouldn't they just want to stay and enjoy the comforts of home?

He looked across the room to find Elizabeth speaking to one of the younger Vanderbilts. For having never met them, she seemed quite at ease, but then she always appeared that way, no matter whom she was with. He hoped she was getting some good tidbits from them.

Another item came up for bid and everyone quieted as the offering started on a painting that was so large, John knew it would only fit in a home like this.

The starting offer was more than the last item had gone for and he tried not to show his amazement as the bids continued to climb into four and then five figures. He couldn't help but overhear one gentleman say to another that his wife had her eye on that painting. The man stuck with it until his wife had that painting and John couldn't help but notice the smug look on her face as she looked at the wife of the last man who couldn't, or wouldn't, come up with the highest offer.

And he couldn't help but be proud for the woman who would go home without the painting as she grabbed her husband's arm and patted it. "You tried."

Whether it was forced or natural, the smile she gave the woman who'd take the painting home that night was bright enough to have her turning away in a huff. Had it been worth that much money to be put in one's place? Somehow he doubted it.

He quickly wrote down the winning couple's name and the name of the painting they won before moving away and mingling with the crowd once more, working himself nearer to his and Elizabeth's designated meeting place. After the next item, they could be on their way out of here.

One more item and she and John could meet up and go on that ride around Central Park. She was happy that this charity event was bringing in so much money—the wealthy who'd been invited to it could well afford it. But there was no doubt that many were here only because Cornelius Vanderbilt II had invited them. And if not for the need to have an event like this covered by the papers and her magazine, she knew that she and John would never have been allowed in.

But just as they liked to help the less fortunate, many of the wealthy were happy to let the world know when they did. Perhaps rightly so, but if at all possible, she'd rather do her good works anonymously.

She'd mingled with many of the younger set of the

family who seemed to go to great lengths to get their own names to appear in the news. Elizabeth supposed she could see how a younger member of such a large and distinguished family might be afraid they'd get lost in the shadow of those who were regularly written about.

All it really did was reinforce her determination to be independent and not have to live that kind of life. She was so consumed by her thoughts she barely noticed when the next item came up for bid. She hoped John had taken notes, as it was over rather quickly. She looked around and saw him heading in her direction when suddenly she felt a tap on her shoulder.

"Say, don't I know you?"

Her heartbeat seemed to come to a standstill as she recognized the man as one she'd seen at more than one event in the past year. "I don't believe we've met. I'm Elizabeth Anderson and I write for the *Delineator*."

"Oh…sorry. I took you for someone else." He let go of her arm and Elizabeth sighed in relief. She wanted to laugh. Obviously, a woman who worked for a living wasn't someone he'd have an association with. She couldn't quite contain her chuckle as she turned to find John hurrying up to her.

"You looked upset a moment ago. Was that man bothering you?"

"He thought I was someone else. Did you get notes on that last bid? I hate to admit it, but I was woolgathering and I somehow missed it all."

He held up his notebook and grinned. "I did. Come on. Let's get out of here and I'll tell you what it was on our drive through Central Park."

Needing no further persuasion, she took the arm he held out and they made their way out of the room.

* * *

As the hack John procured took off from the Vanderbilt mansion, they turned to each other, smiled and
sighed.

"I truly hope this is the last society function I have
to cover," John said, settling into the corner of the seat.
"I know these people do help the poor and are very
good to give some of their money to charity. But still,
that home... I can't understand why any family, even a
large one, would need over a hundred rooms in a home."

Neither did Elizabeth. But her home had several
more rooms than it needed, too. Enough so that she
felt very lonely when her father had been gone and it
was just her and the housekeeper. She could remember
hearing all manner of sounds at night and being afraid
to go investigate.

Mrs. Harper had always reassured her it was just the
house settling. Still, as a young girl, she remembered
hiding under the covers when her father wasn't in town.

When she grew older, she'd prayed for the Lord to
calm her fears before going to sleep. But the loneliness
never really went away. And her home was nowhere
near the size of the Vanderbilt mansion. But it was big,
and if tonight had done anything, it had reinforced the
need to tell John who she really was.

"Elizabeth? You're awfully quiet. Is anything
wrong?"

"No, not really. There is just something I must tell
you and I'm not sure how you'll take it."

"That sounds ominous." He sat up a little straighter
on the seat.

"It's not really. It's just something you don't know
about me and I—"

"You aren't going to tell me you're related to the Vanderbilts, are you?"

She couldn't contain her giggle at that thought. "No. I'm not related to the Vanderbilts. But, I— John, there's no other way to say it. I come from a wealthy family, too. Not nearly as wealthy at the Vanderbilts or Astors, but—"

He was quiet in his corner of the seat and she held her breath as she waited for his reaction. He looked out the window of the carriage and rubbed his chin.

Was he angry that she was only now revealing who she was?

"Ah, that explains it," he finally said.

"Explains what?"

"Why you've always seemed different from the rest of us, why you seemed so comfortable talking to everyone at the Vanderbilts tonight. Why you seem to be comfortable in any situation."

"I wasn't all that comfortable tonight. I've just learned to hide my nervousness well. I don't really know these people. I'm from Boston and...my real name is Elizabeth Anderson Reynolds. My father's name is Edward and..."

John whistled. "You do come from a wealthy family. I'm familiar with that name. But if that's the case, then why are you working for a living and living at Heaton House? Did you get cut out of the will?"

"I don't know. If so, my father hasn't told me. But he wasn't happy with me for wanting to live here in New York City, so it's possible." He might as well know it all. "However, I do have an inheritance from my grandmother on my mother's side of the family. That's what made it possible for me to come here, to make a life of my own. Well, that and the fact that my father didn't like me helping…" No. There was no need to make John think less of her father. "He worried about my going into some of the poorer sections of town and I like helping people. Anyway, he sent me to my aunt in hopes I'd learn what a lady of wealth should do with her time. But he forgot that I take after my mother and my aunt. My aunt understood my need to be independent and make my own way, and my desire to help others. She sympathized with me and with her help, Papa finally let me stay here."

"I see."

His tone was somber and Elizabeth's chest was heavy. He sounded disappointed and she supposed she really couldn't blame him.

"I wish you'd told me all this earlier. Why did you feel the need to—"

"I just wanted to be one of Mrs. Heaton's boarders. I was afraid you'd all avoid me and I wanted so badly to fit in. And then I was afraid that once you found out, you'd all feel I'd somehow betrayed your trust in me. I'm so sorry…" Her voice broke and she turned her head to look out of the window so that John couldn't see the tears in her eyes. She could hear movement and knew that he'd moved closer to her.

He'd heard the sincerity in her voice and he slid nearer to her, wanting to comfort her. "Elizabeth, there's nothing to forgive. You don't owe me any explanations. You'd fit in at Heaton House no matter what your name was. I do wish you'd let us know from the start, but I suppose I can understand why you didn't."

She hadn't set out to mislead them. And he well understood not wanting people to know every little thing about you. He hadn't told anyone about the humiliation he'd felt when his dreams had crashed around him. But this wasn't an easy thing to accept—that Elizabeth was a wealthy woman. Even though she wanted to be like the rest of them, she wasn't. She had that wealth to fall back on and she'd lived a very different kind of life. Would she want to go back to it eventually? And what if she longed for things a normal working fellow couldn't give her?

"Then, are we still friends?"

Oh, what he felt for this woman was more than friendship. There was no denying it. But he had even more reason to distance himself from her now. It'd been hard enough to think he might have a chance with her before, but now—well, he'd vowed never to fall for another woman—especially a wealthy one. And even if he wanted to change his mind, she *was* wealthy and that presented a whole other set of problems. There was no way he could hope to—

"John?" She'd turned to him and he could see tears in her eyes, one escaping to run down her cheek.

He reached out to brush it away. "Oh, Elizabeth, of course we're still friends. I hope we'll always be friends." With all that was in him, he hoped that. For that was all they ever could be now.

"So do I."

Her eyes were sorrowful and he felt the need to reassure her again. He cupped her jaw in his hand and lowered his head. He kissed her on the cheek—as a friend might do—even though what he truly wished was to kiss her lips. He leaned his forehead against hers. "We'll be friends for as long as you want us to be."

That much he could promise. For he wanted this woman in his life and if friends was all they could be, so be it. The rest of the drive through central Park wasn't quite what he'd dreamed it might be, but he was glad to be with Elizabeth.

"When are you going to tell the others?"

"As soon as I can. It's been so hard these past few months, realizing I'd made things worse by not just saying who I was from the start. I became afraid someone would recognize me at one of the society functions we've covered or that I've helped my aunt with and—"

"Your aunt?"

"Yes. You've met her. She's Beatrice Watson."

"I should have known. She has your smile—or, you have hers. She's very nice. And…you were the flower girl that helped her at the masquerade party, weren't you?"

"I was. And I was so afraid you'd find out who I was that night and be angry with me. That was when I knew I had to tell you soon. You and Kathleen first, before anyone else."

He should have felt some comfort that she'd wanted him to be one of the first to know, but there was little comfort in knowing for certain that he was indeed out of her league. "Have you told her?"

"Yes. I told her last night. I can't begin to tell you what a relief it is to have it out. And I feel so bad that all this time my aunt could have enjoyed knowing you all and you could have known her. She would love the atmosphere at Heaton House as much as I do."

"Well, I'm sure that can be remedied now. Mrs. Heaton would be glad to have her for Sunday dinner."

"Oh, I know she would. She's told me to invite her anytime."

"Then she knows?"

Elizabeth nodded. "She does. And so does Michael. I felt I had to tell them when I applied for the room. They understood my reasons for using my mother's last name at the time. But they told me anytime I wanted to let everyone know they would stand behind me."

"They are loyal to us all, aren't they?"

"Yes. I'm very thankful that my aunt had heard of Mrs. Heaton and insisted I board with her."

"So am I." John couldn't imagine not having Elizabeth in his life and he prayed he'd never have to. But the dreams he'd begun to weave would have to come to a stop. "I'll be there when you tell the others, but I don't think you have to worry about it. They know the kind of person you are, Elizabeth. They'll understand."

Elizabeth prayed John was right the next morning as she went downstairs early and sought out Mrs. Heaton. She was in her study to Elizabeth's relief and she looked up when she knocked on the doorframe.

"Why, Elizabeth, dear. You're down very early. Is something wrong?"

"Not really, but I would like to talk to you, if you have time."

"You know I always have time for you. Come in."

Elizabeth shut the door behind her and took a seat across from Mrs. Heaton's desk.

"What is it, dear?"

"Well, I wanted to let you know that I'm going to let everyone know who I really am. I've told Kathleen and John and I want the others to know, as well."

"I see. It became too much to worry about, didn't it?" Mrs. Heaton's blue eyes were kind behind her spectacles. Her auburn hair was done up on top of her head and she looked much the same as the day Elizabeth had come asking for a room.

"It did. I finally realized I'd jumped out ahead of the Lord and made a decision that only complicated my life. The more I came to care about everyone the worse I felt for not being totally honest from the beginning. And the more fearful I was of them finding out and feeling as if I'd somehow betrayed their trust in me."

"Oh, my dear. Elizabeth, they aren't going to think that. You had reasons for not giving your whole name at the time. But I am glad you aren't worried about that any longer."

"So am I. And I'll no longer feel anxious that someone besides me would reveal to anyone I care about who I really am."

"That is perfectly understandable. Are you going to tell them today?"

"I think so. I'd like to get it over with."

"I'm proud of the decision you've made, Elizabeth. There is absolutely no reason you should hide your wealth. I know firsthand what you do to help others, many who don't know where the help comes from." She glanced up at the clock on the wall. "Come, it's time for breakfast. Let's go get this all out in the open so you can live your life the way the Lord wants you to."

Several boarders were already at the table when she and Mrs. Heaton entered the dining room. She breathed a sigh of relief when she was greeted by smiles from John and Kathleen. She fixed her plate and slipped into her chair beside John.

"You all right this morning?" His eyes looked deeply into hers and she nodded.

"I am. Or I will be once breakfast is over."

It was as if the Lord knew she wanted to do this only one more time, for in just minutes, everyone was gathered around the table—something that rarely happened on a Saturday morning.

She gave them time to eat before tapping the side of her coffee cup to get everyone's attention. "I'm not sure there is ever a good time for this kind of thing but since everyone is here…I have something I need to tell you all."

"What is it?" Millicent asked. "You aren't leaving Heaton House, are you?"

"No. But you might wish I would once you hear what I have to tell you."

"No, they won't," Kathleen assured her as the table quieted, waiting for Elizabeth to speak.

"When I came to Heaton House, I was determined to be independent and make my own way. And I wanted to fit in and be considered just like the rest of you. And I am and I plan on continuing to be, if possible. But there were a few details I left out when I was introduced to you all."

She had everyone's attention now. Fear that they wouldn't accept her for who she was gripped her, but she wanted it over with, no matter how they all took it.

She looked around the table and saw Mrs. Heaton's encouraging nod, Kathleen's smile—even Luke seemed to be encouraging, although she wasn't sure if he knew or not. And John, who whispered, "Go ahead. It'll be all right."

The most important ones in her life were still her

friends and that was a blessing she wouldn't take for granted.

She swallowed around the knot in her throat and took a deep breath.

"I am Elizabeth Anderson, but I left off part of my name when I came here. My real name is Elizabeth Anderson Reynolds and my father is Edward Reynolds of Boston. He owns a shipping company and has interests in all manner of other things. I work because I want to, but I don't have to."

"In other words, you're wealthy," Millicent bluntly said.

"I am. Yes."

"Well, that's a relief. I wondered why you always had a little extra cash and offered it whenever one of us was running short. I thought you just managed money a whole lot better than I did."

"You didn't think we'd treat you the same as we treat each other if we knew at the start?" Julia's tone was cool.

"I was afraid you might not. And I so wanted to be accepted by you all."

"Perhaps we would have treated you differently," Julia said. "I don't know, although I would hope not. But still, I wish you'd given us a chance, Elizabeth."

"I'm sorry, Julia. That's all I can say. I wish I'd been totally truthful with you all, too. But I can't go back and do it all over again."

"No. I suppose not." Julia sighed and shook her head. "I'd stay mad at you, but you've been too good a friend for that. Besides, we know you now, and it doesn't matter if you have more money than we do. You're the Elizabeth we love."

"And the one we know we can come to if we come up short at the end of the month," Millicent added. Her smile said she was teasing, but Elizabeth was glad they realized she could and would help any of them.

"So you don't hate me for not telling you everything from the start?"

"Elizabeth, it's not like you committed a crime. I'm sure you've suffered the consequences of not being totally truthful and that you wrestled with it all this time or you wouldn't be telling us now," Ben said from across the table. "We all have parts of ourselves we don't share with others. You are like us in that respect and there's no way we can hold it against you."

"Thank you, Ben." She looked around the table once more. "Thank you all. I'm an only child with no cousins and well, you all mean so much to me."

She hadn't told them everything—not about her broken engagement or her mistrust of men. There was no need to go into all of that, at least not now and not with everyone.

Chapter Sixteen

They set out for the ball game that afternoon in high spirits. Elizabeth felt freer than she had in years, now that she'd told her story and everyone knew who she was.

Her heart was light as she walked along with John and the others, enjoying the mild afternoon. The men had all worn light-colored pants, striped shirts and suspenders, with straw bowlers topping off their outfits.

Elizabeth had chosen a dark green skirt with a pale green shirtwaist. Her hat was straw with a large brim trimmed with flowers. The other women were dressed similarly. She liked dressing like the others and not having to change clothes for every different outing. She'd always thought doing so was a terrible waste of time.

When talk turned to the next weekend and what they'd planned for the day, she tried not to feel jealous, but she so wanted to be part of that weekend. If only her father would cancel his trip and come another time. But she knew that wasn't going to happen and she reminded herself it was only for a few days.

They caught the trolley that would take them to the

polo field where the game was being played. When they arrived, Elizabeth saw there were trees around the area and she thought the doubled-deck grandstand was impressive. A line was forming to buy tickets to get in.

"We're lucky to get here this early, some of the good seats are still left," John said, grasping Elizabeth's arm and leading her up into the grandstand.

The seats they chose were midway over and up so as to be able to see everything. Elizabeth couldn't help but notice several teenage boys on the very top. They all had baseball gloves with them.

"Are they part of the team?"

John chuckled. "No. They're just hoping to catch a home-run ball before it goes out of the park."

"A home run?"

John nodded. "That's when a batter hits a ball outside of the field, where no one on the other team can catch it. The player goes around all the bases, and gets to home without fear of being tagged out. Sometimes the fans get to catch that ball and take it home for a souvenir."

"Oh! That would be fun, wouldn't it?"

"Sure would. I used to be like those boys. Actually caught a few when I was their age."

Elizabeth had a feeling all the men there might miss some of the game, just trying to teach it to the women. "If I ask a question at the wrong time, I'll understand if you don't answer right away."

"Don't worry about that. I want you to learn the game. You'll enjoy it much more if you do."

She was already enjoying it. There was a soft breeze that cooled the afternoon air and she could feel the excitement all around as the team took to the field and the first batter began to swing his bat.

"I do hate to show my ignorance, but which team is ours?"

"We're for the Giants and we're first up at bat. The other team is the Brooklyn Bridegrooms."

"That seems an odd name for a baseball team."

John laughed. "We kind of think so, too. But they are pretty good. They beat us yesterday."

"And the man behind the plate? The one with that funny mask and breast padding? What is he and why is he wearing all that?"

"He's the umpire and that mask is to guard his face, the chest padding to keep the impact from hurting him in case a ball comes at him."

It wasn't long before Elizabeth understood the precautions. A ball whizzed by the batter and right by the catcher's face. She held her breath as he reached out to catch it, and then she released a huge sigh. "Oh, I can see why all that is needed."

John nodded. "They can still get hurt, but not nearly as bad as they could be without the protection."

"I'm glad they have it. What about the pitcher? I'd think he might be afraid of a ball coming straight toward him."

"Probably is. And a few have been hurt, but it's easier for them to get out of the way than for a catcher squatting down behind the batter's plate."

"I had no idea it could be so dangerous."

"It usually isn't. Hopefully today will be just a regular game." He smiled down at her and relief flooded her. He was still her friend after all she'd told him and that alone was enough to make the day special. *Thank You, Lord.*

She tried to follow the game, but when the batter

began to walk to first base without hitting the ball, she finally had to ask. "Why is he getting to do that?"

"He gets to walk. After four balls—that means the pitcher threw balls that weren't over home plate—the batter gets to walk to first base. Good for us because our next batter is really good and we could get two runs out of it."

"Really? I'm sorry. You must be getting tired of answering my questions."

"Elizabeth, don't you know we men love teaching women things?"

"Yes, well, I'm sure you like enjoying the game, too, and I'm taking your attention off of it."

"I'm getting to see the game and teach you about it at the same time. I'm not going to miss anything important. I can watch the game and answer your questions at the same time."

"You're sure?"

"I'm positive."

She smiled at him. "Good. Then maybe by next time, I'll understand it well enough to let you watch in peace."

"Would you want to come again?"

"Oh, yes! It's quite exciting."

John grinned. "Well, there are still a lot of games left in the season. I'm sure we'll come again—if you can tear yourself away from some of those wedding plans."

Elizabeth leaned out and nodded toward Kathleen and Luke, who sat on the other side of John. "It appears Kathleen's enjoying it as much as I am. I think we'll be able to work around ball games."

His smile shot straight to her heart and she could feel her face flush as she looked away just as the batter hit the second ball out of the ballpark.

John jumped up and cheered with the others to watch the batter and the man on first make it all the way in to home base. She jumped up and cheered with him. He turned to her, pulled her closer, knocking her hat eschew, before he quickly dropped his arms. Elizabeth reached up to straighten her hat, color high in her face.

"We're up by two," he said, smiling at Elizabeth. She couldn't help but smile back.

Elizabeth sat back down beside John, trying to get her racing pulse to slow down. She'd nearly been hugged by John, only he'd seemed to think better of it just seconds before both arms had enveloped her. She could tell from the look in his eyes, he'd been acting spontaneously in excitement of the game. Luke was hugging Kathleen and others around them did the same thing. Still, it wasn't something one did in public unless they were engaged or married.

But it had been an exciting moment in all kinds of ways. At least he hadn't apologized, and she hoped that meant he wasn't sorry. She, on the other hand, *was* sorry he stopped himself short of a full hug. She caught her breath. What was she thinking?

She gave herself a little shake and forced her thoughts back to the ball game. Trying to ease any embarrassment John might feel and wanting to let him know she wasn't upset at him, she began asking questions again and they eased back into the game together.

A refreshment boy came around with his tray of cold lemonade and another one followed with freshly popped popcorn and a new snack called Cracker Jack that'd been introduced at the Chicago World's Fair in 1893. It was a box of popped corn and peanuts coated with molasses.

"Have you had these before?" John asked.

"No, I haven't, but I've heard they're very good."

John bought a box of Cracker Jack, two drinks and a bag of popcorn for them to share. The sweet and tart drink went well with the salty treat. And the Cracker Jack snacks were every bit as good as she'd heard they were.

Luke bought the same and they all shared with Ben, Julia, Millicent and Matt. The game ended with the Giants winning six to three.

As they filed out of the polo field, they all tried to figure out where they'd eat dinner. Mrs. Heaton had let Gretchen and Maida have the evening off, as none of them would be there for dinner. She'd gone to spend the day with her children, who'd decided against going to the game. Violet didn't feel up to it and Rebecca, who wasn't a big fan of baseball, thought spending time with her grandmother would be best for Jenny.

At Luke and Kathleen's suggestion, they decided on going to an Italian restaurant they liked. It was still light out and a bit early for dinner, so they concluded it was a wonderful evening for a walk.

The restaurant had a cozy atmosphere, with candles on each table, and they were seated at a huge round table that was just right for eight people.

Kathleen and Luke told them about their favorite dishes, and Elizabeth decided on the spaghetti and meatballs at Kathleen's recommendation. John ordered the same while several others ordered a dish called *fettuccine burro e parmigiano*.

By the time their orders got there, the aroma in the place had them all so hungry, Elizabeth wondered if it would have mattered what they ate—but her dish was wonderful.

"Mmm. This is delicious. I've never had Italian food before."

"Neither have I," John said.

"Luke brought me here one night before we became engaged," Kathleen said. "It's been one of our favorite places ever since."

"I can certainly see why."

"I love this place," Millicent said. "I'll have to write home about it. I'd love to get the recipe for this fettuccine dish."

For the rest of the evening, they all talked, laughed and thoroughly enjoyed themselves.

It'd been a wonderful day and Elizabeth hoped there would be more like it in the future. The chef did give the recipe to Millicent, but it was in Italian and they all chuckled as they said goodbye to the proprietors.

They filed out of the restaurant and headed back to Heaton House.

"I think I'll catch a trolley if I can get one of you men to come with me," Millicent said.

"You mean you're actually afraid to go by yourself?" Matt asked with a teasing grin on his face.

"No, I don't mean that and you know it. But I respect Mrs. Heaton's rules, even if I don't agree with them. Besides, if I took off by myself, one of you would probably tell her and—"

"I'll go with you. Mrs. Heaton's rules are in place for good reason and we wouldn't have let you go by yourself," Matt said. "Anyone else want to get back quickly?"

"I think I'll go, too," Julia said. "I need to press my dress for church tomorrow."

"If you're going, so am I," Ben said. "I certainly don't want to be the odd man here with two other couples."

"Well, we have to stay if you all are going. Kathleen and Luke have to have some supervision," John teased.

"Yeah, well, I'm not sure they're the only ones. You all behave yourselves, you hear?" Ben said. He laughed and caught up with the others who'd reached the trolley stop.

Elizabeth's heart skipped a beat. Was Ben insinuating she and John were a couple? He knew better. But... did he and the others see her and John that way? Would it be so bad if they did? She felt all fluttery at the very idea.

John was glad Elizabeth hadn't insisted on going back with the others. He'd enjoyed the day and didn't want it to come to an end just yet. He wouldn't be seeing as much of her after tonight and he might as well enjoy each minute of the evening.

"I'd like a little time with my fiancé, but if you two are willing to walk far enough behind that we can converse out of your hearing, I suppose you can tag along home with us," Luke said.

John chuckled and looked down at Elizabeth. "I don't know. Think we should let them get that far ahead of us?"

"Long as you keep us in sight, we should be good," Luke said. "No need to hear our every word."

"I suppose they are right," Elizabeth said. She motioned to the couple with her hands. "Shoo. Get along now."

John chuckled as the couple took off. "I guess we can't blame them for wanting some privacy."

"No, we can't. They don't get much time to themselves living at Heaton House. Perhaps that's not a bad thing, though."

"Perhaps. But I know I'd find it hard to have so little time with the woman I was engaged to." He couldn't help but feel envious of his friend, who was leaning close to hear whatever it was Kathleen was saying.

Here the one woman who attracted him in ways he'd never experienced before had just let him know she was wealthy and now he was more certain than ever that she was out of his league. And yet, she was still the same woman she'd been before she told him all that and he couldn't turn his feelings on and off like a lightbulb.

But there was no getting around the fact that she *was* wealthy. And he wasn't. He could offer her nothing she couldn't get for herself.

"John, is everything all right?"

"Yes, of course. It's been a great day and I thank you for spending it with me."

She smiled up at him. "Thank you for asking me to. I loved being out in the open watching the baseball game. And while I may not understand it all, I understood enough to enjoy it, thanks to you. Did you mean it about going again? Because I'd really like to."

"I did mean it. We'll do it again." When he had his feelings for her more in control and thought of her as a good friend instead of longing for more. "You seemed to be more relaxed. How are you feeling after telling everyone?"

"Freer than I ever have, I believe."

"And now you don't have to worry about us finding out who you are, or how wealthy you are and—"

"I do still worry that my wealth might affect some of my relationships, but I'll have to deal with that if it happens. Does it—does it bother you?"

"No." Only that she'd never look to him to provide her with what she wanted. She'd never have to. "I do hope you don't think all men you meet will be after your money, though."

"That might be difficult."

"Oh, Elizabeth, you aren't the kind to—"

"I'm afraid I am the kind of woman who has vowed never to trust my heart to another man."

"Another man?"

She sighed and looked up at him. "John, I have more to tell you."

"More?"

"Yes. There's another reason why I didn't want to go by my real name. I don't think it's anything I need to tell everyone, and I might not be telling you except you brought up the subject, and well, there's really no reason you shouldn't know."

"Please, go on." He might not trust all women, but he felt he had to know why Elizabeth felt she couldn't trust any man.

"I was engaged once. With a man Papa thought was just right for me. But the night of our engagement party, I found out that he was only interested in my money and was really in love with another woman. And even though I decided then and there that I could never trust another man—I wanted to make sure I wouldn't have to deal with that kind of thing again. Men like that seem to come out of the woodwork at the hint of a woman with money of her own."

He'd like to get ahold of that man who'd hurt her so badly and caused her to believe she couldn't trust ever again. No wonder she'd had no callers. She hadn't wanted any. "I am sorry that you had to deal with all of that, Elizabeth. I'm sorry those kind of men are out there. But surely you know we're not all like that."

"I do know that. I just don't know how I can tell if a man might find out who I am and try to present himself as something he's not. Someone who cares only for me and not my money or who will profess he never knew—" She broke off and shook her head. "But you can see why I'm not excited about meeting another of Papa's choices."

"I can." He did, and it made him breathe a sigh of relief at the thought of her spending time at her aunt's. The man would have to be very special to get past her mistrust. "What about me and Ben and the other men from Heaton House? Do you trust us at all?"

She laughed. "Of course I do. But none of you have set your cap for me, so I have no reason not to."

He wanted to ask how she would feel if he told her he *was* interested in her, but he wasn't sure he wanted to hear her answer. "I do understand, in a way. I set my cap for a young woman several years back. She was the daughter of my boss and was wealthy, although I was brash enough to think that one day I would be able to make enough money to take care of her. Her father even seemed to like me. Then some young reporter came to town and swept her off her feet."

He let out a deep breath. She might as well know it all. "I caught him kissing her and pulled him off her. I thought he was taking advantage. Turned out he wasn't and she blamed the fight on me. Her father fired me and…" He shrugged. "With no good character reference coming from him, I came here and started from scratch."

"Oh, John. I'm so sorry—"

"She was just playing with me and probably him, too, until someone who could take care of her in the manner she was accustomed to came along. But I decided then and there never to fall for another woman—especially a wealthy one."

Elizabeth shook her head. "We're quite a pair, aren't we?"

"We are."

"Thank you for opening up to me. I know it must not have been easy."

He smiled down at her. "I knew you'd understand. I figured if you could open up to me, I could do the same. Think we'll ever learn to trust again?"

Elizabeth shrugged. "That is the question, isn't it? We can only hope so."

Hope filled his heart. If they could, was it possible that he and Elizabeth could ever be more than friends?

Chapter Seventeen

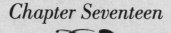

John finally came to his senses two days later. Who was he kidding about he and Elizabeth becoming more than friends? He had only his heart to offer her. And he didn't think that would be enough for any woman, much less one like her. He'd gotten carried away over the past week, letting his dreams interfere with reality. He'd always felt Elizabeth was out of his reach and he'd been right.

He'd promised her they'd remain friends, but could he keep to that when he truly wanted much more? Could he stay at Heaton House, seeing her every day? And what if she did decide to trust again? What if she even decided she could during the coming weekend? What if the man her father wanted her to meet was just right for her? The very thought of it sickened him.

But even if Elizabeth didn't find her father's choice appealing, it wouldn't matter if John ever told her how he felt. How could she trust that he wasn't after her money like her fiancé had been?

John didn't care about her money. He knew that to be true because his feelings for Elizabeth had begun growing when he thought she was just like the rest of them—working to get by, to make a good life for herself. He wished a million times he'd told her how much he'd begun to care about her before she'd revealed she was wealthy. But would she have believed him, or thought he'd found out and been keeping quiet about it?

He expelled a huge sigh. None of that really mattered because, even if the impossible happened and she cared about him, her father would never agree to let her marry him. Not a mere reporter.

He had to stop all these thoughts. It was getting him nowhere. He had a job to do and that had to be his first priority now. His goal was to find out who owned those buildings and get something done about them. He needed to distance himself from Elizabeth.

He hurried up to breakfast, hoping to be gone before Elizabeth came downstairs. He didn't want to see her, didn't want to—

"Good morning, John."

She was at the table with a few others, looking fresh and ready for the day. Obviously, she hadn't tossed and turned as he had. "Good morning. You're down early."

"I woke up early."

"Mmm, so did I." He filled his plate at the sideboard and told himself he'd have to get used to being around her without giving his feelings away.

"Must have been the nice weekend we all had," Kathleen said. "I woke early this morning, too."

John wasn't sure he'd even slept but he wasn't about to say so. "Mmm," he said, noncommittally. He took his seat beside Elizabeth and put all his attention on his meal.

"You seem a bit out of sorts this morning, John," Ben said from across the table.

"Perhaps he just didn't sleep well," Elizabeth said.

"I'm fine. Sorry, I've been thinking about all I need to do this week. If I'm not here for dinner, Mrs. Heaton, please don't worry."

"I won't. But I will have Gretchen save you a plate."

"Thank you. I appreciate that."

"Are you going to city hall today?" Elizabeth asked.

"I am. I'm determined to find out who owns those buildings we've been looking into."

"Is there any way I can help?"

"Thank you, but not really. It's just tedious work, but it will be worth it in the end. I'll let you know what I find out though. Don't worry about that." He knew he sounded curt. He would love nothing more than for her to go with him, but that would only compound his problem where Elizabeth was concerned.

"I wasn't worried. I know you'll keep me up-to-date."

But she sounded hurt and that was the last thing John had intended to do. "I'll be glad to. We're in this together, remember?"

She smiled then and his heart slammed against his chest as he wondered how he was going to manage to distance himself enough in the next week to be able to resume working with Elizabeth on these investigations and also keep his promise that they would always be friends.

"I do remember."

Only friends. He'd do well to keep reminding himself of that fact in the coming days. John finished his breakfast, barely chewing each bite, then pushed back from the table. "I'd better get to work so I have something to share. Have a good day, everyone."

With that he hurried out of the dining room and grabbed his hat from the rack in the foyer. It was going to be a very long week.

Something was wrong. John wasn't himself at all. Was he having second thoughts about all she'd told him? Maybe he'd changed his mind about staying friends. Elizabeth's heart twisted at the very thought. It was going to be difficult enough to keep from caring more for him than she already did, much less think about losing his friendship.

But perhaps it was better that he'd be working late this week. It'd give her time to accept the fact that he didn't trust women any more than she trusted men and to concentrate on the fact that while they were friends, there was very little hope for anything else.

Even if something had seemed to be changing between them these past few weeks. Had it only been that their friendship was growing or was there more? She didn't really know how John felt—and she might never know. But she couldn't deny that she'd begun to feel more for him.

She hurried upstairs and pinned her hat in place, then grabbed her purse and hurried back down and out the door. At least she'd have something to do to keep her thoughts off John—and her father's impending visit—over the next few days. But as thoughts of how he seemed that morning came to mind, she had a feeling it didn't matter what she did. Thoughts of John would always be with her.

She saw her trolley approaching the corner and hurried to meet it. Maybe he'd find out some information quicker than he thought and wouldn't have to work late. But something in his manner made her believe that he wouldn't be home early in any case. And she had to wonder why.

By Thursday, John hadn't come up with any leads on who owned the buildings they'd been investigating and decided to stop by the three buildings again, hoping to find the managers and get some information from them. It seemed his bad luck would continue, until he returned to the first apartment building they'd visited, where they'd helped…Lacy…yes, that was her name, with her rent.

He knocked on the manager's door, Brown was his name—if John remembered right. There was no answer and John decided to go up and see if Lacy knew if he was still the manager or if there'd been any changes. He knocked on her door and waited, but again, there was no answer.

John sighed. He was fed up with loose ends and he was very tired of staying away from Heaton House until well after dinner. All he really wanted to do was to get back to where he and Elizabeth were before she'd told him her full name and how wealthy she really was.

He could no longer deny that before she had, he'd begun to hope for something he'd thought never to hope for again. He knew there was no use wishing for the impossible, but knowing that didn't stop him from thinking about Elizabeth. Didn't stop him from missing her.

He headed back downstairs and that's where he met up with Brown. The man was just coming out of his apartment. Had he been there when he knocked?

"What is it you're doin' back here?" Brown asked when he spotted John.

"I was looking for Lacy."

"I thought you were good friends, seein' as how you paid her rent."

"Would I be looking for her if—"

"You'd be lookin' for her somewhere else. You'd know she moved out before her rent was up again— if you were such good friends with her." Brown took a step forward. "So tell me what it is you're here for."

"I want to know who owns this building."

"What's it to you?"

"He's responsible for the shape it's in. Either that or you are, and the city is real interested to know which one of you it is."

"Why you… I see. You're the one been writing those articles, aren't you?"

"Which articles?"

"The ones tellin' how bad a condition some of the buildin's are in—just tryin' to make trouble for us all. It's you, isn't it?" Brown began to walk toward him in a menacing manner.

John shrugged, trying to ignore the feeling of impending danger. "It might be. You have any answers for me?"

Before John could see it coming, the man's right hook caught him in the eye, making him stagger backward. With his one good eye, he could see Brown getting ready to throw another fist at him.

John had never walked away from a fight and he didn't intend to now. Head down, he bolted forward and caught the guy in the gut, knocking him down. But up Brown came and this time his fist crashed into the side of John's cheek hard enough that he had to shake his head to clear it. At that point it became a real brawl and big as Brown was, only the fact that John was younger and in better shape saved him. When he left, Brown was alive and breathing. But he was moaning, crumpled up in a pile of trash, while a couple of rats scurried down the hall.

As John staggered out of the building, he could taste blood on a lip that was quickly swelling, and could only see out of one eye. He couldn't go back to Heaton House like this so he did the only thing he could think of. He went to Mrs. Oliver's building and up to her apartment where she graciously patched him up.

"Young man, you have to watch it in this neighborhood. There are people who don't like the good you and your friends try to do."

"I know. And I thank you for taking care of me. I hope that my coming here won't bring you any trouble."

Mrs. Oliver shook her head. "It won't. Just you watch out for yourself, you hear?"

He kissed the older woman on the cheek when he left and his determination to help her and others living in those buildings grew stronger than ever.

He didn't want to take a chance of anyone at Heaton House seeing him until he could check out the damage himself. And he needed someone to talk to about his investigation. He stopped at Michael and Violet's place, hoping to get some advice.

"John, what happened to you, man?" Michael asked as Violet came up behind him and gasped.

"Just a run-in with an apartment manager. Don't worry. He's in worse shape than I am."

Violet and her husband exchanged glances.

"I'm glad to hear it," Michael said. "We're just about to eat dinner. Come join us."

"Oh, no, I'm sorry. I should have known it was dinnertime for you—"

"John Talbot, you get in this house and have dinner with us," Violet said from behind her husband. "We have plenty."

"I—"

Michael grabbed his arm and pulled him inside. "No excuses. Come on in. It's good to see you, even if your face is changing colors by the minute."

"Thank you, then, if you're sure you have enough."

John followed them into the dining room to find Rebecca and Jenny already at the table. Michael and Violet's maid, Hilda, set another place for him and John quickly took the seat in front of it. The aroma from the roast waiting for Michael to carve assailed his nostrils and he needed no further prodding to join them.

Jenny looked at him from beside her mother, her eyes wide. "You got hit hard?" the child asked.

"I did." John wondered if she'd seen many fights while living in the tenements.

"Does it hurt much?"

"A little bit." More than that, but he didn't need to make a child worry about him.

"I hope it's better soon."

"Thank you, Jenny. I'm sure it will be."

"Let's thank the Lord for our food and for John to get better, okay?" Michael said, smiling at his niece.

She nodded and after Michael said grace, he began to slice the roast beef while Hilda passed the side dishes around. Once everyone was served, Michael asked, "What brought you by this evening? Did your brawl give you any clues to who might own those buildings yet?"

John shook his head. "No. And that's why I'm here. I thought it might be time to take you up on your offer to help. I keep running into dead ends."

"I'll be glad to. We can talk it over after dinner. Some of the ladies of Heaton House are gathering here to talk weddings again, and they'll be upstairs half the night."

That meant Elizabeth would be there. He'd missed her more than he thought possible this week, getting home after she'd gone upstairs each night. And he did want to see her before the next day. He wasn't sure when she was going to her aunt's, but he didn't want her leaving before at least seeing her, getting to speak to her, even for a few minutes, even looking the way he did. Could it be that his last-minute decision to come here was the Lord's plan? He hoped so.

"Now, Michael, it won't take all that long," Violet assured her husband.

"You say that now, but things seem to change when you ladies get to talking about weddings and babies."

The smile the couple shared had John looking away and tamping down his longing for a relationship like they had.

"Aunt Vi is going to have a baby cousin for me," Jenny said as if he didn't know.

He centered his attention on the little girl and tried not to think of what-ifs. "She is? Just for you?"

"Uh-huh. And I'll be its cousin, too. And Mama will be an aunt like Aunt Vi is."

"I see. And I can tell you're excited about it."

"Uh-huh." Jenny grinned at him. "I can't wait."

"Neither can I," Violet said. "You are going to be such a wonderful help, Jenny."

Jenny nodded her head and grinned. "Mama says I'm a big girl so I can do all kinds of things now."

Talk soon turned to the renovations Mrs. Heaton wanted to make before Rebecca and Jenny moved in. It took them through the meal and dessert. Just as they were leaving the dining room, there was a knock on the door and Hilda answered it.

Kathleen and Elizabeth came in, with Luke bringing up the rear. John watched as Elizabeth noticed him for the first time. Her eyes widened in concern and she gasped. "John! What happened to you?"

He shrugged. "One of the building managers didn't like the questions I asked him."

"Well, I sure hope the other guy looks worse than you do," Luke said. "I can see why you might not have wanted to go back to Heaton House."

"I don't even know how bad I look yet. I didn't want—"

"You look as if you're in a lot of pain," Elizabeth said. "Your eye is swollen shut and your lip is—"

"I'll be fine," John assured her.

"You look awful," Luke stated. "I hope you at least got some answers from the man."

John pulled his gaze away from Elizabeth to answer Luke. "I've not come up with anything concrete and thought it was time to ask for help. Michael and Violet were kind enough to ask me to stay for dinner."

"And we're going to talk things over while you ladies are talking weddings. Maybe you'd like to join us, Luke?"

"Certainly. I was planning on taking up your evening anyway."

John looked back at Elizabeth and smiled. Only when she smiled back did the tightness in his chest ease up. "If you let me walk you back to Heaton House, I'll fill you in on what we come up with."

"I will. Thank you."

"And Luke can fill me in," Kathleen added. "But for now—"

"We have some fittings to do," Violet interjected. "We won't take any longer than necessary."

"Yes, we know, dear," Michael said to his wife. Then he turned to John and Luke. "We have a good hour and a half."

Everyone chuckled as the ladies made their way upstairs and Michael led the way into the parlor.

John followed him and Luke, feeling at peace for the first time in days. He'd avoided Elizabeth all he could and he certainly didn't want to avoid her tonight—not when she would be meeting the man her father wanted her to meet this weekend. He'd have all that time to convince himself he wasn't falling in love with her.

They'd be talking about the investigation tonight, so he should be on safe ground. *Dear Lord, please help me to keep from showing what a struggle I'm having with my feelings for Elizabeth. Help me to quit longing for what can't be and accept that friendship is all there can be between us. I promised her we'd always be friends. Please help me to keep that promise—no matter how hard it might become. In Jesus's name, Amen.*

Once upstairs, Elizabeth had a difficult time keeping up with the conversation, her mind was on John and his injuries. What had he been thinking to confront a manager like that? Still, bad as he looked, she was glad to see him. She'd been afraid she wouldn't see him before leaving for her aunt's—and that he'd planned it that way. But obviously he'd been working hard *and* putting himself in danger.

She'd missed him more than she thought possible. She missed sharing her day, their talks about the investigation and the direction they were taking with their articles. She missed his presence at the dinner table and in the parlor or going out for ice cream.

After hearing how he'd vowed not to give his heart to another and especially not someone wealthy like her, though, she'd realized it was probably for the best that she didn't see so much of him.

But when she'd spotted him here tonight, she thanked the Lord above. She'd planned on staying up until he came in that night just so she could have a few minutes with him before she left for her aunt's the next day. He'd been leaving Heaton House early and not getting home until after she'd gone up for the night. She had the feeling he was drawing away from her as fast as he could.

"Okay, ladies." Violet broke into her thoughts. "I think we're going to make it back down earlier than Luke thought we would," Violet said.

Elizabeth's heartbeat drummed with each step she took back down the stairs and into the parlor. The men stopped talking and stood as they entered.

"We're done." Violet grinned at her husband.

"And in record time." He smiled and put an arm about her as she reached him.

"Are you and John ready to walk Elizabeth and I home?" Kathleen asked Luke.

"We are."

They all thanked Violet and Michael for their hospitality and headed out the door.

Elizabeth's pulse began to race as John fell into step beside her. Kathleen and Luke were up ahead and she had to admit she was glad.

"How has your week gone?" John asked.

"I've been busy with work and helping Kathleen this week." But it hadn't stopped her from missing him. "I guess your week hasn't been great since you haven't been able to find anything. And well..." she said, pointing at his injured face.

"It hasn't been. I should have called Michael in before now. He does this kind of thing for a living after all."

"I'm sure you've done your best. But hopefully he'll be able to help find out quicker."

"That's what I'm hoping. When are you leaving to go to your aunt's?"

"Tomorrow after work."

"And you'll be back when?"

She wondered if he wanted to know so that he would be sure to be gone. "Sunday evening or Monday. It depends on when Papa decides to leave, I suppose."

"Well, I'll be glad when the weekend is over. It's never the same at Heaton House when you aren't there."

"Nor is it the same when you're out late or on assignment." Oh! Why had she said that? She'd been determined not to let him know she'd missed him.

"In what way?" He stopped in the middle of the walk and the expression in his good eye had Elizabeth catching her breath. His gaze dropped to her lips and her pulse raced.

"You two stop dawdling back there," Luke said. "Or we'll have to start chaperoning *you*."

Elizabeth breathed a sigh of relief that she didn't have to answer John's question.

"We're just giving you plenty of room for those private talks you insist on," John teased as they began to walk again.

They reached Heaton House much sooner than Elizabeth would have liked, but perhaps it was best that way. She and John both seemed not to know what to say to each other. She did dread being away over the weekend, but it might be for the best, as well. By the time she got back, maybe she'd be able to hide the fact that she cared deeply for this man from him and the others.

Kathleen and Luke slipped into the parlor and there was no way Elizabeth was going to interrupt their goodnights to each other, especially as everyone else had scattered off to their rooms. Elizabeth was surprised to find that she and John were the only ones in the foyer, suddenly all alone again.

He took a step nearer to her and she could see clearly how the bruise on his cheek was turning purple, while his battered eye was swollen black and blue, and his lip was nearly twice the usual size. Her hand went up of its own accord to gently touch a spot on his face that wasn't bruised. "I'm so sorry you got hurt. You won't be going back there while I'm gone, will you?"

"No."

"Good. You take it easy this weekend." She looked into his eyes and wanted nothing more than to kiss his swollen lips, but that would only bring him more pain. She lifted her hand but John caught it in his and gave it a squeeze.

"If I don't see you before you leave tomorrow, enjoy your visit, but watch your heart around that young man your father is bringing."

Elizabeth chuckled. "After all I've told you, you should know that I will."

"That's what I'm counting on." John dipped his head and she thought he was going to kiss her even in spite of his injuries. But he only looked from her lips to her eyes and back again. Time seemed to stand still for the next few moments and Elizabeth wondered if his heart was beating as hard as hers was.

He raised his head, reached out and cupped her cheek instead. "You're a special woman, Elizabeth Anderson. You take care."

"I will. You, too."

John took his hand away but continued to look into her eyes. "We need to talk when you get back."

"I—" She nodded. "Yes, we do."

He broke their gaze and turned to go downstairs, leaving her pulse racing. The look he'd given her had been… Earlier he'd said things weren't the same with her gone—could his feelings for her be as strong as hers were for him? And if so, could they ever learn to trust enough to find out?

Chapter Eighteen

John took the coward's way out and left for work without going in to breakfast the next morning. He didn't want to run into Elizabeth—didn't want to have to tell her goodbye again—at least not without kissing her as he wished he'd done the night before.

He couldn't stand the idea that she would be gone—would be meeting a man her father deemed acceptable as a son-in-law. Couldn't bring himself to even consider the fact that the man might be acceptable to Elizabeth, as well. It didn't seem to matter that she'd told him she couldn't trust that a man might not be after her wealth. She'd been fooled by one before, wasn't it possible she might be again?

She'd said things weren't the same when he wasn't there and that had given him hope once more that she might have growing feelings for him, too. But even if she did, it didn't mean she would trust her heart to him. But if that was so, it also meant she wouldn't trust someone she'd just met, right?

John expelled a huge sigh of relief. No, she wouldn't.

And it was that thought that carried him through the next few days.

On Saturday, he was still feeling optimistic, but he couldn't help but wonder what this man was like—what Elizabeth's father was like, for that matter. Wonder what they were going to be doing over the weekend. Would they enjoy a picnic like everyone at Heaton House planned to or would they be watching the fireworks from her aunt's apartment windows? He wished he'd asked to take her to her aunt's, now that they all knew about her, but Elizabeth needed time to let her know she'd told everyone about her, too.

But now that he knew her aunt's name… John hurried to the alcove where the telephone sat. Underneath it was the city telephone directory. He quickly flipped through the pages until he found a Mrs. Beatrice Watson, whose address was an apartment at the Osborne, one of the apartment buildings on Fifth Avenue not far from Central Park. He let out a light whistle. It took some money to rent that kind of apartment.

Elizabeth had to be used to a very different life than the kind she lived at Heaton House. And yet she seemed to have no desire to leave. He knew she was happy here and that told him what kind of woman she was. She didn't pick her friends by how much money they had or might have one day. In fact most of her friends now would never have what she did, even if her father did disinherit her.

She was special in every kind of way he could think of and he'd never known a woman like her. And if she truly didn't care about the money…

He shook his head. She still would be suspect of any man who showed interest, whether they had money or not. And he couldn't blame her. But was there a way a man could convince her that he cared only about her? That he wanted to make it on his own and not from his wife's wealth? What would it take to get her to believe it was possible? John didn't know, but he hoped to figure it out, because if any woman was trustworthy, it was Elizabeth Anderson. Of that he had no doubt.

By Saturday evening, Elizabeth was more than ready to get back to Heaton House—back to see how John was doing. He'd filled her thoughts off and on each hour since they'd parted. But her father wasn't leaving until the next afternoon and there was still tonight and tomorrow to get through.

The man he'd brought with him—Richard Thomas III—was nice-looking—a little too much so in her opinion. He kept looking at himself in every mirror he passed and it had gotten to the point that she and her aunt were having a hard time not dissolving into laughter when they caught him at it. He, of course, was oblivious to anything but himself.

And to say that he was cocky was an understatement to say the least. He bragged about all his holdings and where he lived and the last trip he took to Europe and all the money he stood to inherit. Over and over again. She couldn't help but compare him to John, and Richard Thomas III came up short each time she did.

Elizabeth could tell her aunt wasn't impressed with him, either, and even her father seemed to realize he was a bore. Still, she'd been raised with manners and she wouldn't embarrass her father or her aunt by taking her leave—much as she wanted to.

They'd been invited to her aunt's friend's penthouse

suite to watch the fireworks. Elizabeth was pleased that they would be with others. Richard kept trying to get her to himself, but it was easier to stay one step ahead of him in a crowd of people. And that was exactly what she did.

The fireworks were impressive to see from so high up and she did enjoy them as much as she could without being in the company of John and the others from Heaton House. But she couldn't help but think of them all and wonder what they were doing. Had they enjoyed their picnic today? Had John made it home for dinner last night?

She'd mentioned going on a picnic earlier in the day with the hope that she might run into them all, but Richard wasn't a fan of picnics and so they'd eaten at Delmonico's for lunch instead.

It seemed Richard liked to see and be seen by anyone at all who was of the upper class, as he called them. He didn't realize that many of them were gone to the seashore for the summer and was a bit disappointed in the evening.

She had given him no indication that she was interested in him in any way and yet he still seemed to think she was attracted to him. She was thankful he was trying to impress more people than just her tonight and quickly made her escape to one of the windows.

Her aunt came to stand by her, and as they looked out they saw fireworks going up all over the city. "I'm sorry this has turned out to be a taxing weekend for you, dear. Had I known what kind of man he was, I'd have insisted your father leave him back in Boston. The good thing is, I think even he realizes this man is not for you."

"I'm sure that's been with your help, Aunt Bea. And

I thank you for it. I wish Papa would just let me do my own choosing and—" Elizabeth stopped midsentence as she realized what she'd just said. For several years, there'd been no thought of choosing a mate at all. She'd been convinced that she could never trust another man ever again. And yet...

"Your father has mellowed in the past few years, dear. He wants you to be happy. He'll come around. You'll see."

Her father approached them with almost an apologetic look on his face. "Are you two ready to go? Richard is boring everyone with how wonderful he is. If you're to remain friends with these people, Bea, I think we need to get him out of here."

"I'm ready," Elizabeth said.

"So am I."

"I am sorry, Elizabeth. I'd never seen this side of him before. I wouldn't wish him on anyone's daughter—much less my own."

Elizabeth kissed him on the cheek. "Thank you, Papa. I'm so glad you feel the same way I do."

"Well, let's go, then. We'll be leaving first thing in the morning. No need to subject you two to him any longer than necessary."

"Oh, Charles, you can surely wait until after church and Sunday dinner. There's no need to deprive us of visiting with you."

"That's true, Papa. Stay and leave after that."

"Are you sure? I know he's hard to take."

Elizabeth laced her arm through her father's. "We're sure."

"Well, then, that's what we'll do, if you think you can put up with his behavior for that much longer."

"Just knowing you aren't going to try to force him on me is worth that much, Papa." She felt closer to him than she had in years. Perhaps Aunt Bea was right. Was it possible that her father had changed after all this time?

They'd all retired earlier than normal that evening but Elizabeth was not surprised when her aunt knocked on her door shortly after she'd gone to her room. Amanda was right behind her with a tea tray.

"You'd mentioned you had some news to share and I want to hear it before I head to bed. I never go to sleep this early, but I'd had about all I could take of Richard."

Elizabeth laughed. "So have I. And I would like to share some news with you. I would have before now but…"

"I know. We haven't had a moment to ourselves." She sat down on the couch set in front of a fireplace, much like the one at Heaton House, only on a grander scale. "Come tell me. Is it good news or bad?"

"I'll let you decide." But Elizabeth was sure her smile gave her away as she took a seat beside her aunt.

"I can't wait to hear. Let me pour us some tea first."

Amanda left the room and Elizabeth turned to her aunt. "I've told everyone who I really am."

"And how did they take it?" her aunt asked, as if she wasn't sure what kind of reaction to give until she knew.

"They were all wonderful. Truly."

A huge smile broke across her aunt's face. "Oh, Elizabeth, I am so glad. Now you don't have to worry about them finding out on their own. Or what they would think. I'm so pleased."

"So am I." Or at least she was for the most part. She still wasn't sure how it all would affect her and John's relationship, but at least she no longer had to worry about him finding out from someone besides her.

"And now you can meet them all. I'd love nothing better than for you to come to Heaton House with me tomorrow afternoon and meet whoever is around."

"I would love to. I can't wait to meet your friends. I hope they like me."

"Oh, Aunt Bea. It's impossible not to like you, just as it is Mrs. Heaton. You two are very much alike in many ways. I can't wait for you to meet everyone. I know they will love you and you'll feel the same way about them."

"Oh, I have no doubt of that!"

They talked for a while longer before her aunt left and after Elizabeth prepared for bed, she went to the window and looked out. There were still a few fireworks being shot off around the city. She would have loved watching them with John and the others. She hoped the group had a wonderful time even if she hoped John missed her as much as she'd missed him.

She said her prayers before she went to bed, thanking the Lord that her father had seen through Richard and put no pressure at all on her to consider him as a suitor. Perhaps he had mellowed as Aunt Bea said.

Maybe one day she'd be able to introduce him to John and the others.

Elizabeth was most relieved to say goodbye to Richard and her father after Sunday dinner the next day.

"I'd like to call on you again when I'm in the city, if I might," Richard said. He seemed quite confident she'd agree and she almost felt bad about letting him down.

"I don't think so, Richard. I live a different life than

you—we aren't interested in the same things." Which so far seemed to be only him.

"But we'd make a good match and with our fortunes combined, you know—"

"That is where we differ, Richard. I won't be marrying because of looks and fortunes. Life is much more than those things."

"But they make life much easier, don't you think?"

Elizabeth shook her head. "I'm sorry. But you'd be wasting your time. I do hope you find someone just right for you, however."

He seemed quite indignant that she wasn't interested in seeing him again. "You aren't at all what your father described."

Elizabeth raised an eyebrow at him. "Nor are you what he described to me."

"Well, then. I'll just go thank your aunt for her hospitality."

"That would be very nice of you." As he turned and walked away, the relief Elizabeth felt escaped in a long sigh. Hopefully her father wouldn't be bringing anyone else to the city for her to meet for a very long time.

As they left, her father insisted they didn't need to accompany them to Grand Central. "I've told your aunt it's not necessary. You've had enough stress for one weekend. I am sorry, my dear. But I'm glad I got to spend some time with you. I know it would have been better had I come alone and that's what I'll do next time."

"Thank you, Papa. That would be wonderful."

Richard and her aunt joined them in the foyer and they said their goodbyes. Elizabeth had to laugh when her aunt leaned against the door and let out a huge breath.

"I am so glad that visit is over. Perhaps the young man just hasn't been raised to think of anything other than himself, but I can't abide that kind of person for too long."

"Thankfully, neither can Papa. Hopefully he'll think long and hard before trying to matchmake again."

"Oh, I've told him to leave me out of those plans from now on. He did seem quite contrite about it all."

"Yes, he did." For once. But would it last? Only time would tell. She hugged her aunt. "Are you ready to go meet my friends?"

"I certainly am. Let's freshen up, gather our things and be on our way."

In little under an hour they were in a hack and on their way. Elizabeth had called Mrs. Heaton to let her know she was bringing her aunt with her and to please let the others know so that if they wanted to meet her, they'd be there.

She knew Aunt Bea would get a warm welcome from Mrs. Heaton and hoped the others were around to add to it. Especially John. Between his working all last week and her being gone over the weekend, it felt like weeks instead of days since she'd seen him.

The hack pulled up at Heaton House and the driver helped them out. But Mrs. Heaton was out of the house before they'd even taken a step.

"Elizabeth, dear, it's good to have you home, and, Mrs. Watson, I'm so pleased to invite you in. I hope you'll feel welcomed to come see your niece anytime at all."

"Why, thank you, Mrs. Heaton. I know Elizabeth

loves it here and I'm very pleased that we can all get together."

Elizabeth relaxed as they walked inside and into the parlor where most everyone had gathered to meet her aunt. She blinked back the tears that threatened to fall. No one could have better friends than these. The only ones missing were John and Luke.

"I'm sorry we're late. I lost track of time and Luke came down to let me know we had company."

Elizabeth's pulse fluttered as John dashed into the parlor, his gaze seeking hers. His bruises had faded somewhat and the swelling had gone down on his eye and his lip.

"It's all right. You're all here now," Mrs. Heaton said as she poured the tea.

"I feel I know you all, as Elizabeth has told me so much about you," Aunt Bea said. "I am thrilled to meet you all in person and put a face to each name. And let's see if I can guess who these two latecomers are." As Luke had hurried to stand by Kathleen, Elizabeth knew she'd get him right. And the only one left was John.

She walked up to him and said, "And you must be John Talbot. I recognize you from some of the benefits I've been at that you've covered for your paper. I'm pleased to meet you in person."

"And I can say the same, Mrs. Watson. I can see the resemblance in you and Elizabeth now."

"I'm very proud of the articles Elizabeth has done for the *Delineator,* but I've also read your articles about the tenements in the *Tribune.* They are very good, just as Elizabeth has told me they were. She told me how you've even put yourself in danger for them, and I can see for myself that you have. That is unfortunate, but you are doing a very good thing, bringing attention to the awful state of those buildings."

"Why, thank you both." He turned to Elizabeth and her pulse raced as his gaze lowered to her mouth, lingered a moment and then rose to meet her eyes.

Once they'd finished their tea, Mrs. Heaton insisted Elizabeth's aunt stay for Sunday night supper and everyone seemed pleased when she accepted. The gathering began to break up, as they knew they'd be spending time together later that evening.

"I want to give Aunt Bea a tour of the house, if you don't mind, Mrs. Heaton?"

"You go right ahead, dear. We'll see you at suppertime."

Elizabeth showed her aunt around the first floor, through the dining room and into the kitchen, around to the small parlor and they peeked in Mrs. Heaton's study before heading upstairs. "I can't show you the bottom floor, for that is where the men's rooms are. They aren't allowed past this floor and we aren't allowed on their level."

"It sounds as if Mrs. Heaton has some very good rules."

"Oh, she does. We can't be out after dark unless we are in a group or have an escort."

"I knew I sent you to the right place," Aunt Bea said as Elizabeth opened the door to her room. "Oh, Elizabeth, this is very nice. I can see why you love it here so much."

"I love your home, too, Aunt Bea."

"I know you do. But it's good for you to be around people your age and I'm glad to get to know them after hearing about them the past few years."

They sat down on the settee in her room and her aunt settled in a corner of it. "But there is one thing you haven't told me...."

"What is that?"

"That you are smitten with John Talbot."

Elizabeth inhaled sharply. Were her feelings that obvious? "I wouldn't say that—not exactly. We've become friends and—"

"Elizabeth, my dear, I saw the way the two of you looked at each other when he came into the room. I'm certain everyone downstairs could, as well."

Elizabeth jumped up. "Oh, no, Aunt Bea, surely not."

Her aunt chuckled. "Oh, Elizabeth, definitely, yes. He seems very nice. And even if you don't want to admit how you feel about him, it's plain to me that you both care a great deal for each other. Although, I believe that you're both trying to deny it."

Elizabeth's heart dipped before settling into pounding against her ribs. Her aunt had always been able to read people well. Could she be right? Was it possible that John was fighting the same kind of feelings she was?

Sunday night supper was quite enjoyable that night. John had been in the parlor when Elizabeth and her aunt came back down and he'd escorted them to the dining room. Mrs. Heaton had set a place for Elizabeth's aunt near where she sat and after John seated her, he pulled out Elizabeth's chair and then took his seat beside her. For the first time in days things felt right again.

Mrs. Heaton filled Elizabeth's aunt in on all the things her boarders had been doing to help those less fortunate.

"It appears you and your boarders are those on the front lines of this struggle, Martha. You know we can raise all kinds of money, but without others being there, seeing what is needed and helping the money get there, it does no good."

"Very true, Bea. I'm very proud of them all."

"As you should be. And I'm sure your good example has contributed to everything they do."

"Oh, I don't—"

"You are exactly right, Mrs. Watson. Mrs. Heaton is a wonderful example to us all," Kathleen said.

By the time supper was over, John felt sure they'd be seeing more of Elizabeth's aunt.

"I suppose it's time I took my leave. I've had a wonderful time and I've so enjoyed meeting you all and I look forward to visiting again. I can see why my niece loves it here so much. May I use your telephone to call for a hack to take me back home?"

"I'll make the call and I'll be glad to escort you back," John said.

"Oh, would you? That way Elizabeth can ride with me and you can see her back safely."

"That would be my pleasure." He liked Elizabeth's aunt more by the minute.

"Then by all means, call the livery company."

"Bea, please come visit anytime," Mrs. Heaton said. "You are always welcome here."

"Thank you, Martha. I will be taking you up on that invitation. I do sometimes get lonesome. And the same goes to you, you'll be welcome at my apartment anytime."

By the time everyone had said goodbye, the hack John called for had arrived. He helped them both in and took the seat across. It didn't take long at this time of night for the hack to arrive at the Osborne and John asked for it to wait while they saw Elizabeth's aunt inside.

"No need to see me all the way up," Mrs. Watson said. "I know Elizabeth had a trying weekend and is probably ready to call it a night. Besides, the doorman is right here and I'm safe."

"I'll at least see you to the front door."

The two women hugged and John helped Elizabeth's aunt out. He walked her to the door the doorman had already opened for her.

"Thank you for seeing me home and now Elizabeth back, Mr. Talbot. Please come back with Elizabeth or stop by anytime."

"Thank you. I'd like that." He tipped his hat to her and hurried back to join Elizabeth, this time taking a seat beside her.

She seemed a bit surprised but smiled at him anyway. "Thank you for escorting Aunt Bea home."

"It's been my pleasure. I wanted a chance to speak to you anyway, so I can't say I had no motive in my offer."

"Oh, what did you want to speak to me about?"

"I wanted to know how your weekend went. Your aunt said it'd been a stressful one."

She chuckled. "It was difficult at first but it's over and I don't think Papa will be bringing anyone else up here—at least for a while."

"What happened?"

"Nothing. And that's a good thing. By last night even Papa was sick of Richard Thomas III. He was a total bore, only interested in himself, his money—and my money. Thought we'd make a great match."

"You nipped that in the bud, I hope." If not, perhaps he would.

"Without a doubt. I'm not going through that again. At least this time I was wiser and knew right away what kind of man he was. Maybe I'm getting better at that. Or do I have to believe that every man who shows an interest in me is the same?"

"Deep down, you know they aren't, Elizabeth. And I'm sure you are getting better at seeing it." John certainly hoped so. For if she did, surely she'd realize he didn't care about her money. He cared only about her. But after the weekend she'd had, he didn't feel it was time to broach that subject. Not when she was tired and seemed disgusted with men in general.

Until then, perhaps he'd be better off keeping a distance. Until the right time came when he could pull her into his arms and convince her that there was one man out there who cared about only her.

Chapter Nineteen

With John digging deeper into city hall's records and Elizabeth working on her next article and helping Kathleen with her wedding plans, the month seemed to fly by. On the fourteenth, John had brought them the bad news that Cornelius Vanderbilt had suffered a stroke. While he was expected to pull through, for the next few weeks the papers had been full of what-ifs. What would happen to his empire if he didn't survive? Who would he leave his vast fortune to?

August was upon them before they knew it and at least John wasn't missing dinner any longer. Their relationship seemed to have an added awareness of each other, and Elizabeth felt as if she were waiting...but for what she didn't know.

For John to tell her how he felt about her, or the right time to tell him how she felt about him? But she had to admit she was enjoying the subtle change in the way they interacted with one another. It was as if they each knew something the other didn't, and together they knew something no one else did.

"Want to take a walk with me?" John asked after dinner that evening. "We could get the key to Gramercy Park. It should be nice and cool."

"I'd love to," Elizabeth answered, her heart skipping a beat. It'd been a while since they'd spent any time alone. "Did you want to ask any of the others?"

John shook his head. "I think Kathleen and Luke are going to Colleen's this evening and Ben said something about going to Michael and Violet's."

She was both nervous and a bit excited about getting to spend some time together. She waited while John got one of the keys from the table drawer in the foyer, wondering if he had anything in particular he wanted to talk to her about. But as they headed out the door and down the street, it didn't really matter. It felt good just to be by his side.

They crossed the street and walked along the iron fence that surrounded the park. The scent of all kinds of flowers met them at the gate while John unlocked it, and then shut it behind them. Only residents of this area had keys to Gramercy Park and it was a very nice oasis for those who lived in the homes and buildings out around it.

They walked a bit, the shaded pathway cool and relaxing. "I wanted to know how things are going with you. How is your aunt doing?"

Aunt Bea had come to Sunday dinner a couple of times since they'd met her and everyone seemed quite taken with her. She'd traveled some and they loved hearing her stories. "She's fine. Papa is coming into town in a few weeks. You know, I'm beginning to think he might move here. And I'm a bit suspicious that he's sweet on Aunt Bea."

"Really? Would that bother you?"

She shook her head. "No, not at all. I think it would be wonderful if they fell in love. They both seem so lonely at times. Papa appears to have mellowed some. He even called Heaton House yesterday to let me know he'd be coming to town. He's never done that before."

"He's not bringing anyone for you to meet this time, is he?"

"No. Not that I know of."

"Good. That's good."

Elizabeth chuckled as her heart skipped a beat. "Yes, I think so, too. I might see if he'd like to come meet you all. Or maybe mention it to him for another time. I think he'd like to see where I live and—"

"You don't think he'd try to get you to go back to Boston?"

She shook her head. "I don't think so. I believe he's realized I'm not going to do that and I think Aunt Bea has been working on him. Maybe he's realized that as much as he is out of town, we didn't really have much of a home life."

They'd come around the park and John stopped at a bench. "Would you like to sit for a bit?"

Elizabeth was in no hurry to end the outing. "Yes, that would be nice." She sat down and John joined her on the bench.

"That must have been hard on you—being alone so much after your mother passed away," he said.

"It was. I was always afraid in that big house when Papa was out of town. Our housekeeper was very nice and assured me over and over again that we were safe, but I'd hear all kinds of noises and hide myself under the covers. I was old enough to know what she said was true. It wasn't like I was a young child. But I was just so lonely after Mama died.... I don't think Papa ever understood fully, though. Maybe having the house to himself has helped. I don't know."

"I'm sorry you were so lonely, Elizabeth. I do understand, though."

"I know you do. And you were much younger when your mother passed away. I must sound like a child."

"No. You sound like someone who was hurting. Your father probably was, too, but didn't know how to handle missing your mother and maybe it was easier for him just to be gone."

"Perhaps. I'm sorry now that I wasn't looking at things from his perspective."

"That's not always easy to do."

"Thank you for listening to me, John. I don't think I've ever told anyone about how lonely I was. Not even Aunt Bea. She was hurting, too, and—"

He reached out and touched her cheek. She couldn't seem to keep herself from covering his hand with one of hers. John turned his hand and grasped hers, bringing it to his lips.

Their eyes met, and the realization of how much she wanted him to really kiss her had Elizabeth suddenly jumping up from the bench and turning this way and that—

John stood and gently grasped her arms and turned her to him. "Elizabeth. I didn't mean to upset you. I—"

"You didn't. But—" She couldn't let him say he was sorry for the tender moment. She didn't want to hear that. "It's just getting late and we should get back."

"But—"

She slipped her hand through his arm. "Thank you

for being so understanding about a schoolgirl's fears and heartaches."

"Anytime." He led the way out of the park. "I mean that, Elizabeth. I've opened up to you in ways I never have with anyone else and I'm here for you anytime you need to talk—about anything."

His words warmed Elizabeth's heart as he locked the gate behind them and they headed toward Heaton House.

Julia was playing the piano when they arrived back and they joined the others in singing around it. Elizabeth kept her eyes on the sheet of music in front of Julia. If she looked at John she was sure that he'd see the longing on her face. She wasn't ready to admit how much she cared about him—not when she really didn't know how he felt about her—other than as a very good friend. This man who she'd sparred with for over a year, had suddenly become the person she shared all her deepest hurts and fears with. He was truly her best friend. But she could no longer deny she longed for more. They'd both been hurt, but if she were beginning to trust him the way she had tonight, was it possible that she could trust him with her heart? And would he want it?

As John headed back to city hall the next day in the sweltering heat, he couldn't quit thinking of the night before. Had Elizabeth not jumped up from the bench when she did, he would have told her how much he cared for her and then kissed her in a way that convinced her he meant every word. But she *had* jumped up and he didn't know why.

Was she upset because she thought he might? No. He didn't think so. For a moment as they'd looked at each other he was almost certain she would have welcomed his words and his kiss, but now… He whooshed out a breath of frustration. The woman had his insides all topsy-turvy.

And yet, she'd told him things she'd never told anyone else—that had to account for something. She wouldn't have told him all that she did, if she didn't trust him to keep it to himself, would she? Surely not.

And if she ever realized that, could she at some point realize she could trust him with her heart as he—John stopped in his tracks and let out a ragged breath before finishing the thought…as he knew he could trust her with his.

But would any of that make a difference in the long run? Her father might have mellowed but that didn't mean he was ready to see his daughter marry a newspaperman who had no wealth of his own to offer her.

John shook his head as he reached city hall and headed downstairs. He didn't know how Elizabeth really felt, but it was getting to the point to where he was going to have to find out. One thing he knew. If she didn't want him, it'd be hard. But he'd get through it. The Lord would see that he did. And that should give him the courage to tell her how he felt and leave it all in His hands.

For now, though, he had a job to do and the good thing about searching through so many records was that he had to block out all thoughts of anything else to make sure he didn't miss anything. He rubbed the back of his neck and got to work.

When he left that afternoon the heat was oppressive, and he was glad all the windows on the trolley were rolled down. The movement created a breeze that made the heat almost tolerable. He'd finally found some information that might lead to finding the owners of a couple of the buildings, but some of it was more than a little disturbing to him and he needed to speak to Michael. He got off the trolley at his office building.

Michael was as concerned as he was at what he'd found and promised to get right on it. It was with a heavy heart that John caught the next trolley to Heaton House. By the time he got there he couldn't deny he was frustrated.

He didn't know what he'd do if his suspicions turned out to be right.

John seemed very quiet that night and Elizabeth couldn't help but wonder if it had anything to do with the evening before when she'd insisted they get back to Heaton House.

Now she wondered what would have happened if she'd stayed? Would the evening have ended with a kiss? With her telling him about her feelings for him? She'd opened up about everything else in her life to him. But she hadn't given any of that a chance because she was afraid to find out that he might not care for her the way she did him. And they seemed to have taken a step backward in their relationship and she wasn't sure what to do about it.

And now probably wasn't the time to do anything. Everyone seemed out of sorts. The heat was awful and according to the papers, several people had already been taken to the hospital. She hated to think what it was like for those in the tenements who couldn't open their windows to let what breeze there might be come through.

Or those in such cramped spaces air could barely circulate if there was a breeze.

Mrs. Heaton had brought home fans of all kinds and put one at each place setting. "I know these won't cool you while you're sleeping, but at least they might help when you're awake. And drink a lot of water—I've been told it helps. We've plenty of ice. I ordered extra from the icehouse, so take advantage of it. I've opened all the upstairs windows, to help let the hot air escape. You might want to hang damp towels in front of your windows tonight, it will help to cool the air if there is a breeze."

"At least some of the office buildings have ceiling fans in them," Elizabeth said. "Hopefully they'll be available for homes before too long."

"That'd be a blessing," Mrs. Heaton said. "It is a little cooler in my garden, so make use of it and of course Gramercy Park is available."

Mention of the park had her glancing at John only to find his gaze on her. There was a look in his eyes that she'd never seen before and her breath caught in her throat. Why did he look so…perplexed?

"John, is something bothering you?" she found herself asking.

"I'm just concerned. I'm afraid if this heat lasts much longer there will be deaths in the city."

His remark stopped any other conversations that were going on around the table.

"I fear the same thing," Kathleen said. "I hope the city opens the fire hydrants in the tenements before long, at least for a few hours so the children can play and cool down during the day. I'm most worried about the elderly, though. This has to be hard on them."

"True. And then again, many of them have gotten through worse," Mrs. Heaton said. "We need to keep praying that this heat wave ends soon."

No one wanted to go upstairs too early as the heat up there was worse than downstairs and they went as a group to the soda shop. There were lines to get in and no seating at all, so they ordered cones and ate them on the way back to Heaton House.

Elizabeth couldn't get the people they'd met in the tenements out of her mind. "John, do you think Mrs. Oliver and the others will make it through this awful weather?"

"I hope so. I pray so. Maybe I can go check on them tomorrow."

"I'd like to go along, if you don't mind?"

He hesitated a moment and she wondered if he were going to turn her down. "Of course I don't mind. My only concern is how hot it is. But I understand you wanting to go, so dress cool as you can. It's bound to feel like an oven in those buildings."

"I know." She finished her ice cream cone, thinking about all the people who didn't have the opportunity to have one. How spoiled she was! She prayed for them all as they continued home. It was one of the quietest outings they'd ever had.

John and Elizabeth set out early the next morning but it wasn't much cooler than it'd been the day before. The heat wasn't dropping at night and he knew that spelled trouble for the city. He was glad Elizabeth had chosen light clothing both in color and in weight. She looked lovely this morning—as always. "Did you sleep well?" he asked.

"Not too bad. I hung a wet towel over one of the windows and it did help. How about you?"

"I did the same downstairs. Although, I think we have it better as we're partly below ground and that keeps it cooler down there. I feel bad about that."

"No need to. At least the room height upstairs helps. Most of it hovers near the ceiling, I think. The people in the tenements aren't as lucky. Their ceilings aren't as high."

"No, they aren't. Did you see the morning's paper?"

"No. What did it have to say?"

"There have been some deaths already and the fear is that there will be many more before this heat lets up." He didn't mention that most of them were expected to come from the tenements. He prayed that none of those came from the buildings they might visit that day.

They were both glad to see that the hydrants had been opened and children were lined up to get to play in the water and cool down. But as they took the stairs to Mrs. Oliver's apartment, the heat rose with each step.

John knocked on Mrs. Oliver's door and they looked at each other as they waited. They each seemed to be holding their breath as they heard the locks being taken off. He heard Elizabeth's breath release at the same time his did. Mrs. Oliver peeked around the corner and smiled at them.

"Oh, come in, come in. I've been hoping I'd see the two of you again. And I'm glad to see that nice face of yours looks normal again, Mr. Talbot." She motioned for them to come in. "I'm sorry I don't have anything very cool to offer you—"

"Oh, please don't worry about that, Mrs. Oliver,"

Elizabeth said. "We only wanted to come make sure you're all right."

"We're fine dear. Thanks to your young man. Having those windows open has saved us, and I thank the good Lord for bringing you here to get them open for us, Mr. Talbot."

"You're more than welcome, ma'am. Do you know about others in the building?"

"So far everyone is getting along. It's very kind of you to check on us. I do know that there've been a few deaths on the block, but not in this building so far."

"We're very thankful for that. Is there anything we can get to make it easier on you?"

"You've already done it, young man."

"Well, we'll come back and check on you again."

"Thank you. I'll be fine but you're welcome anytime."

They took their leave and John was sure that just as his did, Elizabeth's heart must feel lighter—knowing that at least Mrs. Oliver and those in her building were faring well.

As the afternoon went on, John fought the urge to tell Elizabeth what he'd found out the day before, but he had no concrete answers to the questions he knew she'd ask yet, and until he did, there was no sense in worrying her.

Chapter Twenty

It was nine days and nights before the oppressive heat wave came to an end. In that time four hundred and twenty people died and most of them were from the tenements. It was heartbreaking for the whole city.

Thankfully everyone in the buildings where John and Luke had opened the windows made it through. Elizabeth's father came in on Friday and she went to dinner at her aunt's. John assumed she'd stay the weekend with them.

Mrs. Heaton had asked Michael, Violet, Rebecca and Jenny over for dinner and as soon as they arrived, Michael pulled John aside. "I have news. We'll discuss it in Mother's study after dinner, all right?"

"Certainly." John started to ask if it was what he'd thought it might be but decided there was no sense spoiling dinner if it was. He'd find out soon enough.

Mrs. Heaton asked Michael to say the blessing and he asked them all to pray with him. "Dear Father, we thank You for this day, we thank You for the end to this awful heat wave, We ask that You give strength and comfort to those families who've lost loved ones. We pray there are no more weather related deaths from this heat. We ask you to forgive our sins and to bless this food, Father. In Jesus's name, Amen."

For the next hour, John put thoughts of what Michael had uncovered out of his mind and enjoyed the company. It helped to keep from missing Elizabeth and thinking on what she was doing.

But by the time they'd finished dessert, he was more than ready to find out what Michael had to say. After making their excuses, Michael gathered the briefcase he'd brought with him from the table in the foyer and the two men headed to Mrs. Heaton's study.

They took a seat in the two chairs flanking the empty fireplace and John got right to the point. "Tell me what you have."

Michael handed him some papers. "This is the party who owned all three of those buildings until about a year and a half ago when he sold them off. They are all owned by different people now." He handed another paper to John. "And you were right. Elizabeth's father is the owner of one of the buildings you two have been investigating. He's owned it for over a year."

John closed his eyes and shook his head. "I truly hoped I was wrong."

"So did I. But it may not be as bad as it looks. He might have bought the property without ever checking what condition it was in. Many investors do that. Or have others do it for them and unfortunately they aren't always told the truth."

John nodded. He could only pray that was the case.

"You have to tell Elizabeth, you know that."

"I do. But I think I'd rather cut off my right arm

than have to tell her that her father owns one of those awful buildings."

"Yes, well, at least you took care of the windows and no one lost their lives during the heat wave. And this is your chance. This is your big story, my friend. It will get your name on the front page if you use it. I'm sure of it."

So was John. But if he broke the story…and mentioned Elizabeth's father, it could cost him all he held most dear.

"I won't be able to speak to Elizabeth about any of it until tomorrow. She's at her aunt's tonight. Her father is in town and I…" He shook his head. "I'm not sure what to do."

"Take it to the Lord, John. He'll guide you."

"I will." And he had faith the Lord would guide him. But, still, John feared the outcome might result in a broken heart and broken dreams.

Michael clasped his shoulder as they left the study. "It will work out. If you need to talk, you know where to find me."

"Thanks, Michael. I'll keep that in mind." Right now he needed to talk to the Lord and then sleep on it. Hopefully by the morning he'd know what to do.

John had spent that night and the next morning going over the papers Michael had given him, trying to figure out how he was going to tell Elizabeth about her father owning one of the buildings. And he was running out of time.

He'd just come out of the parlor, planning to go for a walk, hoping to ward off some of his frustration, when Elizabeth walked in the door. "Elizabeth! I'm surprised to see you back so early. Is anything wrong?"

"No. Everything is fine. I'll be going back later for dinner, but I took the opportunity to come home for a bit. Now that everyone here knows who I am, and I'm seeing more of Aunt Bea, I don't feel I have to stay all weekend. Besides, I had the feeling the two of them wanted some time together."

"Oh? Then you think you were right in assuming your father is sweet on your aunt?"

She grinned. "I do. Where are you off to?"

"To get a bit of fresh air now that it's not quite so hot."

"Want some company?"

It appeared his time was up. He couldn't take a chance on Elizabeth finding out about her father from anyone but him. "Sure, I'd love you to come along. Want to go to Gramercy Park?"

"Wherever you want to go."

John grabbed the garden key from the drawer and they slipped out the door. She took his arm and smiled and he wished with all his heart that he didn't have to tell her what he must. He hoped there wouldn't be many people in the park and that they could find a quiet spot to talk.

When they entered the park, John was pleased to find it almost empty. They walked around to a secluded bench where the shade was thick and cool. He motioned for Elizabeth to take a seat and then sat down beside her.

"It's nice and peaceful here," he said.

"It is. I've come to love this park."

"So have I." He couldn't help but remember the night he'd very nearly revealed how he felt about her. Oh, how he wished he had, right then and there.

"I have an invitation for you," Elizabeth said.

"You do?" She'd take it back once he told her what he had to.

"I do. Aunt Bea has been reading your stories and she want's Papa to meet you. She told me to ask you to come for dinner tonight."

John's heart felt as if it was being torn right down the middle. "Oh, that…was very nice of her."

"So will you come?" She smiled a smile that dug itself deep into his heart.

He had no choice but to tell her the truth and the time was now. "I'd love to. But first I have something to tell you, Elizabeth, and I don't think you'll want me there once I do."

"What do you mean? What do you have to tell me?"

"Michael and I know who owns the buildings."

"Oh? Why would that upset me? Who owns them?"

"Until about a year and a half ago, a man named Adam Worthington owned the three that we've been looking into."

"I'm not familiar with that name. Should I be?"

This was even more difficult than he'd thought it would be. He reached out and took one of her hands in his. "No. Not him. But the man who bought one of the buildings…the one Mrs. Oliver lives in…that man is your father."

She looked dazed as she shook her head. He could see horror at the thought and then disbelief in her eyes. She jerked her hand out of his grasp and jumped up. "No! I know my father has his faults, but he'd never let anything he owned fall into that kind of disrepair. He'd never buy something in that condition to begin with. If for no other reason than he wouldn't want others to think less of him. He can't own that building!"

"I'm sorry, Elizabeth, but he does own it. We have the proof." The pain in her eyes shot like an arrow into his heart.

She turned to him. "And now you're going to make your dreams come true, I suppose! This is the break you've been waiting for—a front-page story with my father's name splashed across the top of it!"

In that moment, John was certain his dreams of a future with her were over. But he couldn't think about that now. She was overwrought and he only wanted to help her. "Elizabeth, I—"

"It can't be true, John! I don't believe it." She shook her head as she grasped her arms and paced back and forth.

John stopped her pacing by gently taking hold of her arms. She tried to pull away, but he gave her a little shake and looked into her pain-filled eyes. "Elizabeth, it is possible your father didn't know how bad it was. Living in Boston, maybe he hasn't even seen the property. Michael says many investors don't really know what they've purchased. They go through brokers and trust what they tell them."

He saw hope fire up in her eyes and he prayed what he'd said was the truth. And if it was, he remembered what it was like to be accused wrongly and not be able to explain. He didn't want that to happen to Elizabeth's father. "I'll go with you to speak to him if you want me to."

She covered her mouth with a shaking hand and nodded. The tears in her eyes were almost his undoing and all he wanted to do was make her feel better. "Do you want to go now or wait until later?"

"Now. Will you…will you get the papers or whatever it is Michael found?"

"I will."

They hurried back to Heaton House in silence until they arrived there and Elizabeth turned to him. "I'll wait here. I don't want to answer a lot of questions from anyone. Just hurry, please."

John nodded and did exactly that, praying all the way that this wouldn't turn into a disaster.

Elizabeth didn't want to believe what John had just told her. Her father truly did seem to have mellowed and she felt they were on their way to a better relationship.

She couldn't believe any of it was true. But if he owned that building and didn't try to make it better… *Oh, dear Lord, please…* She couldn't even form the words of what she wanted to pray, but she trusted that her groans were heard and understood.

John was back in only a few minutes and they were on their way. Acting protective of her, he gently grasped her arm and led her to the trolley stop. But Elizabeth pulled her arm away. The very thought that John might get that front-page spread he so desperately wanted with an article that could ruin her father's life made her ill.

Once they got on the trolley and took a seat, John pulled some folded papers from his jacket pocket and handed them to her. She quickly looked through them. The evidence was there. She couldn't argue with it. She swallowed around the knot in her throat as she folded the papers and handed them back to John.

The ride to the Osborne was quiet. Elizabeth had no words. She didn't know what to say about anything. At least John didn't try to get her to talk, and for that she was thankful. Her throat was so full of tears she couldn't speak if she had to.

The doorman opened the door for them and Elizabeth led the way to the elevator. It took them to the sixth floor. She could tell John was impressed with the interior of the building and she could only hope it didn't intimidate him. Deep down, she knew he wasn't out to hurt her family, only to get to the truth.

She knocked on the door and Amanda opened it to them. "Are my father and Aunt Bea in, Amanda?"

"They are. They're in the parlor taking tea."

"Thank you." She turned to John. "Are you ready for this?"

"As I'll ever be. Are you? We can wait a few days, you know."

"No. I've got to know if he knew what condition it was—is—in. I want to get it over with. Come on." She led the way to the parlor.

"Elizabeth, dear!" Aunt Bea said. "You're back early."

"I am. And I brought John with me."

"Why that's wonderful. John, it's good to see you again."

"Thank you, Mrs. Watson, it's good to see you, too."

"You're very welcome. We'd been talking about what you two are doing to help others and I thought Charles should meet you.

"Charles, this is John Talbot, Elizabeth's friend and the reporter she's been working with. John, this is Elizabeth's father, Charles Edward Reynolds."

The older man held out his hand and John shook it. The handshake was firm and short, and the appraisal he gave John was intense. "I've heard quite a bit about you from Bea, Mr. Talbot. Glad to make your acquaintance."

"Glad to make yours as well, sir."

"Aunt Bea, John and I have something we need to talk to Papa about. Could we—"

"Oh! Of course. I'll just go talk to Amanda about our dinner." Elizabeth's aunt smiled and John felt sure she had no idea what they were going to tell Elizabeth's father and expected an entirely different subject to be brought up. A conversation he would love to have as a matter of fact, but that dream seemed to be dying right before his eyes.

Once Elizabeth's aunt left the room, her father looked from his daughter to John and back again. "Either of you want to give me an idea what this is all about?"

"Yes, of course, Papa. Let's sit down and we'll explain," Elizabeth said.

John took a seat on the couch beside Elizabeth and her father took the chair nearest her.

"I'm waiting. What is it you have to tell me?"

"Well, Aunt Bea told you about the buildings in the tenements that we've been investigating."

"Yes. What about them?"

"It's taken a while to find out who owns them and John even called in Mrs. Heaton's son, Michael, to help. He's a private investigator."

"I see. But what does all this have to do with me?"

John saw her father sit up a little straighter in his chair. Was he beginning to put things together? Elizabeth bit her bottom lip and looked at John. "Papa—"

"Mr. Reynolds, sir. We found that one of those buildings belongs to you."

"And what proof do you have?"

Elizabeth turned to John. "Give him the papers, please."

John pulled out the folded documents and handed them to her father. The man snatched them out of his hand and quickly looked over them. His shoulders seemed to slump before John's eyes. John could hear Elizabeth's quick intake of breath as she watched her father.

"That is your name. It is your property, isn't it, Papa?" she asked

"It is."

"Oh, Papa, how you could own a property in such deplorable condition and not do anything about it?" Elizabeth asked.

The man jumped up from his chair. "How dare you accuse me of not taking care of my property."

"I've seen it, Papa. I've taken pictures of the inside. I know what it looks like—"

"Enough!" Her father turned to John and his face hardened as he approached him. "I know where this is leading! You're trying to turn my daughter against me! I should have known."

"Papa!" Elizabeth stood as well and John quickly stood by her side. "That isn't true at all!"

"Oh, Elizabeth, you know nothing of the way men think."

"You may be right about that. I thought I knew you, Papa, but this has nothing to do with the way men think. It has to do with you owning a derelict property—one people live in—children live in—"

"I should never have let her move here!" Her father turned his wrath on John. "This is what comes from associating with the likes of—"

"Papa!"

John had had enough. "Sir! Perhaps if you'd spent more time with your daughter instead of making trips to invest in property you knew nothing about, you would know this is breaking her heart!"

"How dare you reprimand me!" He came toward John, his fist clenched, but John stood his ground.

Elizabeth slipped in between them just before her father reached John. "John, perhaps it would be better if you go back to Heaton House and let my father and I straighten this out."

"I don't want to leave you alone with him."

"You think I'd harm my daughter? Why, you—"

"He won't hurt me." Elizabeth touched John's arm. "Please—"

"And she isn't alone, John," Mrs. Watson said from the doorway. "I'll make sure Elizabeth is unharmed. I'm sorry you can't stay for dinner with us."

"Bea! How much of this dribble have you heard?"

"Enough."

"Go. Please," Elizabeth said, her eyes full of tears.

John gave a curt nod and looked at her aunt. "I'll see myself out."

"Thank you."

John took one last glance at Elizabeth before taking his leave. She looked as miserable as he felt—if that were even possible. He felt his dream crashing hard and fast as he walked out the door.

Chapter Twenty-One

"Now, please, tell me what this is all about, Charles. I think I deserve to know since this is my home and—"

He huffed out a breath and closed his eyes. "It appears this young man you are so fond of has convinced my daughter that I buy run-down properties and leave them that way as a regular practice."

"Oh, Papa! You know that is not true. You *do* own one of the buildings. But for your information, Papa, John told me it was possible you didn't know what bad shape it was in when you bought it, or were ever made aware that the property has never been improved upon. He thought you should have a chance to tell us if that were the case."

Suddenly Elizabeth realized that sick as she might be that her father could be ruined by all of this, John wasn't the one at fault here. And no one—*no one*—had ever stood up for her the way he just had with her father.

"Humph. Still, he brought up my being out of town too much and spending my time buying these kinds of properties—and neglecting you."

"Now, Charles, you've freely admitted to me that you regret not spending more time with Elizabeth."

"Is that true, Papa?"

"Yes, it is. And I'm sorry for it. But I can't undo it, can I?"

"You've acknowledged it and apologized. That helps more than you know."

"But he had no right to accuse me of buying these kinds of properties—"

"Charles, he did not say that exactly," Aunt Bea said.

"Just how much did you hear, Bea?"

"I started listening when you started yelling, and I heard enough to know that John Talbot did not accuse you of anything. In fact, he actually assumed you did not know anything about them. Either you did or you didn't, and Elizabeth deserves to know the truth. Which is it, Charles?" Aunt Bea asked.

Elizabeth's father dropped down in the nearest chair and put his head in his hands. "I never even checked it out. Instead, I relied on a broker I'd never used before. He said it was like the others in the tenements."

"And you didn't ask exactly what that meant?"

"No. I'm sorry, Elizabeth, I know you must be very disappointed in me. I—I suppose my name will be splashed all over the *Tribune*."

"I don't know. It's possible." It was John's story, the one that would put his name on the front page of the paper. The story would make his career—exactly what he'd been working for. Yet she knew his purpose was not to expose her father—but to report the truth. It wasn't his fault Papa was one of the owners they'd sought to find.

"Papa, I think that you should see what condition this

place is in. You need to know what we are talking about. And then you need to figure out what to do about it."

He nodded. "Of course. When do you want to take me to see it?"

"Right now would be good."

The next few hours were spent in the tenements, in the building her father owned. They went from one floor to another and in as many apartments as they could so that her father could see for himself why she and John had been asked to find out who owned the building in the first place.

By the time they arrived back at her aunt's, Elizabeth knew her father would do all he could to make amends, to bring the building up to a better standard for the people living in it. She'd seen his expression turn from disbelief to total disgust from the time they entered the building until they left. He'd spoken with several of the tenants and made promises she knew he intended to keep.

"I'm going back to Heaton House. I need to speak with John," she said once her father had helped her aunt out of the hack.

"That's a good idea, dear," Aunt Bea said. "Please tell him we'll do dinner another time."

"I will." But he might not want to come after the way she'd acted in the park and the way her father had treated him. She certainly couldn't blame him if he didn't. *Dear Lord, please let him forgive me.*

"I'll be staying over to take care of things—fire the manager, look into what needs to be done," her father said. "I'd like to speak to Mr. Talbot, too. Ask his forgiveness for my treatment of him earlier."

"I'll tell him, Papa."

Her father leaned into the hack and kissed her on the cheek. "I love you, Elizabeth. And I'll be making amends to you, as well."

She held her tears in check, but whispered, "I love you, too, Papa."

John slipped into Heaton House and was glad no one was around. He made it to his room unnoticed, dropped down into the easy chair, and leaned his head back. He wondered how things were going with Elizabeth and her father. Would she be back or would she stay the night?

After the way she had reacted when he'd told her about her father, he was sure he could forget ever telling her how much he loved her or asking her to marry him. After today, her father would never allow her to marry him without disowning her. And John couldn't allow that to happen.

And now he had another decision to make. Should he keep quiet or break the story of his career? One that would have Elizabeth's father's name attached to it and would surely break her heart. He ran his fingers through his hair then got up and began to pace the room.

He couldn't do it. He couldn't make his dream a reality—not with this story. Not with something that would cause Elizabeth pain. Her father would make things right, John was sure of that. He knew what kind of woman Elizabeth was and she would never let him get by without making amends for what he'd let those tenants go through. And wasn't that the real reason to get to the bottom of who owned the buildings? Not to ruin a man but to help the tenants?

John sat back down and prayed for guidance, leaving the Lord to take charge. If he were meant to break a big story, the Lord would give him another one. Peace settled over him and he knew it would all work out one way or another.

There was a rap at the door and he heard Luke say, "John, you in there?"

"I'm coming." He opened the door to his friend.

"Elizabeth asked me to see if you'd meet her in Mrs. Heaton's study. Said she needed to speak with you. And she looks pretty upset."

John shut the door behind him and hurried down the hall.

"Is something wrong with you two?" Luke asked.

"I don't know."

He took the stairs two steps at a time, stopping only long enough to take a deep breath before he entered the study. Elizabeth was at the window, looking out on the evening sky. She turned just as he spoke her name.

She looked devastated and he hurried to her side. "Are you all right?"

She nodded. "I am. Or I will be—if you will forgive me for what I said in the park this afternoon. I am so sorry for that, John. And I'm sorry about the way my father treated you today, too. He's asked me to tell you he'd like to speak to you, to apologize for how he acted toward you."

"Then you got him to see—"

She nodded. "I did. With Aunt Bea's help. And then I took them to the building. He hadn't known what shape it was in, but that's no excuse at all. He should have and he realizes that now."

"Good. I'm glad. Are things better between the two of you now?"

"Yes. I… John, I have to ask." She bit her bottom

lip and looked up at him with tear-filled eyes. "I know this is your big chance and I don't want you to lose it, but..." Her voice broke before she continued, "Please don't destroy him. He's my father and I do love him."

She looked so heartbroken, her tears beginning to run down her cheek. John grasped her upper arms and looked into her eyes. "I know you love him, Elizabeth. I'm not going to ruin your father. I'd already decided not to break the story before you got home. Hopefully we can convince the owners of the other two buildings to make amends, too. And as for my big break, it's in the Lord's hands. He's taught me that there are more important things in life than having my name on the front page of a newspaper."

The relief in her eyes was all he needed. "Oh, John, thank you. I—"

"Shh." John placed his fingertip on her lips. He'd given up on one dream, but he wasn't ready to give up the other—not now and not unless he had to. "You are more important to me than any byline ever will be, Elizabeth. I love you. I have been falling deeper and deeper in love with each passing day. I'd never do anything to hurt you."

The light in her eyes gave him hope and the courage to continue, "I know that you might not believe me, but it's true. I was in love with you before I found out who you are. I don't care about your money—you can give it away for all I care. I just pray that someday you'll realize you can trust your heart to me."

"John. I...I do realize that. And I feel the same way about you. I knew you were trustworthy a long time ago and I don't know what got into me today. I am so sorry for what I said to you. Please forgive me."

"There is nothing to forgive—I knew you were distraught with the news I gave you."

She touched his cheek with her fingertips. "Oh, John, I love you with all my heart."

Pure joy filled John's heart. But there was still a question he had to ask. "Do you think your father would ever accept me as a husband for you?"

She brushed at her eyes and released a half chuckle. "It doesn't matter. *I'm* the one who has the say in who I marry, and if you are asking me to marry you, I'll say yes right now."

His heart soared with love for this woman as he asked, "You will?"

"I will. Besides, how could my father possibly refuse when you're going to save his reputation?"

John chuckled as he drew her fully into his arms. "Elizabeth Anderson, I love you with all that is in me."

"John Talbot, I love you the very same way and I thank the Lord for letting me realize you are a *most* trustworthy man. There is no other man I'd trust my heart to. Only you."

John claimed her lips with his, and did his best to fully convince her of just how much he loved her now and for always.

Epilogue

Kathleen made a beautiful bride as she and Luke exchanged wedding vows in the parlor at Heaton House. But Elizabeth's thoughts were on the man beside Luke. The wink John flashed her as they listened to their friends say their vows sent her pulse racing furiously.

Her heart flooded with joy just thinking about her own upcoming wedding. When she and John had announced their engagement last month, Mrs. Heaton had joked that she should add a line reading Love Finds You Here on the Heaton House sign out front.

The past few weeks had been the happiest Elizabeth had ever known. Her father had given her and John his blessing, and as soon as Kathleen and Luke got back from their wedding trip, she and John would start planning their own.

Elizabeth's father had realized that she and John were going to help those less fortunate for the rest of their lives, and he'd put them in charge of overseeing the work on the building he owned—and the new manager.

John and Michael had talked with the owners of the other two buildings and they'd agreed to start work on them immediately in order to keep their names out of the papers.

John's next articles had been about the changes being made in the tenements as opposed to the men who owned them and he seemed content to have moved up to page two.

As the minister pronounced Luke and Kathleen husband and wife, they kissed and then turned to the friends and loved ones who'd come to share their day. Kathleen's sister Colleen was there with her policeman beau. It would surprise no one if they were married before long.

Mrs. Heaton, along with Michael and Violet, and Rebecca and her daughter, Jenny, sat beside them on the left. Elizabeth prayed Rebecca would find someone special soon.

She spotted the other boarders—Julia, Ben, Matt and Millicent in the row on the right, and behind them, Elizabeth's father and her aunt. If she wasn't mistaken they'd soon be married, too, but she knew they'd be there for her and John's wedding come December, and she couldn't be happier for them.

Love was definitely in the air and as Elizabeth took John's arm and they followed Kathleen and Luke into Mrs. Heaton's dining room to cut the cake, she thanked the Lord above for her friends and family.

But mostly she thanked Him for the man at her side, for showing her how special John was and for teaching them both to learn to trust again and to step out in faith to give their hearts to each other.

Once they'd stood with the happy couple long enough for Millicent to take some photographs, John pulled her back out into foyer and down the hall to Mrs. Heaton's study.

"What it is? Has something happened?" she asked her fiancé.

He grinned and shook his head. "No. I just wanted a moment with you to myself. I realized that I haven't told you just how much I love you yet today. I think I'll show you instead."

John pulled Elizabeth into his arms and did just that—kissing her soundly, leaving her no doubt that he did indeed love her. It only seemed right to reciprocate. She kissed him back.

* * * * *

Dear Reader,

While I was writing both *Somewhere to Call Home* and *A Place of Refuge,* Elizabeth Anderson, another of Mrs. Heaton's boarders, became one of my favorites. She'd been helpful in each story, first to Violet, befriending her when she first arrived, and then to Kathleen when she was brought to the boardinghouse. It was always obvious that Elizabeth cared for others and was involved with the Ladies' Aide Society along with Mrs. Heaton, doing as much good as she could.

And over time, it became obvious that she and John Talbot had a special kind of relationship, even if most of what was heard was their sparring with each other. By the time I finished *A Place of Refuge,* I felt Elizabeth and John were ready for a story of their own. I hope you've enjoyed reading their story as much as I enjoyed writing it, and I hope you'll be looking forward to Rebecca's story next. I can't wait to get started on it!

Thanks so much for reading *A Home for Her Heart!* Please let me know what you thought of it and feel free to connect with me at my website, www.janetleebarton. com, or email me at janet@janetleebarton.com, or in care of Love Inspired Books, 233 Broadway, Suite 1001, New York, NY 10279.

Blessings,
Janet Lee Barton

Questions for Discussion

1. When Elizabeth first came to Heaton House, she wanted to be accepted by the other boarders and didn't want them to know she was rich. Would you have felt the same way, or would you have been open about who you were? Why or why not?

2. Once she started caring about the people at Heaton House, she felt bad about not letting them know who she was. And then she was afraid to tell them because she didn't know how they would take the news that she didn't have to work for a living. Would you have felt the same way? Why or why not?

3. Both John and Elizabeth have been hurt in the past and are determined not to fall in love with anyone again. Have you ever felt the same way? Did you ask for the Lord's help in getting past it?

4. When Kathleen suggests they work together to bring attention to the conditions in many of the tenements, neither of them are thrilled about it, but they can't refuse her request. Have you ever been in that situation?

5. John seems to be interested only in getting ahead at his newspaper when the book begins. Do you think he is?

6. Does Elizabeth have reason to think he is "full of himself," or is she being judgmental?

7. And when do you think Elizabeth begins to see a change in John? Why do you think he begins to? Have you seen people change for the better over time?

8. About the time John realizes he cares deeply for Elizabeth, he finds out she's wealthy and that she's vowed never to fall in love again. What do you think he feels at that time? Does he have good reason to?

9. Both try to guard their hearts from one another, but it doesn't seem to help. Do you see the Lord working in their lives at this point? Do you think they see He has a plan for them?

10. Did you agree with John's decision not to destroy Elizabeth's father's reputation? Would you have done the same thing? Why or why not?

REQUEST YOUR FREE BOOKS!

2 FREE INSPIRATIONAL NOVELS
PLUS 2
FREE
MYSTERY GIFTS

Love Inspired
HISTORICAL
INSPIRATIONAL HISTORICAL ROMANCE

YES! Please send me 2 FREE Love Inspired® Historical novels and my 2 FREE mystery gifts (gifts are worth about $10). After receiving them, if I don't wish to receive any more books, I can return the shipping statement marked "cancel." If I don't cancel, I will receive 4 brand-new novels every month and be billed just $4.74 per book in the U.S. or $5.24 per book in Canada. That's a saving of at least 21% off the cover price. It's quite a bargain! Shipping and handling is just 50¢ per book in the U.S. and 75¢ per book in Canada.* I understand that accepting the 2 free books and gifts places me under no obligation to buy anything. I can always return a shipment and cancel at any time. Even if I never buy another book, the two free books and gifts are mine to keep forever.

102/302 IDN F5CN

Name	(PLEASE PRINT)	
Address		Apt. #
City	State/Prov.	Zip/Postal Code

Signature (if under 18, a parent or guardian must sign)

Mail to the Harlequin® Reader Service:
IN U.S.A.: P.O. Box 1867, Buffalo, NY 14240-1867
IN CANADA: P.O. Box 609, Fort Erie, Ontario L2A 5X3

Want to try two free books from another series?
Call 1-800-873-8635 or visit www.ReaderService.com.

* Terms and prices subject to change without notice. Prices do not include applicable taxes. Sales tax applicable in N.Y. Canadian residents will be charged applicable taxes. Offer not valid in Quebec. This offer is limited to one order per household. Not valid for current subscribers to Love Inspired Historical books. All orders subject to credit approval. Credit or debit balances in a customer's account(s) may be offset by any other outstanding balance owed by or to the customer. Please allow 4 to 6 weeks for delivery. Offer available while quantities last.

Your Privacy—The Harlequin® Reader Service is committed to protecting your privacy. Our Privacy Policy is available online at www.ReaderService.com or upon request from the Harlequin Reader Service.

We make a portion of our mailing list available to reputable third parties that offer products we believe may interest you. If you prefer that we not exchange your name with third parties, or if you wish to clarify or modify your communication preferences, please visit us at www.ReaderService.com/consumerchoice or write to us at Harlequin Reader Service Preference Service, P.O. Box 9062, Buffalo, NY 14269. Include your complete name and address.

LIH13R

SPECIAL EXCERPT FROM

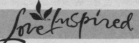

*Get ready for a Big Sky wedding…or fifty! Here's a
sneak peek at
HIS MONTANA BRIDE by Brenda Minton,
part of the **BIG SKY CENTENNIAL** miniseries:*

"**B**ad news," Cord said. "That was the wedding coordinator. She's quitting."

"Ouch. So now what?"

"I'm not sure."

"With no coordinator to help, will you call off the wedding?" Katie asked.

"No." There was too much at stake. The town needed this wedding and the money it would bring in. They had a bridge in need of repairs and a museum they couldn't finish without more funds. "I'll just figure out how to pull off a wedding for fifty couples, maybe get some media attention for Jasper Gulch and hopefully not mess up anyone's life."

"I think you'll do just fine. Remember, it's all about the dress."

"How long are you going to be in town, Katie?" He placed a hand on her back and guided her up the sidewalk.

"I'm not sure. I'm supposed to be helping my sister, but she seems to have escaped and left me here." She sighed and glanced at him.

"Do you think that as long as you're here…"

They were standing in front of the massive wooden doors that led to the church. She had a slightly red nose from the cool morning air and her lips were tinted with pink gloss. As long as she was there, she could be a friend. That wasn' what he'd planned to say, but the thought framed itself as a question in his mind.

She was studying his face, waiting for him to finish.

"Maybe you could help me with this wedding?"

"I thought maybe you wanted me to run interference and keep the single women at bay. 'Hands off Cord Shaw,' that kind of thing." As she said it, somehow her palm came to rest on his shoulder as if they'd been friends forever.

It was the strangest and maybe one of the best feelings. It tangled him up and made him lose track of the reality that he was standing in front of the church. The door could open at any moment. And for the first time in years, a woman had made him feel at ease.

Can rancher Cord Shaw and Katie Archer pull off Jasper Gulch's latest centennial event without getting their hearts involved? Find out in HIS MONTANA BRIDE by Brenda Minton, available October 2014 from Love Inspired.

Big Sky Cowboy

by LINDA FORD

JUST THE COWBOY SHE NEEDED?

The last thing Cora Bell wants is a distracting cowboy showing up on her family's farm seeking temporary shelter. Especially one she is sure has something to hide. But she'll accept Wyatt Williams's help rebuilding her family's barn—and try not to fall once again for a man whose plans don't include staying around.

Since leaving his troubled past behind, Wyatt avoids personal entanglements. He just wants to make a new start with his younger brother. But there's something about Cora that he's instinctively drawn to. Dare this solitary cowboy risk revealing his secrets for a chance at redemption and a bright new future with Cora by his side?

Montana
Marriages

Three sisters discover a legacy
of love beneath the Western sky

*Available October 2014 wherever
Love Inspired books and ebooks are sold.*

Find us on Facebook at
www.Facebook.com/LoveInspiredBooks

LIH28281